He held up a hand to stop her.

"I shouldn't have described it as run-down. It's just...in the middle of nowhere. And you're doing everything alone as far as I can tell. While recuperating from injuries. Doesn't seem like the brightest—" He caught himself. "It seems like a lot to take on."

"It is a lot. But I love it here, and I won't let my scars keep me from living the life I want."

They stared at each other for a moment. Tony swallowed hard. "Good for you. Not everyone can move on like that." He dropped his gaze to the floor, and she thought he was going to say more, but he turned away. "I gotta get back to work."

He headed out of the kitchen, his head still down. He'd seemed amazed that she actually wanted to live out here on her own, but he was also in the middle of nowhere. Why was Tony here in Gallant Lake? He'd been living and working in the city for years. Was he trying to move on from something, too?

Or hiding from it?

Dear Reader,

Most authors will agree that our characters can surprise us. That was the case with this book. When I originally envisioned the story, I assumed Tony was going to rescue Olivia, who's been left badly scarred from an accident that changed her life. But Tony ended up having his *own* trauma to deal with, and I thought maybe Olivia would have to rescue Tony instead. How to choose?

Then I remembered the ending scene from one of my favorite rom-com movies, *Pretty Woman*. When Richard Gere's character asks Julia Roberts's what happens after the prince climbs the tower and rescues the princess, she smiles and says, "She rescues him right back."

And that's what happens in this story. Tony and Olivia rescue each other by pushing back against their fears and taking a chance on love. Rescuing is a theme throughout this book, as Olivia rescues animals, from horses to chickens. It's all about caring enough to want to make a difference.

It wouldn't be a Gallant Lake novel without a wide circle of friends and their *many* opinions. I can't believe this is the *eighth* Gallant Lake Stories book and the *tenth* book I've written set in this Catskills resort town. Thank you, readers, for loving this place as much as I do!

Thanks also to my wonderful editor, Gail Chasan, and all of my own supportive friends. Of course, I can't imagine doing *any* of this without the love of my real-life romance hero, Himself. I'm forever grateful he came into my life and gave me my very own happily-ever-after.

Jo McNally

Skyscrapers to Greener Pastures

JO McNALLY

HARLEQUIN
SPECIAL
EDITION

HARLEQUIN® SPECIAL EDITION™

Recycling programs for this product may not exist in your area.

ISBN-13: 978-1-335-72468-7

Skyscrapers to Greener Pastures

Copyright © 2023 by Jo McNally

For questions and comments about the quality of this book, please contact us at CustomerService@Harlequin.com.

Harlequin Enterprises ULC
22 Adelaide St. West, 41st Floor
Toronto, Ontario M5H 4E3, Canada
www.Harlequin.com

Printed in U.S.A.

Jo McNally lives in upstate New York with one hundred pounds of dog and two hundred pounds of husband—her slice of the bed is very small. When she's not writing or reading romance novels (or clinging to the edge of the bed), she can often be found on the back porch sipping wine with friends while listening to great music. If the weather is absolutely perfect, Jo might join her husband on the golf course, where she tends to feel far more competitive than her actual skill level would suggest.

She likes writing stories about strong women and the men who love them. She's a true believer that love can conquer all if given just half a chance.

You can follow Jo pretty much anywhere on social media—and she'd love it if you did—but you can start at her website, jomcnallyromance.com.

Books by Jo McNally

Harlequin Special Edition

Gallant Lake Stories

A Man You Can Trust
It Started at Christmas...
Her Homecoming Wish
Changing His Plans
Her Mountainside Haven
Second-Chance Summer
Expecting His Holiday Surprise

The Fortunes of Texas: The Wedding Gift

A Soldier's Dare

Visit the Author Profile page
at Harlequin.com for more titles.

This book is dedicated to the girl
who's been by my side (or at my feet) throughout
my publishing journey. My husband's "other blonde."
She's our goofy, adorable, perpetually shedding,
ice cream–loving rescue dog.

To Tully-girl, with love.

Chapter One

Olivia Carson grimaced as she tossed hay into two of the six stalls in the old barn. Mornings were always the worst for her. Especially damp, cool May mornings like this. Her bones ached, and the tangle of scarred skin from her thigh to her arm was tight and painful. But chores needed to be done, and the barn was more orderly and calm than the inside of her house.

The dappled gray gelding in the first stall shook his head up and down as if agreeing with Olivia's unspoken thoughts. She couldn't help but laugh.

"You know it's the truth, Scout." She leaned against the stall door and waited for the big quarter horse to drop his head over the top for his morning ear scritches. "You have a nicer home than I do right now, and I have no one to blame but myself."

It wasn't like her to be overly trusting—especially

not with her house—but what did she know about con-struction? What had gotten her into such trouble was not speaking up when she saw an issue. Or, in the case of her contractor, Larry Goodman, allowing him to patronize her with nonsensical explanations of why she wasn't *really* seeing what she was clearly seeing. And what she was *seeing* was herself being ripped off.

Scout pulled away from Olivia to drink from the water bucket, and Olivia rested her arms on top of the stall gate to watch. When the horse was finished, he whipped his head back and forth in agitation and stomped a front hoof.

"Yeah, yeah. I keep telling you not to bite the hand who feeds you." But Olivia stepped away, knowing the old gelding sometimes forgot how good he had it and reverted back to the abused animal who'd been rescued from going to an auction a year ago.

Her most recent rescue was in the next stall. Misty looked up from her grain bin when the hay hit the floor, then went back to her grain after a soft huff of acknowl-edgement. Hugely pregnant, the palomino was either completely unflappable or just too tired to care. Olivia hadn't decided yet, since the sweet girl had only been here a few months.

Olivia made sure the barn cats had food in their dish, then she fed the chickens in the yard and headed back to the square white house that was supposed to be her home. It *was* her home. It just didn't feel very homey.

She whistled for Ginger, and the curly-haired dog came galloping around the corner of the house to join her. Judging from the burrs stuck in her coat, the labra-doodle had been off chasing rabbits through the brush out back.

"Come on, dog. Everyone else has eaten. It's time for *our* breakfast."

She opened the front door of the hundred-year-old house and looked straight through to the back door, thirty feet away. Sure, she'd wanted a more open floor plan than the place originally had. But not quite *this* open. Half-built walls showed where the new rooms *would* be. Someday. The framing was done. Or done-*ish*. Electrical? Sort of, although she was giving lots of side-eye to the new wiring. Plumbing? Again…sort of.

The kitchen and downstairs bathroom were functional. Mainly because Larry hadn't touched them yet. But upstairs? She glanced up the stairway and wrinkled her nose. Upstairs was a *totally* open floor plan these days, bathroom and all. Nothing but two-by-four studs from one exterior wall to the other. After seven months of work—during which he often didn't show up for weeks at a time—Larry had done a lot of demolition and very little construction. Olivia straightened her shoulders and headed for the kitchen with Ginger at her heels. This was a Scarlett O'Hara moment—she'd worry about all of that tomorrow.

Right now she wanted to warm herself up with a bowl of oatmeal. And maybe wash it down with half a pot of coffee. Then she'd do her morning stretches and put lotion on her scars—doing both helped maintain what flexibility she still had. After that, hopefully she'd feel up to cleaning the stalls. Dr. Jupta insisted the more she moved, the better off she'd be "in the long run." Never mind how much it hurt in the here and now. It was all just a part of her life now. Pain and memories.

Ginger was waiting patiently by her dish, giving the silent laser-eye treatment to communicate her impending starvation if Olivia didn't feed her. The animals were her reason to crawl out of bed every morning, whether she wanted to or not. She filled the bowl, then made some microwave oatmeal and sat at the kitchen table with her phone and a mug of coffee.

She scrolled through the headlines and caught up with her emails as she ate. An incoming text pinged on the phone as she was putting her bowl in the dishwasher. It was from Julie Walker, the manager at the Gallant Lake Resort and Olivia's friend,

When she'd moved to the farm, Olivia had not been looking for a social circle. She'd basically wanted to be a hermit. But she'd quickly learned that no one in Gallant Lake wanted to see people isolate themselves. They'd made it clear that she had friends here, and she'd eventually given in to their persistence.

Olivia had never really been hermit material, anyway. Her new friends understood why she avoided being in public. She didn't like the stares and whispers over her appearance. She just wanted to live her life, such as it was now, in peace.

J: Good morning! Just a reminder that Bobby will be there around noon to come up with a plan for your place.

Olivia muttered a curse. There was no question that she needed the help. And Julie's brother was an excellent contractor. If she'd known that *before* hiring Larry, her house might actually be done by now. But it was embarrassing to have people see how deep she'd let Larry get with the work before realizing how completely over his head he was. Her phone pinged again.

J: You up? Everything okay?

She tapped her response.

O: Yes to both. Just headed upstairs to do my stretches.

J: You coming in for a massage this week?

O: Thursday morning. Wanna do lunch?

J: Duh! Of course! Good luck with Bobby—he's crazy busy these days, but I'm sure he'll work something out. You get your money back from that other asshat yet?

Her jaw tightened, making her teeth ache from how hard she'd been clenching them lately. When she'd told her former contractor she thought they should part ways a few weeks ago, Larry had insisted that what she'd paid him only covered supplies and labor for what he'd done so far. She highly doubted that, but when she'd asked for receipts, he'd gotten loud, accusing her of not trusting him. And she didn't! He'd left with a vague threat that she'd better not complain about his work to anyone because any so-called problems were all in her head, and if there *was* an issue it was *her* fault, and if anything, she owed *him* money. By that point, she was just glad to see him drive off.

O: Don't worry about Larry. I'm sure Bobby will be fine.

Julie's brother was soft-spoken and seemed to have a laid-back approach to life. Olivia was sure she'd feel comfortable having him around the house, which had never been the case with Larry.

Sure enough, when Bobby pulled in an hour later, he sort of ambled over to where she was working in the garden. He brushed a shock of dark blond hair from his forehead and flashed a smile that lit up his blue eyes. Bobby Brown felt...safe. She had no doubt he was one of the good guys.

"Hey, Bobby," she greeted him as she straightened. "Thanks for stopping. I hope Julie didn't pressure you too much."

Ginger came bounding over to greet Bobby and got an enthusiastic head scratch as a reward. Then she was off again. Endless energy.

He gave a soft laugh. "No pressure at all. It was a sisterly request for a favor, which she knows I'd never turn down."

He looked up at the house, which seemed perfectly normal from the outside, if a bit dull, she mused. White clapboard siding highlighted with white trim and a white porch and white front door.

"It looks solid enough. New roof?" he asked.

She nodded, taking off her gardening gloves and leading the way to the front porch. "I had that done before I moved in." Thank God she'd hired a reputable roofing company, not Larry, for that. "The foundation seems solid, but honestly the basement creeps me out. It's a little musty down there."

"Might just need a dehumidifier. I'll take a look while I'm—" His voice faltered when she opened the door. "Wow...did you *buy* it like this?"

Her face heated. "No. I hired someone to remodel and...well, it didn't work out."

Bobby's eyes were wide. He stood at the base of the staircase and turned to take it all in. "Damn, Olivia. This is…unbelievable." He looked up the stairs and spied more framed-only walls. "He gutted both floors?"

Humiliation coursed through her. She felt like such a fool. Bobby must have noticed her discomfort, because his voice softened.

"Hey—none of this is your fault. Julie told me you hired Larry Goodman from a reputable online-recommendation site." Bobby looked around, then smiled at her. "I don't think anything here is unfixable. It's just a much bigger job than I was thinking." His smile dimmed. "And it won't be cheap. Please tell me you didn't pay him for everything up front."

"Not everything, no. I have the money to cover the rest of it." The insurance settlement from her accident had been substantial, even though it had taken a lawsuit to get it. It was enough for her to be able to afford the small hillside farm in the Catskills, and to modernize it while she reestablished her website-design business. She didn't *want* to lose the money Larry had taken, but it wouldn't change her plans drastically.

She walked Bobby through the house, explaining what she'd envisioned. The biggest project was opening up the old living room, butler's pantry and entrance hall to the kitchen as one large open space. The former parlor at the base of the stairs would become her office. She wanted a master suite along the back wall of the upstairs, with two smaller bedrooms in the front.

Her hip was beginning to protest going up and down the staircase more times in one day than usual, so Bobby went into the basement alone. She'd considered bringing the master suite downstairs to avoid the stairs, but there were only so many concessions she was willing to make for her injuries. Besides, there was a lot more space upstairs for the suite she'd envisioned, complete with a deep soaking tub and multihead shower with room for a bench. And Dr. Jupta said the stairs were good for her—she needed to keep moving. As if responding to that thought, Ginger barked at the door. She went to let her in, knowing in half an hour the dog would want to go back out again.

When Bobby came back upstairs, he looked grim. *Uh-oh.*

"What is it? What did you find?" The home inspector had assured her the foundation was fine when she bought the farm last year.

Bobby blinked, then smiled, but it looked like a sad smile to Olivia. Oh, no—why was he sad?

"It's nothing terrible. You need a better drain system down there and a new sump pump. After that, a dehumidifier should do the trick." He gave her a wink. "The good news is your furnace and hot-water heater are fairly new, and both are energy-efficient." He looked around and sighed. "I don't want you to live like this any longer than you have to, but this is a big job, and I've got a couple other big jobs lined up ahead of you. I'm not sure when I can get a crew here to do the work. It could be a few months…"

His forehead furrowed as he stared at the space that would someday be her office. She could tell he was doing some sort of math or planning in his head. Then he brightened, snapping his fingers.

"You know what? I might have just the guy for this."

"One guy? A minute ago you said a crew."

"I can't get my crew here full-time for weeks, but if I can get Tony Vello to run lead on this, he could do a lot of the work on his own. My guys could pop in as needed." He nodded to himself. "He needs the work, and you obviously need the job done sooner rather than later."

A thread of concern shot through her. "Why does this Tony guy need work?"

"He's not destitute or anything. He's just new to the area. But he's got the experience. His dad and his family build skyscrapers in New York City."

"I'm not looking to build a skyscraper."

"He's got the skills for this, Olivia. One of his uncles builds houses in Jersey. Tony did some work over at the ski lodge for Matt and Jillie last week, and did a great job." Bobby shrugged. "It's either him or wait a few more months. Look, I trust the guy, but I promise I'll stop by and check his work on a regular basis."

Bobby and his sister, Julie, had lived in the small resort town of Gallant Lake all their lives. They loved the town and its people. Julie was one of the first people to have taken Olivia under her wing as soon as they met— which had been *after* she'd hired Larry, unfortunately.

It wasn't until Julie had stopped by a week ago with a plate of pastries from the Greek bakery in town that the truth had gotten out there. Larry had left Olivia with a mess. Just because she'd been letting some friends into her life didn't mean she'd been ready to share everything with them. Especially something so embarrassing. If Bobby was willing to vouch for this Tony guy…

"Okay." She looked around to remind herself she had to do *something*. "I trust you, Bobby. And if you can keep an eye on things while he's working, it would make me feel that much better."

"No problem." He kneeled to give Ginger a hug, sending the dog into ecstasy. "And remember, this is only a referral. If you don't like Tony, tell him you're not interested and that's that." He gave Ginger one more pat, then headed out the door with a wave. "You won't hurt my feelings any." Hopefully Tony would be as honest and skilled as Bobby was, and as nice to be around.

If not, no matter how much she hated the thought, she'd have to fire him and start all over. Again.

Chapter Two

"You want me to do a full remodel job?" Tony Vello stared at his friend, who was sitting next to him at the Chalet, Gallant Lake's townie bar and pizza joint. Bobby took a sip of his beer, raising an eyebrow at Tony.

"You told me you wanted work. This is work." Bobby set down his beer. "The homeowner's in a bind. The guy she hired made a muck-up of the whole thing—two floors of poorly framed-in rooms and shoddy wiring."

Tony huffed out a laugh and drank his ginger ale. "You make this job sound more and more appealing all the time."

It was true he wanted work. But he was hoping for some basic carpentry, like framing a house or something. Mindless work like hammering nails all day to silence the ghosts in his head. He'd promised his counselor at Terra Springs Recovery Center that he'd limit his stress in order to give sobriety his best shot. Rebuilding some woman's house—fixing another guy's mistakes—wasn't exactly *mindless*.

He'd stumbled across Gallant Lake by accident two weeks ago. Traffic between Albany and metro New York had been backed up for miles that day, thanks to a wreck in the middle of a construction zone. Sitting still made him twitchy, so Tony took the first exit he came across and started driving west, looking for a detour. He came over a small rise and saw the valley, the lake and the town itself. *Quaint* had never been his style, and he'd gotten more of it than he'd wanted at Terra Springs—the addiction-recovery center was perched near the top of a mountain in the Adirondacks.

But there was something about Gallant Lake that had made him park his truck and walk down the sidewalk, looking into the tidy little storefronts. He'd run into Bobby in front of the Greek pastry shop—literally. Bobby had been coming out the door with an armload of white boxes when Tony walked around the corner and straight into the guy, sending bakery boxes flying.

By the time Bobby finally agreed to let Tony replace the pastries, they'd discovered they both worked in construction, even if in vastly different forms. Bobby directed him to the Gallant Lake Resort for a place to stay, telling him to ask for his sister, Julie, and she'd give him a family discount. Within days, Tony was thinking this town might be a better place to continue his recovery than going right back to the bosom of his well-meaning, but high-octane, family.

He'd helped Bobby with a job at the local ski resort last week, and had dropped some hints that he'd like to take on more work. Nothing long-term. Nothing taxing. Just something while he decided what to do next. He'd explained his situation to Bobby, so he'd know Tony wasn't some vagabond. He was trying to stay sober, he wasn't ready to go back to Staten Island, and he needed busy work.

He was *not* in the market for a one-man remodeling job.

"Look," Bobby began, "my sister likes Olivia Carson, and I do, too. She's quiet, kind of a loner. Not the type of client who'll drive you crazy. Do the work you can handle on your own, and I'll bring the gang over there for the big stuff." He paused. "At least meet her and get a sense of the job. The work will keep you busy for a month or so, and that's what you said you wanted."

He was right. It was exactly what Tony was looking for—staying busy to finish clearing his head before he started doing steel work again. He pulled out his phone.

"Give me the address. I'll check it out."

No one would *ever* accuse Tony Vello of being some small-town country boy. In fact, he could almost hear his cousins laughing at him as he turned his truck up the winding gravel drive. Luca and Paulie would be pretending to play banjos or something, as if this was a scene out of the movie *Deliverance*. Anything north of Tarrytown was "the boondocks." A year ago, he'd have been laughing right along with them.

But a lot had changed in a year.

If a job on this hillside in the Catskills would keep him busy—and help him avoid going home—he could handle staying in the boondocks a while longer. Anything to keep from letting his family know he might never be able to return to his job there.

The driveway curved to the right at the top of the hill, exposing a four-square farmhouse with a large red barn behind it. It was more open up here than he'd expected after driving through the trees and overgrowth along the driveway. There were twin fenced-in fields behind the barn that stretched to the woods farther up the slope.

He'd pictured an older woman when Bobby was talking about this quiet loner, Olivia, so he was a little surprised at the size of the place. Maybe her husband had died or something, leaving her to run the farm on her own. His jaw tightened at the thought of the other contractor taking advantage of an old widow lady.

He parked his truck and got out, stopping for a moment to soak in the silence and the warm late-May sunshine. Before his life had been upended, he would have been working thirty stories above the streets of Manhattan by this hour, listening to the steady hum of traffic, sirens and people below. By contrast, the only sound up here was the soft shush of a breeze rustling the new leaves on the trees. And the sound of a barn door being rolled open. He turned toward the sound and froze when he spotted a woman his age—maybe younger—staring at him, her hand still holding the edge of the big door.

She had long, honey-colored hair falling down her back in soft waves. Despite standing in a barn, she was wearing a dress. A loose blue dress that flowed from her shoulders to almost her ankles. And...rubber boots. She was tugging off a pair of leather work gloves. It was an intriguing mix. Her intense blue eyes were wide, staring at him with suspicion.

This must be Olivia's daughter, or maybe even granddaughter. Tony knew his presence could be intimidating. He was a big guy, and his dark Mediterranean looks sometimes bothered those who'd watched too many Mafia movies. He gave a friendly I'm-not-here-to-harm-you wave.

"I'm Tony Vello. Bobby sent me up to talk to Olivia about some work at the house. Is she around?" The woman didn't move. Patience was *not* one of Tony's strong points. He started to turn away. "Okay, then. I'll just go knock on the door."

"I'm Olivia." Her voice was as cautious as her expression. "I didn't expect you today."

He shrugged, trying to wrap his head around this slender, ethereal woman being his potential client. So much for that little old lady he'd imagined. "Bobby said you needed the work done sooner rather than later. Do you want me to come back?" She was in a dress, so maybe she was going somewhere. But she had those rubber barn boots on. Bobby said she was a *loner*, not some eccentric hippy.

She hesitated, then shook her head. "No. I was just cleaning stalls. I'll show you the house." She tossed the work gloves onto a hay bale near her. She'd been cleaning stalls in a *dress*? He followed her toward the house, noting she was wearing a long-sleeve thermal top under her dress. It looked like her preferred fashion was "bag lady chic." He hoped she could pay for the work she needed done.

She was clearly not afraid of hard work. But there was a frailty to her he couldn't identify. It wasn't until she reached the steps to her front porch that he noticed she had a slight limp. When she was walking across the yard, he'd assumed her ambling gait was due to those tall Wellingtons. But she gripped the railing tightly with her right hand, almost pulling herself up the stairs.

He was still trying to process the puzzle of Olivia Carson when she opened the door and turned to him. "It's a bit of a mess, I'm afraid."

Holy...

Tony stood in the doorway and stared at the skeletal shell that was the interior of her house.

"What the...?" He stepped inside, glancing up the staircase. It was the same upstairs. "You just let this guy rip out *everything*?"

She straightened. "I didn't *let* him do anything. I *hired* someone I thought was a professional to do a job. Can you finish it or not?"

She was defensive. Angry. Meanwhile, Tony felt his own rage rising on her behalf.

"*Finish* it?" He gestured around. "I'll have to *fix* it first. That open span needs a major support beam. And that wall right there is supposed to be load-bearing, but look at the gap between the top of the framing and the beams supporting the upstairs."

She looked up, skeptical. "It's only an inch."

Tony stared at her. "*Only* an inch? Trust me, if that upstairs floor starts sagging, you'll notice that inch in a hurry up there." He looked around, his mouth still open in stunned surprise. "Did you even check the man's references? Has he ever built more than a dog-house before?" He turned back to Olivia. "Please tell me you didn't *pay* him."

Her cheeks went pink under her pale freckles. "Well,

not *everything*, but he needed a deposit and enough to cover supplies."

"Son of a…" Tony's jaw went tight. He hated shady contractors. This guy, whoever he was, had taken this woman's money and nearly destroyed her house. But browbeating her wasn't going to change anything. He sucked in a sharp breath and pulled out his phone to start taking photos and notes. "Do you have plans of what this is *supposed* to look like?"

She nodded. "In the kitchen."

The plans weren't *plans* as much as sketches. Nicely done. Almost framable. But they were just pretty little pencil sketches of what the finished product was supposed to look like. Nothing showing electrical or plumbing. No supply list—nothing.

"Did you draw these?" She nodded, and he rolled his eyes. "Cute, but completely useless. You need actual blueprints. How did you ever get a building permit without…" His eyes fell closed. "Tell me you got a permit."

"Larry said he took care of that."

"Yeah, I'll just bet he did. He either paid off someone at the zoning board, or never applied in the first place. Because there's no way you qualified for a permit with these things as a plan." He tossed the sketches back on the table, then scrubbed the back of his neck with his hand. "Things have to be done to code, and this…" Tony pointed to electrical wires stapled to a two-by-four with the staple running *through* the plastic that protected the wires, which were hopefully *not* live. "This is not even safe, much less to code."

She stared hard at him, her blue eyes turning to steel. Her mouth worked back and forth as if she was fighting to hold something back. It reminded him of his cousin Joey's wife, Helen. She'd finally learned to speak up in the brash Vello household or forever be ignored. He leaned on the nearest framed wall, hoping it would hold his weight, and folded his arms on his chest.

"Just spit it out, Olivia. If we can't communicate, there's no sense in me even starting."

She lifted her chin. "You make it sound like this is all my fault. And maybe it is, but..." Her voice was sharp now. "Look, I asked him about adding a beam for the great room. I asked about the wiring. I'm not some idiot just because I can't build a house. He told me not to worry about it." She swept her arm around at the disarray. "That's why *you're* here. But I don't think this is going to work out—"

Tony pushed away from the wall, cursing to himself. Helen had told him more than once that the Vellos were "a lot" for people who weren't used to a noisy, competitive, tough-talking Italian family. And this woman standing in a wreck of a home wasn't some New York City developer who could take a good raking over the coals and call it *business*. He raised a hand in apology.

"I'm not angry *with* you. I'm angry *for* you. There's a difference." He paused, and her eyes softened a bit. Still ice-blue, but no longer ice-hard. He couldn't help wondering what made her buy an entire farm on her own. He gestured toward the staircase. "I can get this done, but it'll take a while. I'll have to work around Bobby's schedule, because I can't do things like install that fourteen-foot support beam by myself." He gave a heavy sigh, looking around again. "It's a solid house. It's not like it's going to come down around your ears or anything. Let me work up an actual plan and a quote, and if you approve both, I'll turn this around... if you let me."

There was something about the willowy blonde, in her flowy dress and rubber boots, that had piqued his curiosity. She'd seemed soft-spoken at first, but she'd shown her backbone when she'd defended herself and had almost sent him on his way. She was absolutely *nothing* like the loud, bold, funny women he'd dated on Staten Island, that's for sure. Maybe that's what intrigued him.

But Tony wasn't looking for some woman to *date*. He wasn't going to hang around Gallant Lake long-term, and he sure as hell wasn't getting involved with some farm lady with actual chickens running around her yard. But since his employer happened to be beautiful and...interesting, that could make the job more enjoyable.

Olivia's eyebrows gathered together, matching her pursed lips. Then she nodded and shrugged at the same time, as if she'd had a silent debate with herself and had come to a reluctant conclusion. She looked at the sketches, then back to him.

"Run the numbers for me, and if it makes sense, you're hired." She paused. "But only because Bobby Brown vouched for you. And I won't pay for anything without receipts and documented hours."

He let out a soft laugh. "Good for you. I like a woman who can learn from her mistakes."

The corner of her mouth twitched into the slightest of smiles. It was gone before he was even sure he'd seen it.

"Just make sure you're not another one, Mr. Vello."

Chapter Three

As she watched the sun setting the following day, Olivia *still* wasn't sure whether she'd been amused or irritated by Tony's comment about learning from mistakes.

She was in her favorite seat—the big porch swing with cushions and pillows galore. The nearby table held her coffee mug and a small plate with cheese and crackers. She'd had a big bowl of leftover pasta for lunch, so this was dinner. Favorite food in her favorite spot.

The farmhouse faced toward the north. That meant less sun on the porch, but the views of the valley made up for it. When the leaves were off the trees in the winter, she could see the blue waters of Gallant Lake in the valley. On a late spring day like today, the lake was hidden, but she could still see the Catskill Mountains marching northward in rich shades of deepening green.

There were times when she'd questioned her choice

to move up here alone on the quiet hillside, removed from close neighbors. She'd never heard of Gallant Lake, New York, but when she saw the farm online, she just had to see it for herself. It hadn't disappointed. What's more, the farm had brought her a sense of peace and security she hadn't found anywhere else since the accident. She shifted in the chair, wincing at the pull of the burn scars on her back. She wasn't looking to be a wild-haired hermit or anything. She just found the setting, nestled into the trees near the top of the sloping hill, to be a sanctuary of sorts.

Until her contractor had ruined it for her.

She glanced over her shoulder to the wooden screen door. Well, he'd ruined the inside. Maybe big, loud, opinionated Tony Vello with the long, dark hair hanging over his mahogany eyes was the guy to fix it. His city brashness had grated on her, but she couldn't find any lies in what he'd had to say. Including the comment about learning from mistakes.

Her phone buzzed in her pocket. It was Bobby's sister, Julie.

"Hey, Jules." Olivia took a piece of cheddar with a cracker, nibbling on the corner of it.

"Hey, yourself. Bobby said you hired his pal Tony."

She took another bite of cheese before answering. "Technically, I told him to write up a quote first. I'm not giving the guy a blank check after meeting him once."

"Lessons learned, eh?"

Olivia hesitated when Julie used Tony's words. She supposed it was better people think she was improving herself and not making the same mistakes all over again. It still stung.

"Liv?" Julie asked. "You okay? What'd you think

of Tony? Bobby likes him, but I've only met him once. He's got that tall-dark-and-handsome vibe, for sure."

"I'm not interested in his *vibe*, Julie." A lot of women might find Tony's dark good looks and confident swagger attractive, but Olivia wasn't looking for love, just a livable house. "Bobby vouched for his skills, and he seemed to know what he was talking about."

I like a woman who can learn from her mistakes...

"Bobby said he has a ton of experience. He's worked residential construction and now he's with his family's company that builds freakin' skyscrapers in Manhattan."

"If he works for *them*, what's he doing in Gallant Lake picking up remodeling jobs?" Olivia probably should have asked him that question herself. What if he was a problem employee and had been fired? What if he'd stolen, or cut corners, or got in a fight...? She closed her eyes in frustration with herself. Had she just trusted the wrong guy *again*?

"I'm honestly not sure," Julie answered. "Bobby said he was looking for a change of pace. Maybe building skyscrapers isn't all it's cracked up to be."

That was fair. Lord knew, city life wasn't for everyone. It certainly hadn't worked out for Olivia. Ginger came up the steps and plopped dramatically at her feet with a loud sigh. Olivia laughed, then explained why. "This dog is such a drama queen. She just finished her evening perimeter check and came up to tell me all is well."

"Ginger's a good girl," Julie chuckled. "I'm glad you have her, being up there all alone."

"The last thing I am is alone. There's an animal every five feet up here." As she spoke, a group of chickens appeared, pecking away at bugs in the grass. Someday she'd build them a real chicken coop. For now, they were free-range, which meant she had to hunt every morning for eggs.

"How are the new kittens doing?"

"Getting frisky. The gray one managed to climb out of the box today—he must have stood on someone's back to do it. I'm hoping I can keep them relatively contained for another week or so."

The police chief, Dan Adams, had called her after finding six tiny kittens on the side of the road near where their mother had sadly been struck by a car. She'd fostered young kittens before, and knew the drill. The vet had provided kitten formula, and she was feeding them every few hours with nursing bottles with tiny rubber nipples.

"You're a sucker for strays, my friend..." Julie paused. "By the way, I mean that as a *good* thing. You've got a big heart.""Yeah, and an even bigger feed bill, between the horses and all the other critters around here."

"You love it," Julie laughed. "Just take good care of that little orange and white cutie in the litter, because she's mine! I don't know how Fluff will handle it, but hopefully she'll just ignore her the way she does anything else she doesn't like...which is everything." Fluff was Julie's consistently malevolent calico cat.

They ended the call with a promise to meet for lunch the following week.Olivia thought about what Julie said about her big heart being a good thing.

But was it, really? Sometimes she wondered.

She went for a massage the next morning. A regular massage schedule helped keep her damaged muscles flexible and her scarred skin soft and supple.

When she got home, Tony's pickup was parked in front of the barn. He was sitting on the tailgate, scrolling through a tablet. Olivia frowned as she parked her own small blue truck next to his much larger black one.

"Did we have an appointment?"

He set down the tablet and slid to his feet. "No, but I worked up the estimate and came right over because, well… I didn't get your number. If it's not a good time…"

"No, it's fine. Let me just check on Misty and we can go inside." She headed for the barn, her long skirt sweeping around her ankles. She normally wasn't big on surprise visits, but shame on her for not making sure he had her phone number. It was a good thing she was feeling extra mellow after a marvelous massage. Hopefully Tony's estimate wouldn't break the bank, and he'd be able to get started soon.

"Who's Misty?" He was following close behind her, but he came to an abrupt halt when Ginger came dashing off the porch and running their way, barking wildly. She loved seeing new people. "Whoa…"

Olivia kneeled on one knee to greet her dog. "I told you I'd be back, silly girl!" She glanced up at Tony and realized he was frozen in place, staring at Ginger with…well, if not *fear*, then at least a fair amount of concern. "Are you afraid of dogs? Ginger's more likely to knock you over with her clumsiness than attack you, I promise."

"I'm not afraid of dogs…in general." He swept his hair back off his face. "It's just that most dogs I know are guarding construction sites, and they're not clumsy *or* friendly." Ginger decided it was time for Tony to pay attention to her. She turned to him, tongue lolling out and tail waving like a fluffy flag. Tony held out his hand for her to sniff, but he still didn't seem at ease with the dog.

Olivia turned back to the barn. "She must have been off chasing rabbits when you were here before. She'll probably be your shadow if you're working here, so you'll have to get used to her. And to answer your other question, Misty is a horse. Oops…watch your step." She pointed to the four chickens trotting across their path.

Tony muttered something and checked the bottom of his shoe. "What is this, a zoo?"

Olivia rolled her eyes. "No, it's a farm—with farm animals like chickens, dogs, cats and horses." She went into the barn and both horses swung their heads over the stall doors, ears up, looking for a snack. "Meet Scout and Misty." She dropped a flake of hay in each stall, stopping to point at the gelding. "Don't get too close to Scout, the gray one. He was abused and sometimes forgets he doesn't have to bite humans to defend himself anymore."

"Getting too close is *not* going to be a problem." Tony was at least ten feet back from the stalls. "I can handle the idea of friendly dogs, but I do *not* do horses. I don't want to be around any animal that outweighs me by a thousand pounds."

"You don't have to be *stronger* than they are… just smarter." She opened the door to Misty's stall and examined her very round stomach. The skin was stretched tight, and she gave the mare a light finger massage, paying forward the massage *she'd* had earlier. She leaned over to look at Misty's udder, which was unchanged.

"Is she sick?" Tony was still standing back, watching through the open door.

"Not sick. Just very, very pregnant." Olivia stepped out and closed the stall door.

"When is she due?"

"That's the question of the hour. She's my most recent rescue, and we're not sure when she was bred. Her owners thought it was a good idea to pasture her with a stallion, and we have no idea when they...you know." She winked. "The vet and I both think she's due in the next three or four weeks." She walked past him to the barn door. "Let's go over this estimate of yours."

They went into the house and sat at the kitchen table. Ginger had followed them, and flopped down onto the floor at Olivia's feet. Tony used his tablet to go over his projected costs for supplies and labor. It wasn't quite as bad as she'd feared, but...it was a lot. Fortunately, it was still within the budget she'd set aside for the overall project...barely. He thought he could be done in four to six weeks. Longer than she'd hoped, but he'd be working alone most of the time.

"I know you've already paid a chunk of money to the first guy, so I did my best to keep it reasonable." Tony scrolled through a series of screens to the summary page. "Unfortunately, some of the work I'll be doing will be *fixing* what he screwed up."

Olivia frowned. "What about the permits you were worried about?"

"Bobby has a friend in the zoning office. So did Larry, but *his* friend was the kind who'll take a hundred-dollar bill to look the other way. Technically, the permit he got covers everything, but the plans were pretty vague. We promised to have town inspectors come out at each stage of the reno—electrical, plumbing, whatever—and they agreed to leave the existing permits in place. That way everyone's ass is covered, including yours." He stopped, wincing a little. "Sorry if that was too…"

"Graphic? No problem. I like having my ass covered when it comes to business." And everything else, for that matter. But they'd taken the metaphor far enough. "Speaking of business, I work from home, so I'll need to have a functioning workspace with power and Wi-Fi somewhere at all times."

He hesitated, and she could have sworn he started to roll his eyes. "Of course. What do you do?"

"I help people with online marketing, but mostly I design websites." She looked to where she wanted the office to be, on the far side of the staircase. "My computer's set up on a card table upstairs for now, but it's far from ideal. And I need to protect the equipment from too much dust."

"Are you asking me to rebuild this house and *not* create dust?"

Olivia didn't appreciate being patronized. "That is not at all what I said. I'd just like to have the office finished first, so I can close the door for privacy and cleanliness." And hopefully keep the foster kittens corralled.

Tony scowled, staring at his plans as if she'd just ruined everything for him. "I shouldn't drywall anything downstairs until all the upstairs wiring and plumbing is complete, along with the ductwork for heat. I was going to start with plumbing the upstairs bathrooms and work my way out and down from there."

She lifted one shoulder. "If you want to get paid, I

need to be able to work. There's a guest bedroom above where the office is going, so you don't have to worry about plumbing."

Tony looked at her sketches still stacked on the table. "The office is going to be in the old parlor, right?" She nodded as he pulled out the drawing of the office plans. His heavy eyebrows knitted together. "Fine." His tone didn't sound like it was *fine* at all. "I'll get that room as enclosed as possible, but then I need to finish the upstairs before I come back down here. Hopscotching around will make the process longer."

"Are you saying you're already changing your estimate?"

Now just one of his eyebrows rose, along with one corner of his mouth. It suddenly hit her—he really *did* have a tall-dark-and-handsome vibe going on. For all Larry's faults, at least he hadn't been a spicy Italian distraction. Tony shook his head.

"I guess you really *did* learn from your mistakes—you're going to micromanage the sh—I mean…the daylights out of me, aren't you?"

"I can't micromanage a man doing a job I don't know how to do. But I'll be watching the budget very closely."

"Fair enough. As long as we don't have any surprises, doing the office first won't change the cost." He looked around the downstairs again. "Today's Thursday… I'll need tomorrow to get supplies together. I'll start on Monday morning?"

"Fair enough," she agreed, echoing his words. "Monday it is."

They remembered to exchange numbers this time, and he headed out to his truck with Ginger at his heels.

He'd seemed afraid of the dog when he got here, but now he stopped by the truck and scratched Ginger's ears. Olivia smiled. Ginger had that effect on people. Tony had made a comment about her so-called zoo when the chickens appeared, and he hadn't even seen the foster kittens yet. They'd been blessedly asleep in their blanket-covered box in the pantry. Hopefully Tony Vello could handle working with a curious dog and a litter of rowdy kittens looking over his shoulder.

And hopefully *she* could work with a hot Italian contractor in the house for the next six weeks.

Chapter Four

Tony ran power to the last outlet in Olivia's eventual office the following Thursday. He hadn't planned on spending four whole days doing electrical work, but that Larry guy had made a mess of basically everything he'd touched, including the electrical box. So Tony had to start at the box, which he upgraded, then he reran *all* the electrical all over again. He didn't want to start drywalling the office until he knew he wouldn't need to get into those walls to correct anything else.

He'd added three more outlets than she'd requested, figuring if it was going to be an office, she'd need more than the minimum code required. He'd also run the wiring for the spare room above the office, so it would be ready when he got up there. It was a lot of tedious work, but it meant the house was safe, and he could move forward more quickly with the rest of the job. He was just securing the last outlet to the two-by-four stud when he heard familiar footsteps behind him.

"You're still working on outlets?" Olivia sounded perplexed, and maybe a bit annoyed. He'd learned her temperament was nowhere near the ethereal, flower-girl image she gave off with her long hair and flowy dresses.

He'd been kneeling in the corner, and he rocked back onto his heels to look at her. "I told you the problem with the wiring started at the box, so I had to redo everything. Like...*everything*."

"Why couldn't you finish up the office first, like you said you would?" She was in the doorway, such as it was—there was no door. Her arms were folded on her chest. Working here this week was like having a nosy mother-in-law poking at him. *What's that? Why are you doing it that way? Are you sure this is going to work?* He wasn't used to having someone looking over his shoulder all the time.

For someone who said she wouldn't micromanage stuff she knew nothing about, she was doing a really good job of doing exactly that. He pushed up to his feet, stretching his back with a sigh. "This will still be the first room done, but, as I just explained—again—I had to fix the bigger problems first."

Her blue eyes narrowed as she looked around the room, probably looking for something else to interrogate him on. He'd learned she had a bottomless pit of questions to ask—all day, every day. "You added more outlets?"

"I know they weren't on the sketch, but I thought you might—"

"No, I like it." Her arms dropped to her side. "Thank

you." *Whoa*. Did she just say she *liked one of his decisions*? He was about to comment on it when she continued. "But maybe ask first before making any more changes to the plans I sketched."

He ran his hand through his hair, shoving it back behind his ear. At some point, he really was going to need a haircut, before it started brushing his shoulders.

"Olivia, you didn't sketch *plans*. You sketched artwork of your dream rooms. You're going to have to trust me to make those pictures a reality while also making sure the work is done safely. I'm not Larry. And frankly, if you bugged *him* this much, I'm wondering if he just gave up and figured he'd never please you anyway, and stopped caring."

It was a step too far. He had no right to insult the woman. But her constant hovering was getting on his last nerve. And this was supposed to be a job to *relax* those nerves.

Her cheeks went a soft pink, but she didn't back down. "I don't know you, so I have no idea if you're a Larry or not. And frankly, maybe my questions are keeping you from *becoming* a Larry. If you know I'm watching what you're doing, then…maybe you'll stay on your toes and not cheat me."

He bristled, ready to tell her he'd never cheated a client in his life and maybe she should find someone else. But he froze when he saw something small, gray and furry scurrying in the corner of the office. He grabbed for the hammer hanging on his tool belt. He'd always hated rats.

Olivia leaped forward, her arms raised to stop him from pounding this rat, or at least throwing something at it. "No, that's Ross!" She ran for the critter, scooping it up with one hand, before turning on him in fury. "What the hell is *wrong* with you?"

He could see now that she was holding a tiny kitten, not a large rat. It was smoky gray, with wide blue eyes. A lot like Olivia's blue eyes right now, except she was glaring at him like he was a kitten-killing monster. He couldn't blame her. He must have looked like a complete fool, ready to beat a flippin' kitten with a hammer.

"Uh...sorry. I thought it was a rat..." His voice trailed off. No matter what he said, it wouldn't make him look very bright.

Olivia's eyebrows shot up. "You think I have *rats* running around my house?"

"I don't know!" He gestured toward the kitten. "It's gray and furry. You have rats out in the country, don't you? We damn sure have them in the city. Some of the ones I've seen on work sites are as big as full-grown cats. And I don't like them one bit."

"Yeah, I can see that." She nodded at the hammer he was still gripping. "Who do you think you are, *Thor*? Were you really going to throw a hammer at it?"

He eased his white-knuckled grip on the hammer and slid it back into his belt. "Only if I needed to." He looked at the little kitten squirming in her arms and realized he'd lost all chance of leaving this conversation with his dignity intact. Then he saw another ball of fur climbing over the footer and into the office space. "Oh, great, there are more of them."

Olivia turned to see the orange-and-white kitten, with a black one following closely. She laughed, and Tony felt a weird jolt of electricity pulse through his arteries. Her giggles as she tried to scoop up the newly-arrived kittens left him weak-kneed. Which made no sense. For one thing, he didn't like cats. For another, he didn't like giggling farm women with long blond hair and gauzy dresses. But something loosened inside his chest, if only for a moment, as he watched her childlike delight in capturing kittens. She glanced over her shoulder.

"Can I get a little help here? They've clearly figured out how to escape their box. This is when the trouble begins, I'm afraid. Joey, don't bite your brother! Chandler, come back here right this minute!" Her expression when she turned again was less amused and more… irritated. "Are you just going to stand there? I promise they're not *rats*, you big coward."

Did she just call him a coward? He was stuck somewhere between laughter, offense and embarrassment, but he did finally move in to help. She shoved the orange kitten into his hands, then handed him a squirming tiger with four white paws, a white bib and longer fur than the others.

"Take Chandler, Monica and Phoebe, and I'll grab the others." She picked up the three remaining kittens, then stood. She took one look at him and started to giggle again. "They're not going to murder you, I promise."

He was staring down at the three kittens clutched in his hands. None of them wanted to stay there. The orange one was crawling up his T-shirt, tickling his skin with tiny needlelike claws. The gray cat was doing somersaults in his cupped hand, then attempted to launch himself from his fingertips.

"It's not me I'm worried about," he answered. "They seem bent on self-destruction. Where's their mama?"

He'd really like to reunite them with her and get himself out of this situation where kittens were crawling on him.

"No mama, I'm afraid." She seemed to have her three kittens under control against her chest. She nodded toward the door. "I'm fostering them. I didn't realize they were so close to being able to escape their box."

Tony followed her into the kitchen. There was a low plastic tub near the table with towels inside and a small improvised litter box in one corner. He set his kittens inside. Phoebe, the orange one, immediately started wiggling her bottom while staring up at the rim of the tub. Sure enough, she made a leap and caught the edge with her front claws, her back legs pedaling against the side as she tried to get herself over the top.

"This thing will not contain your horde." He looked around. "I've got some flashing I can duct-tape to the sides to make it a little taller, but now that they've learned they can get out, they're going to keep trying." That was one reason he didn't like cats. They were too damn smart. It was creepy. And in this case, as Phoebe pulled herself up by sheer willpower, it was pretty impressive. He caught her and dropped her back into the bin. She didn't hesitate to try jumping again.

"The sooner you can get that flashing, the better," Olivia said. "They're determined little devils."

"Right." He went to his truck and grabbed the roll of six-inch aluminum flashing and some duct tape. It was leftover from the job he'd done at the ski lodge. He went back inside and stopped at the kitchen door.

Olivia was giggling again, trying to keep all six kittens in a box they were no longer interested in inhabiting. As soon as she'd pluck one off the edge, another would jump up. She was kneeling by the box, talking to her foster cats in a voice that was half-scold, half-croon. And one-hundred-percent sexy.

"Oh, no you don't, you little rascal." She held the orange kitten in front of her face. "I know you're an independent little diva, but I can't have you running around loose just yet. If anything happened to you, your new mama, Julie, would be very unhappy with me. You don't want to get me in trouble, do you?" Olivia planted a kiss on top of the mewling kitten's head. "Stop complaining and let me kiss you. You know how much I love you, baby."

Tony thought for a minute that he'd have to turn away to keep from physically embarrassing himself. Her voice. Those words. The pursed lips planting a kiss. Damn if it didn't make his jeans suddenly tight in certain private areas. It took some willpower, but he managed to get himself under control before she sensed his presence and turned with a bright smile.

"There you are—Uncle Tony to the rescue!" The combination of the smile, the laugh and the unguarded softness of her blue eyes. *Hot damn.* He knew she was pretty, but now? Right now she was hotter than any woman he'd ever seen. He blinked, commanding his body once again to stand down. This was ridiculous. The last thing he needed was any kind of relationship, or even a quick fling, with some woman in Gallant Lake. Much less a woman who'd spent most of the week questioning his every move. She was his *client*. Besides, it was the kittens making her act all soft and sweet, not him.

He refocused on why he was here—the work. He

ran the flashing around the top of the box, creasing the corners and taping it all together, then finished things off with a few layers of duct tape around the top edge. "This should help save you from cutting yourself on it, but be careful, anyway." The kittens were already flinging themselves up the sides of the box. "It won't be long before they're big enough to clear this."

"I know." She was sitting on the floor on the opposite side of the box. "There's a pet fostering group in White Plains and the director said she'd loan me a multilevel cage with a top and doors. I'm supposed to pick it up this weekend."

Tony sat on the floor, too. He'd been kneeling far too much this week, and was beginning to feel like an old man. "You foster kittens often? Isn't it hard to give them up?"

She watched the kittens, who seemed to have worn themselves out. One by one, they were curling up together in the corner of the box. "All of my animals are rescues, and yes, fostering them to be rehomed is tough. Giving them up will probably crush me, but I can't keep them all."

"*All* the animals? The horses? And chickens?" He'd never heard of a rescue chicken.

Olivia nodded. "All of them. I grew up on a farm, but I didn't start rescuing until I got this place. Scout, the gray gelding, was the first. He'd been badly abused and beaten. Someone tried to rehabilitate him, but he'd given up and was sending him to auction. A neighbor heard about it and asked if I'd take him since they knew I had the barn and pastures. I was hoping to get a horse, anyway, so I took him on. The chickens came from an old guy down the road. He was selling his place to go live with his granddaughter." She winced as she shifted her weight. He'd seen her do that a few times this week, as if she was in pain from something. "And I have some friends with a maple-syrup stand on the far side of town, and they alerted me to Misty. A neighbor of theirs was looking to get rid of their horses because they couldn't afford them."

"So now *you* have to feed them and take care of them because someone else got in over their heads? That doesn't seem fair. Why should they be *your* problem?" He felt angry on her behalf again. It seemed like Larry wasn't the only person who'd taken advantage of Olivia Carson.

Her eyes went round. "They're not my *problem*. I'm rescuing them from possibly going to be dog food. I consider that an honor."

"Dog food? Does that really happen?" He'd heard that horsemeat was in dog food, of course, but it somehow never connected that it might be from beautiful horses like the ones in Olivia's barn.

Her jaw dropped. "Of course, it happens! When you take a horse to auction, sometimes the first thing they do is walk it onto scales and weigh it, and the bidding starts at whatever the current rate is per pound."

"How would anyone let that happen to their horse?" His family wasn't big on owning animals, large or small. Horses scared him. But the idea of anyone sending a beautiful horse to slaughter turned his stomach.

And Olivia had come to their rescue. She was even more interesting than he'd first thought.

Olivia nodded sympathetically at the look of horror on Tony's face. "It's terrible, but it happens more than you think. Horses are expensive to keep, and times have been tough for some people. Sometimes they just run out of budget and energy, and they can't rehome them."

It was interesting to watch the big, tough, city guy absorbing the realities of country life. He was sitting cross-legged on the kitchen floor across from her, with the kitten box between them. His hair hung over his forehead, and he kept pushing it back. It was something she'd seen him do a lot this week.

She straightened. There was nothing wrong with keeping an eye on her contractor, as long as she focused on the *work* he was doing, and not his dark eyes and the stubble that outlined the straight lines of his jaw. The way his heavy eyebrows lowered when he was concentrating...

He was still scowling. "People shouldn't get animals if they can't take care of them. They should take responsibility and figure something out." He leaned forward to peek into the box. "It shouldn't be up to folks like you to pick up their slack."

All six kittens were now sound asleep. She should have picked up the crate for them last week, but they were barely bumbling about then. She forgot how fast kittens grow.

"I don't mind. I've always loved animals, and it makes me feel good to help them. I grew up on a farm, so this is just normal life for me." Tony was staring at her with an intensity that made her skin twitch. Then he blinked and looked away, scrambling to his feet as if he'd just remembered something he urgently had to do. He cleared his throat roughly.

"I should, uh, get back to it, I guess. I want to start

drywalling in the office on Monday." He looked down at the box, his jaw moving back and forth tightly. "Keep them outta my way, okay? I don't want to step on one by accident, or have them bite into a live wire—"

"Or have you throw something at them?" Olivia was teasing, but Tony had retreated back into Mr. All Business.

"I wouldn't have actually thrown it once I saw what it was." He was almost pouting. Clearly not in the mood for jokes all of a sudden.

She started to stand, and he reached his hand out to help her. She put her hand in his without thinking about it. As soon as their fingers touched, a tingle of… something…traveled up her arm. Tony always seemed so in control, but there was an energy there, pulsing under his skin.

Unfortunately, she'd given him her left hand without thinking, and he gave a pretty firm tug instead of just steadying her. She came to her feet, but couldn't hold back the hiss of pain. She hadn't done her stretches today, and the tight skin of her scars didn't like being pulled on.

"I hurt you." His voice was still gruff, but his eyes showed nothing but concern.

"No, I'm fine."

"You're *not* fine."

She pulled back her shoulders and smiled, ignoring the pinpricks of white-hot pain sliding down her side. It was like ringing a bell—a jolt of pain, then it gradually retreated back to normal.

"It's an old injury. I really am fine."

"What kind of injury?"

She didn't like talking about the night that changed

her life's trajectory. But whether it was the bluntness of his question or the genuine curiosity in his expression, she found herself telling him just a little.

"Car accident. A little over two years ago. I still have some aches and pains from it, and I probably always will. It is what it is, right?"

"And you thought buying a run-down rescue farm alone after that was the best plan?"

Olivia bristled. "This is *not* a run-down farm. You said yourself this house is solid. And the barn is in great shape. I work hard to take good care of this place—"

He held up a hand to stop her. "I shouldn't have described it as run-down. It's just…in the middle of nowhere. And you're doing everything alone as far as I can tell. While recuperating from injuries. Doesn't seem like the brightest…" He caught himself. "It seems like a lot to take on."

"It is a lot. But I love it here, and I won't let my scars keep me from living the life I want."

They stared at each other for a moment. Tony swallowed hard. "Good for you. Not everyone can move on like that."

He dropped his gaze to the floor, and she thought he was going to say more, but he turned away. "I gotta get back to work."

He headed out of the kitchen, his head still down. He'd seemed amazed that she actually wanted to live out here on her own, but *he* was in the middle of nowhere, too. Why *was* Tony in Gallant Lake? He'd been living and working in the city for years. Was he trying to move on from something, too?

Or hiding from it?

Chapter Five

"Hi, Hank! How are ya'?"

Tony was talking to a parrot. Add that to the list of unusual—at least for him—things he'd done since arriving in Gallant Lake. Carrying tiny kittens in his hands. Sitting alone on the front steps of an old farmhouse to admire the morning light with a cup of coffee, like he'd done yesterday at Olivia's. And now he was talking to a parrot in a hardware store.

Hank was a fixture at Nate Thomas's hardware store on Main Street. The bird's custom-built enclosure took up a lot of wall space that could have gone to merchandise, but Nate didn't seem to care.

"Shut up, you jerk!" Hank hollered. Tony chuckled.

"Shut up yourself, bird."

"Sale! Sale! Sale! Sale!" Hank ruffled his turquoise feathers, spreading his wings out to shake them before settling back on the perch. "Buy something, damn it! Buy something, damn it!"

Nate walked up next to Tony, shaking his finger at the bird. "Be nice, Hank."

Hank let out a squawk that sounded a lot like laughter. "Be nice. Be nice. Buy something, damn it!"

Tony laughed. "You've got him earning his keep."

Nate shook his head. "You should have heard him a couple years ago—he started every morning cursing up a streak as blue as his feathers. I hired a kid who thought if the bird was going to yell, he should yell something good for business, and he introduced Hank to marketing." He clapped Tony on the back. "I bet you're here for those drywall screws, right? They just came in."

The hardware store had been in Nate's family for something like five generations. These days he did more business with his antiques than he did with actual hardware, but he could order whatever smaller items local contractors needed. Outside of Hank's floor-to-ceiling enclosure, the place was divided between hardware shelves, antiques for sale and a Gallant Lake history display across the back. Next door, Nate's wife, Brittany, had her real-estate office and more antiques. There was a display of T-shirts with an image of Hank on them near the cage. Apparently he'd become quite the tourist attraction, so it made sense to cash in on that.

Nate set the case of screws on the counter and took Tony's card to cash out. "How's the work coming up at Olivia's place?"

"It's coming, but there's a lot of work left to be done." He'd started hanging drywall in the office yesterday, and today Bobby was coming over to help do the ceiling. "She wants the office done first, which is not the logical progression, but she's the boss."

As much as he'd joked with her about learning her lesson with the first contractor, he was afraid he'd created a monster. He tried to be patient with her questions, but he wasn't used to doing residential work, where homeowners were just...*there*...all the time. With commercial construction, you got your orders and plowed ahead with them. His uncle trusted him to get the job done right.

Until the crane accident changed everything. After that, he'd found himself under close scrutiny, and for good reason. He didn't trust himself, so he couldn't blame his family for not trusting him. And, of course, there was the drinking.

"Yeah," Nate said, "Olivia got ripped off bad by that first guy. Brittany said Liv was really embarrassed by the whole thing. No one even knew how bad it was until Julie dropped in one day and saw the house was gutted. That's when she called in the troops." He looked up at Tony and winked. "That's small-town lingo for summoning the helpers. No one goes through trouble alone in Gallant Lake, not even someone as private as Olivia Carson. The women in this town won't stand for it."

Tony knew all about that. Bobby had introduced him to the local police chief, Dan Adams, on his second day here. Dan hadn't spent much time with him at all before he introduced him to Melanie Brannigan. And Mel took him under her wing.

Turned out Mel had battled substance abuse herself, and Dan told her he had a feeling she might have that in common with Tony. Either that police chief

was a pretty smart guy, or Bobby had shared some of
Tony's background with him. Mel still attended meetings regularly. Even better, she'd started a small support group in Gallant Lake that met at the Methodist
church on Sunday evenings. She gave him a schedule
of other groups nearby.

And then Mel had introduced him to Nora Peyton.
Nora owned the Gallant Brew—the local coffee shop
on Main Street. There was a furnished loft above the
café that just happened to be vacant. And just like that,
he'd found friends, support and a place to live within
three days of arriving in town.

Nate tipped his head to the side. "How are you handling small-town living? Do you miss running around
on those steel girders? I don't know how you do it."

There was a time, not that long ago, when he would
have said those skyscrapers were his whole life. But
now…just the thought of stepping out there with no
walls and no floors made his skin grow tight. He shook
his head and reached for the case of screws. "Nope.
How did Olivia end up on that farm alone, anyway?
Was it her family's place or something?"

"She bought it on her own. Moved here from Maryland. She told Brittany she wanted to go back to her
roots or something like that. I guess she grew up on a
horse farm." He shook his head. "The place was struc-
turally okay, but overgrown and neglected. She went
right to work on it, though, and brought it back to life.
Did most of it herself, too, until she started making
friends here. Even then, she's pretty independent."

"I get that impression, too." He thought about her
cleaning stalls every morning and working in her garden, often in her long cotton dresses and long-sleeved

shirts. She'd rescued the farm, just like she'd rescued all the critters on it. "She was moving pretty slow yesterday—she mentioned having an accident. Was that after she moved here?"

He'd clearly hurt her when he'd helped her up from the kitchen floor last week. He'd hated knowing that, but he hadn't pulled her that hard. Yesterday he'd seen her pause by the staircase. He could tell she was bracing herself for the climb upstairs. He'd asked, but, of course, she'd said she was fine.

Nate's smile faded. "Her car accident happened in Maryland, before she moved here."

"What happened?"

"I don't know much, other than that she doesn't like talking about it." Nate's look was pointed, and Tony got the message. He could relate—he didn't like talking about what happened to him, either.

"I was just curious. Seems like a lot of work to take on for someone who has…limitations."

Nate chuckled softly. "She has that soft look about her, but she's one tough lady. A couple of the guys and I helped fix up the pasture fences, and she was right there with us, hauling posts. She even tried swinging a sledgehammer, but we took it away from her after a few tries. The scars limit how far she can raise her arm, and…" Nate looked up at the ceiling and sighed. "And I've said all I'm going to say, because I'm clearly not cut out for *not* sharing stories."

The word *scars* sent a visceral reaction through Tony. It was one thing to think she might have broken some bones and have some aches and pains, but if she had scars severe enough to limit motion… It unsettled him. Made his chest tight and cold. He'd seen guys hurt. Watched his best friend die. He was torn between wanting to know more about what happened to Olivia, and not wanting to be pulled down that particular memory lane. Or, even worse, pulling *her* down one.

He headed out to his truck and drove back to the farm, trying to push down the shadow of that day on the tenth floor on East 77th Street. The day that had sent him into a drinking binge that nearly killed him. Opening that door might tempt him to reach for alcohol as his painkiller again. He couldn't risk that. Let Olivia keep her past to herself. He'd do the same. It would be best for both of them.

Over two weeks into this project, and Olivia was already *way* past wanting it to be over. She'd known Larry was in the house when he was working, but not in the same way that she knew Tony was in her house. Tony had a pulsing energy, with his quick moves, sharp voice and general impatience with…everything that made the whole house shimmer with his presence.

Right now she was happily working in her new office space, with the new door closed, and Tony was upstairs working on plumbing or…something. He may as well have been right here in the room with her, though. She could hear him mumbling to himself—and occasionally cursing—as he moved around up there. The guy couldn't even have a conversation with *himself* quietly!

But he was getting the job done. Her office, while still unpainted, was looking great. Every edge was finished cleanly, every corner was square—something Larry rarely managed. And Tony had added things, like the extra outlets, that made the finished product even better than she'd anticipated.

She loved her office, and it *should* have made her working hours more efficient, but here she was, sitting and staring into space, thinking about Tony Vello instead of working. She gave herself a mental shake and straightened in her seat. This website for a restaurant over in Kingston had to get done, and had to look good.

Her biggest project to date had been for the Gallant Lake Resort and Spa. That redesign and monthly maintenance had put her on much more secure professional ground as she worked to reestablish her business. The resort owners, Blake and Amanda Randall, had then asked her to create a unique online presence for each of their other four resorts. Now, she was expanding from Gallant Lake with a strong foundation.

She heard a thud from upstairs, followed by a string of expletives, followed by a silence thick with tension. Was he okay? He was probably fine, but she shouldn't just assume that, right? What if he was bleeding up there? If that was the case, he'd probably call for help. Unless he couldn't. She'd just heard him swear a blue streak. But...what if that was with his last breath?

"Tony?" she called out. "Everything okay?"

"*Nothing* in this damn house is even close to being freakin' *okay.*" His voice was cracking with anger. That seemed to be his general happy place—being ticked off. There was a pause. "Never mind. It's fine." His anger seemed to have abated. "Just another easy job that just turned to sh—" His volume had decreased enough that she couldn't hear the rest, but she could guess. He was still muttering up there, and she heard the power drill fire up.

There had been a few times this week where she'd asked him if he was okay after he had a temper tantrum, and each time he'd looked at her in surprise and said he was fine. Apparently he was one of those people whose anger flashed hot, then immediately dissipated. Olivia, on the other hand, held on to frustrations and let herself stew until it was either too late to deal with it, or until she blew up.

Maybe it was better to be like Tony, and just let it out whenever she was the least bit annoyed. But that had to be stressful, too, just in a different way. Between the two of them, she wondered who was more likely to give themselves a heart attack.

A-a-a-a-nd…she was doing it again. Thinking about Tony instead of doing her work. *Get to it, Olivia.* That was the problem with being her own boss—she also had to discipline herself. She slid her chair closer to the desk, with its two giant monitors, and did her best to get her mind back on how to market steamed lobster and Kobi beef. She was just getting into the creative zone when she heard heavy footsteps thumping grumpily down the stairs. She'd learned his walk and knew he was aggravated again.

There was a sharp rap on her office door before it opened. The man had no patience. He stepped in, saw the monitors behind her and grimaced.

"Sorry to interrupt your work." He paused to look into the kitten cage, where they were all blessedly asleep. "I ran into a roadblock that I can't fix without a trip to White Plains in the morning. I texted Nate, but he doesn't have the part I need, so I'm done for the day." He gave a quick grin. "Didn't want you to think I was quitting early without telling you."

She'd accused him of just that the previous week. He'd gone out the front door and hopped into his truck without a word in the middle of the afternoon. Olivia had run out to the porch and called out to ask him where he thought he was going. Turned out he was running to Nate's hardware store to pick up more PVC piping and was coming right back.

They'd had a brief, sharp exchange about her micro-managing him before he'd conceded his communication skills *could* use some work. This was him working on it. She returned his smile.

"I appreciate the heads-up." She looked at her watch. It was after three. *Damn.* She'd promised Mel Brannigan that she'd stop by the Five and Design Boutique to pick up some cotton dresses she'd ordered. "I actually have some errands to run myself. I'll see you in the morning."

She headed into town shortly after Tony left. Mel—a statuesque former model—was locking the shop door when she saw Olivia hurrying up the sidewalk in her direction. Mel let her in and locked the door behind them. She had the dresses wrapped and tied with ribbon.

"I think you'll like this material," she said, pulling out a corner of yellow calico for Olivia to touch. It was brushed, so it was extra soft.

"Oh, that *is* nice. Thanks for thinking of me."

Mel brushed it off. "Not only is it my job, but it's just what we do here. You know how it is in small towns—you grew up in one, right? We take care of each other."

Olivia nodded. She *did* know how it was. She'd avoided being around people when she first moved here. She didn't like their stares, and she didn't like explaining things over and over. But Julie, Amanda and the other women in town were making her see that she didn't have to be a hermit. She may not want her scars on display, but she could find a way to have friends.

She paid for the dresses and left the shop with a promise to join Mel for coffee sometime soon. Across the street from the shop was a small park on the lakeshore. There was a freshly painted white gazebo there. A young mother was sitting on the gazebo steps, watching two small toddlers run around. When one of them got too close to the water's edge, the mom stood, and Olivia could see she was pregnant. The young boy ran back to her.

"My grandsons are nothing but sheer energy." Nora Peyton came out of her coffee shop, the Gallant Brew, and stood next to Olivia. "I don't know how my daughter is going to keep up with three of them, although the newest will be a girl."

Olivia smiled. "I can't believe you're going to a grandmother of *three*, Nora. You're only…"

"I'm forty-six, hon. And Becky and Michael got off to an early start. She had the first when she was eighteen. But they've made it work, God bless 'em." Nora turned to Olivia. "I hear my tenant is doing some work at your place."

It took her a minute to realize Nora was talking about Tony. That's right—he was renting the loft above the coffee shop. "Um…yeah. A *lot* of work. His personality may not be stellar, but he's doing a good job."

"What's wrong with Tony's personality? He has coffee here every morning and seems like a great guy."

She bit her lip. Small towns meant everyone knew everyone, so you had to be careful what you said. "I should have said his personality is…different. Big. Loud."

Nora chuckled. "That I can believe. He's a New York City boy, through and through. But his heart is good."

Olivia thought about the way he'd checked on the kittens. "I think you're right, Nora. I'll try to give him the benefit of the doubt." She looked out at the lake, shimmering in the late sun. "It's so pretty. But I need to get going. I have a website to finish. I'm going to pick up a calzone or something at the Chalet and get back to the farm."

Nora put her hand on Olivia's arm. "Come down some morning around ten and have coffee with us. Not Tony—he's long gone by then. But the ladies of Gallant Lake usually gather in the café after our morning rush to chat about business and families and life. You know everyone—Mel, Mack, Amanda, Brittany, Jade. Sometimes Jillie Danzer joins us. You'd fit right in." She paused, giving her a warm, meaningful look. "We'd love to have you."

It was time she started being part of things in Gallant Lake.

"I might just do that. Thanks."

The Chalet was quiet. It was still early for dinner, and it was a weeknight. She parked and went in, waving at Jesse behind the bar.

"What can I get ya, Liv?"

"I'd love a sausage calzone to go, with extra sauce on the side and a Caesar salad." It had been weeks since she'd brought home a take-out meal. It felt indulgent. Look at her, acting like a confident grown woman.

She sat at the bar, but turned down Jesse's offer of

a drink. She scrolled through her phone while waiting for her food.

"Olivia?" She spun on the barstool to face Tony. He looked just as surprised as she felt.

"Tony…uh, hi." Before either could say more, Jesse came out with two brown paper bags. He sat one in front of Olivia and the other in front of Tony.

"Meatball sub with a side order of chicken wings, right?" Tony nodded, handing over his payment. He glanced at Olivia.

"Looks like we had the same dinner plans—eating take-out alone."

Jesse pointed toward the door. "We've got picnic tables out on the side lawn. You could eat takeout *together* if you want."

He moved down the bar to pour a beer for another customer while Tony and Olivia stared at each other. The only logical thing to do was for them to leave, get in their separate vehicles and go to their separate homes to eat.

Tony looked as if he agreed, and then he spoke. "It's a nice evening out there. I'm game if you are."

"You want to eat together?"

"It's either that or both eat alone. I don't know about you, but I'm getting a little sick of that." He gave her a pointed look. "It's just a meal. And we both paid for our own, so it's not like it's a date or anything."

"Sure. Why not?" She walked toward the door, feeling uncharacteristically bold.

He was the one who suggested it, but he seemed surprised at her acceptance. He stepped ahead and opened the door for her.

Yeah, I'm surprised, too, but here we are.

Chapter Six

Tony kicked himself all the way to the picnic table. This was blurring a line between client and contractor, which meant it was probably a mistake. Their relationship had settled into a professional tidiness once he started showing visible progress with the place. He'd gotten her settled in her office—Bobby and one of his guys had helped relocate her office furniture in there—and they'd given each other space. She still liked to pop her head into a room without warning to make sure he was working. What she didn't realize was that he was always acutely aware of where she was in the house.

Usually, no matter how quiet she tried to be, he heard her distinctive step, with that slight hitch to it. Not always a limp, but not quite a full stride. And sometimes he just…sensed her if she was near. He couldn't describe it, really. It was just a prickling sensation he'd feel skittering across his skin. He'd look up and there she'd be. Watching him with those baby blues and acting like she was surprised he was even there.

Oh, sorry, I was looking for my headset...

No, she was checking up on him. And that was okay, as long as she didn't play twenty questions and interfere with his progress. He understood where her skepticism came from after that last guy had screwed up so many things.

But she seemed to be trusting him more and more. The visits had decreased, and in a weird way, he found he missed them. There was something about the woman that fascinated him—her earth-mother vibe juxtaposed against her hi-tech office setup and internet-based career. At first he'd thought she was a bit of a snob, standoffish and suspicious.

As days went on, though, he started seeing Olivia as more...*contained.* She kept herself in a protective little bubble. She didn't show fear or anything like that. In fact, the opposite. He'd seen her handling the large horses and taking them out to pasture and back into the barn with cool authority. She lived her life, as solitary as it was, with a detachment that felt intentional, but not unfriendly.

Something else that didn't seem unfriendly was the way she was walking in front of him. Yes, the slight limp was there, but it wasn't preventing her hips from swaying nicely back and forth under that dress of hers. Her hair was pulled back into a heavy braid that hung past her shoulders. She was, as usual, wearing a loose-fitting dress over a soft shirt. The dress was long, its blue floral fabric swirling around her ankles.

He forced himself to look away, taking in the trees

behind the restaurant and the area of grass where the tables were. As they reached the table, he could see that they had a nice view of the lake from here, even if they would also be looking at the parking lot. But it wasn't as nice a view as when Olivia scooped up her skirt to sit on the bench seat.

Oh, yeah. This meal was a *big* mistake. But there was no way out of it now. He sat across from her and they both pulled out their meals.

"Oh, wait," he said. "We need something to drink. I'll get it. Water? Lemonade? It won't be as good as yours, of course."

Her eyebrows rose. She'd offered him lemonade several times while he was at the house, and it was delicious. She used actual lemons and sugar, and it was the best lemonade he'd ever had.

"Thanks for the compliment." She smiled. "Water's fine for me." He jogged back inside and grabbed two bottles of water for them. When he sat, she looked over and tipped her head. "You could have bought yourself a beer, Tony."

Tony frowned. He hadn't thought much about needing to navigate refusing alcohol. He cleared his throat.

"Water's fine."

"I'm just saying I wouldn't mind if you had beer or whatever. Feel free."

His counselor had assured him that a lot of people didn't drink for a lot of different reasons, including plain old personal preference. The key was not getting emotional or defensive about it. Be calm, cool and direct.

"I don't drink."

She froze for a moment, then gave a quick smile. "Oh. Okay. I don't really drink, either."

There was a heavy silence when they started eating. It's not like they had anything in common to talk about, other than her house.

Then she started to giggle. Her laugh suited her. Light. Honest. "I didn't even think about you being Italian, from the city, and here we are at a small-town pizza joint. Your parents would be shocked."

"My parents are gone." He said it as gently as he could, not wanting to upset her. "I lost them when I was ten. But my Nonna would approve of this meal—they do a good job here."

Nonna Vello would probably like Olivia. It was a surprising realization. Nonna didn't like many of the women he'd brought home in the past. He tended to go for the flashy, party girls. Bold? Yes. But bold in appearance, fashion and humor than the type of boldness that had led Olivia to buy a damn farm on her own. A farm.

It was unlikely that he'd ever settle down with the good-time gals he'd been dating. It was *far* more unlikely that he'd try to bring a quiet farm woman like Olivia into his hectic family and intense lifestyle in the city. And him moving to some farm was even less likely. Gallant Lake was just a stepping stone that would lead him back to his old life. Eventually.

"Tony? Are you okay?" Olivia's voice broke into his thoughts.

"What? Yeah, why?" He took a bite of his sandwich.

"Uh…because I just asked you twice if you wanted some of my extra sauce and you just stared at your plate without answering."

He straightened, his fork halfway to his mouth. He'd been daydreaming longer than he realized. "Oh. Sorry." He looked at his fork, then raised it and grinned. "This delicious meal mesmerized me."

Olivia rolled her eyes. "Yeah, okay. *Do* you want more sauce?"

"No, thanks."

She reached for her water, and the bottle started to tip. She made a sharp move to catch it, then winced and took a sharp breath.

"From your injury? The accident?"

"Yeah." She pushed a stray strand of hair behind her ear. "It's fine. Gosh, what a beautiful day."

"Car accident, right?"

She leveled a firm gaze at him. "That is *not* dinner conversation."

"Okay." They ate in silence for a moment, then Olivia set down her fork.

"Now *I'm* sorry. That was rude." She sighed. "It's not a forbidden topic or anything. Yes, it was a car accident." Her words came more quickly. "A drunk driver crossed the yellow and hit us head-on. I was in the hospital a long time. It—it changed my life in every way imaginable."

The color had drained from her cheeks. She was only talking about this because he'd asked. She'd said "hit *us*." But she only talked about herself being in the hospital. If someone had died…

Well, he knew exactly how that felt.

"I'm sorry that happened." Time to pivot. "So tell me your favorite thing about Gallant Lake."

Her mouth quirked up into a smile. "Besides the Chalet? Smooth change of subject."

Then she told him things about the town that she loved, including many he hadn't seen or heard of yet. A llama farm. A maple-syrup stand. The greek pastry shop, which Tony had been visiting pretty regularly. The owner, Jade, was a magician in the kitchen. She'd put the best Italian bakers in Little Italy to shame.

Olivia told him how much she enjoyed the lake, which she could see from the farm in the wintertime. There was a hiking trail up Gallant Mountain, but she hadn't tried it. He knew it had to be because of her injuries, but he didn't say a word.

"Honestly," she said, taking a sip from her water. "The best thing about Gallant Lake is the people. They can be annoying as all get out, because they are *relentless*. But their hearts are so damn *good* that it's impossible to be mad at them. They make great friends, and I say that as someone who doesn't make friends easily."

He couldn't let that tidbit slide by. "Why not?"

Olivia only paused for a moment. "I used to have a lot of friends, but that was before the accident. My best friend was killed in the crash, and a lot of the others drifted away while I was in the hospital, including my fiancé. People think tragedy is contagious, I guess." There was a breeze coming up, and it kept blowing her blond hair across her face. She brushed away several strands again. "But enough about me. In fact, too *much* about me. Why are you in Gallant Lake and not on some skyscraper somewhere? Isn't that what you do?"

"It's what my family has done for generations. The Empire State Building? My great-great-grandfather was one of the foremen on that."

Olivia sat back, one eyebrow rising toward her hairline. "I didn't ask about your family. I asked about *you.* You were an ironworker, right? You're not some mobster hiding from the law in small-town America, are you?"

Once again, she'd proven she wasn't as meek as she often appeared. This earth-mother woman was savvy.

"Because all Italians have to be mobsters?" She began to apologize, but he stopped her. "I know you didn't mean it that way. I'm deflecting again." He chewed his lip, knowing it hadn't been easy for her to tell as much of her story as she had. He should at least try to fill in the blanks for her.

"You're not the only one who had...an accident," he said slowly. "It was on the jobsite. People were hurt. A man died."

"I'm so sorry..." She barely breathed the words. Yeah, he was sorry, too. But being sorry didn't change a damn thing. It sure didn't bring Tim Murphy back. He sat straighter in his seat.

"I'll go back to the family business, but I had to, uh, take a break." *To sober up.* He didn't need her worrying that her contractor was a drunk, so he skipped that part of the story. "I found Gallant Lake by complete chance, met Bobby and decided I wanted to do a few residential jobs before I head back. One of my uncles builds houses in New Jersey, so I cut my teeth on work like carpentry and finishing work."

"So why not go build houses with your uncle?"

He huffed a low laugh. "Italians may not all be mobsters, but some of the stereotypes are accurate. Like the ones about loyalty. Doing what your family expects of you." His shoulders sagged in sudden exhaustion. "It's the way it's done. I work for another uncle in the city. Uncle Rocco and Aunt Mary raised me after my parents died"

Tony couldn't imagine the uproar if he ever told Rocco Vello that he was stepping away from Vello Brothers Construction for good. They were barely tolerating his leave of absence over the past few months as he worked to get his life back on track. If it hadn't been Nonna insisting that he go away to get himself straightened out, his uncle probably would have refused to let him go. After all, "real men" didn't need therapy.

When he'd called to say he was staying in a small Catskills town to do some carpentry work, Uncle Rocco almost had a stroke right there on the phone. He'd stammered and stuttered and swore more than once, even though Tony could hear Nonna in the background scolding him. Rocco didn't understand—which was fair, since Tony had such a hard time explaining it, even to himself. How do you tell the macho, tough-talking uncle who raised you that you'd developed a fear so intense it might make *ever* coming back impossible?

"And there he goes again, zoning out right in front of me." Olivia chuckled as she started folding up her serving box and napkins, then stuffed them into the take-out bag. "I think you really *have* had a long day. Go home and get some sleep, Tony."

He blinked, realizing he'd been lost in his thoughts again. Not about her—about himself this time. "Damn. I'm sorry. Hey, thanks for joining me for dinner. It was nice to have company, even if I was sort of a downer."

"We both had sad stories to tell." She smiled as he stood and gathered up his own containers and trash.

"But it was nice. And a better view for me than a construction zone."

He grimaced. "I'm doing my best to give you a home again, Olivia. I'll be a little late in the morning—I've got to make that run to White Plains."

"No problem. I have a doctor's appointment tomorrow morning, anyway, but I'll be home by ten or eleven."

Tony knew where the house key was hidden, so if he got there before her it wasn't a problem. Ginger knew him well enough to let him in with nothing more than a greeting bark and a leap on his chest for petting. He was getting used to the dog supervising his work even more than Olivia did.

"I saw that fancy kitten condo in your office—pretty slick."

"They'll outgrow it before I know it. I usually try to give them an hour or two outside the cage every morning and evening, too. They love playing hide and seek between all the framed-in walls." She sighed with a laugh. "And this week they figured out how to climb the stairs, so they keep me on my toes."

"I saw them upstairs the other morning. My favorite is that gray one... Ross, right? He likes hiding around corners and attacking my legs when I go by. He climbed right up my jeans last week." They were both laughing as they tossed their trash into the outdoor bin. He was taking half a dozen wings home for a late night snack.

A hawk soared overhead, and they stopped to watch it. Actually, Olivia watched it, and he watched Olivia. The warm breeze was still lifting soft strands of hair that had broken free of the braid. Her face was turned upward, and the evening sun made her skin seem as golden as her hair. Gallant Lake sparkled in the background, waves catching the sunlight that was also making the mountains on the far side of the lake glow with a summery haze.

He could get used to this.

What?

No, no, no. Tony Vello didn't do lakeside picnic tables with women in long cotton dresses who had chickens and horses. He didn't talk about kittens. This was not his real life. It was just a stopover. He was going back to New York. He straightened and marched toward his truck, suddenly angry with...something. Everything.

"See you tomorrow." He almost barked the words over his shoulder to Olivia.

"Um...okay. 'Bye." She sounded bemused behind him, and he managed not to look, other than giving a quick wave as he sped out of the lot. Like he was running away.

He'd been doing a lot of that lately.

Olivia let out a groan as she slid into her truck. Dr. Jupta had definitely put her through her paces this morning, testing her flexibility against her milestones from a year ago. She'd made some small gains in most measurements, meaning she was close to full mobility in nearly everything but waist flexibility. The scar tissue kept her from doing twists, especially from left to right. Attempting it left her with burning pain that lingered, threatening to flare again if she made a wrong move.

The doctor was kind, but honest. "Olivia, you're

at an impressive level right now. You've worked hard to get here. But this is probably as good as it's going to get. You're not at a hundred percent, but considering the injuries and the burns, you being in the ninety percentile is damn close to a miracle. You should be proud."

And she *was* proud. She was also frustrated at the idea of settling for anything less than perfect. She leaned back against the headrest and sighed. That driven woman who always had to be the best was her *former* self. The teen who pushed herself to win horse-show championships. The student who was the high-school valedictorian and on the dean's list in college. The woman who found the perfect job, met the perfect guy and planned the perfect wedding. Sure, she'd met with resistance once in a while, but she'd always been a winner.

Until she met a set of circumstances that couldn't be conquered. Twisted metal and flames. A lost friend. A fiancé who wasn't so perfect after all. A canceled wedding. A hospital bed, agonizing surgeries and physical therapy.

As good as it's going to get...

Old Olivia would have lashed out at those words. Defied them. Fought the very idea of not being one hundred percent. But new Olivia had learned to be more pragmatic. She started the drive home, remembering she'd told Tony she'd be there by midmorning.

New Olivia had lost enough in life that she never wanted to go back to her old ways. Sure, she wanted her business to do well and she wanted a comfortable home and a nice life on the farm. But she didn't have the need to be at the *top* anymore. Being at the top was dangerous. It literally meant there was nowhere to go but down. Nothing to do but lose.

She pulled into the farm and went to check the horses before going into the house. It was a bright, sunny day, so she'd put them in the south pasture that morning. Misty was moving normally, but Olivia noticed her udder, or bag, had started to fill a bit. Baby time was getting close—maybe in the next week.

The chickens were scattered around the yard, as usual. Someday she'd get a coop and put up a fence to contain them, but they seemed happy with their freedom. Ginger was sprawled across the top of the porch stairs. Her tail thumped slowly as Oliviaapproached. All the critters were content. It was time for her to find that peace and contentment, too.

She glanced at her watch. She had time for a quick shower, because she'd worked up a stress sweat at her appointment. She should also have time to give the kittens a half hour or so of playtime before Tony arrived. *As good as it's going to get...*

She'd lost a lot, it was true. But she was building a life here, and the life was good. Or, at least, good enough. And probably more than she deserved.

After her shower, she changed into one of her "work dresses." Her scars had been stretched and prodded that morning, so she wanted something soft and loose to wear. Cotton dresses weren't standard farm clothing, except perhaps if she'd been Amish. But they were comfortable, and she wasn't trying to impress anyone. The only person who routinely saw her like this was Tony, and she *definitely* didn't care about impressing him. He was her contractor, and nothing more. Even if they'd had dinner together last night. That was a co-incidence, not a date.

And it was probably a mistake. There was no need to tear down that wall between client and contractor. They'd been functioning just fine in their separate roles.

She went into the office and let the kittens out of their fancy cat-condo cage. They bounded out, wrestling at her feet before they tore off to cause trouble. It was no surprise that Ross was the first to work his way up the stairs. The others followed. He was the chief mischief-maker of the group. There wasn't much they could get in trouble with up there, so she sat to check her emails.

Now that she and Tony had shared a bit of their personal stories over a meal, she was thinking of him differently. He was still loud and pushy and short-tempered—he'd proven that with his odd burst of anger as he abruptly left her standing in the parking lot. But she'd learned that he'd lost something, too. An accident at work. Someone died. He'd been more tight-lipped about his past than *she* normally was, which was saying something. But she *had* opened up to him a little. Even her closest friends in Gallant Lake didn't know every detail. It was weird that grumpy Tony was the person who'd somehow managed to get her talking, however briefly.

She checked her emails—nothing pressing. Then she grabbed a can of sparkling water and looked at her planner. The afternoon was blocked out for finishing a proposed website design for a tour-boat company up north in Lake George. Fifteen minutes passed before she remembered the terrors…er, kittens were still loose upstairs. And it was suspiciously quiet up there.

They were no longer in the hallway, so she went on the hunt. Both guest rooms were empty. Olivia stopped in the second one to admire the work Tony was doing. The outer walls had been insulated and drywalled, and he was supposed to start closing in all the interior walls by next week, as soon as the plumbing was finished in both bathrooms. She heard a small *meow* come from her room, reminding her why she'd come upstairs.

Chandler and Rachel were the only kittens she spotted. She looked around, leaning over to check under the bed, and found Monica. She could still hear soft mewling, so they couldn't be far. But the upstairs was wide open, and she couldn't see them. Then she noticed the loose screen in the open window above the bed. They'd become quick little climbers in the past few days.

She'd seen the corner tear in the screen, but hadn't thought much about it. The nights were cool enough that the bugs weren't too bad yet. There was no way the kittens could have…

Meow. Meow. Meow.

The cries were coming from outside. Her heart fell. Olivia's pillow was right under the window, and they must have figured out a way to jump up to the windowsill, then wriggled through the tear in the screen. Little devils. She kneeled on the bed and looked out onto the porch roof, which was luckily directly below the window. Sure enough, there were the three missing kittens, wandering the roof.

She removed the torn screen and called them, but Phoebe was the only one who came bouncing close enough for Olivia to grab. She set her on the floor.

Ross and Joey were having too much fun exploring this big, new world. The breeze rustled the leaves in the oak tree that shaded the porch. The sound sent the kittens even farther away from the window. They paid absolutely no attention to her calling and *cush-cush-cushing* to them. *Just like a man.*

Cats might have nine lives, but she knew these tiny kittens were unlikely to survive a fall from the edge of the porch roof, which they kept approaching, as if to taunt her. *Fine.* She'd just have to go out there and get them herself. She'd never been afraid of heights, and the porch roof wasn't *that* far off the ground. Maybe fourteen feet? She grimaced as she started to twist herself through the window, hiking her dress up high enough that she could crawl. Not the brightest move when no one was around, but Ross and Joey were bouncing their way farther away again. Waiting wasn't really an option She crawled onto the roof and started calling to them.

Seeing her on her hands and knees got their attention, and Joey started doing a sideways bounce in her direction, being careful to stay just out of reach. They thought she was here to *join* their fun, not spoil it. She was so focused on getting close to them that she barely registered the sound of Tony's truck pulling in. He couldn't do anything from the ground, but hopefully he'd come upstairs and—

"What the *hell* do you think you're doing?" His voice was so sharp that she flinched, her hand sliding a little on the shingles. He was on the lawn, hands on his hips, scowling furiously up at her. "Don't move!" he yelled. "Don't move a muscle, Olivia. I… I'm coming to get you."

She didn't need him to get *her*, but she did need his help with her delinquent kittens. Just then, Joey came within reach and she snatched him up. Startled, he hissed and struggled, but she wasn't about to let go. With one hand clutching the kitten, she turned back to the window, where she was surprised to see Tony looking out.

He was silent, his eyes round and his face pale. It was as if he'd rushed to the window, then become frozen there. He didn't attempt to come out on the roof, so she hobbled closer, ignoring the hissing, biting bit of fluff in her hand. Tony didn't reach out. The only movement she saw was the color draining from his face.

"Take him, Tony." She held out Joey, but Tony just stared. It finally dawned on her what was happening. Tony was terrified. Of *heights*? It was a first-story roof. Joey bit her finger again, his tiny needle teeth sinking in. Her voice sharpened. "Tony! Take the cat!"

He blinked, then reached out. He took Joey, and cursed when he got clawed for his efforts. She started to turn back for Ross, but Tony clutched her arm with his free hand.

"Come back inside. Right now." His voice was raw with fear. Wasn't this guy an *ironworker*? Didn't he build *skyscrapers*? Ross spied a bug moving across the shingles and began to stalk it. Olivia tried to tug her arm free, but Tony held fast.

"Let me go, Tony. I need to get Ross before he gets too close to the edge and falls." She pulled again, but Tony's grip just tightened. She was annoyed, until she looked into his eyes and saw how deep his fear went.

She tried to sound as calm and reassuring as possible. "I promise I won't fall."

"You can't promise that." His eyebrows were low and bunched together, and there was a flicker of anger in his eyes. Not at her, though. It was like he was watching something else play out.

Someone died...

The accident he'd mentioned at dinner. He said it was on a jobsite. He must have seen it happen. Way up in the air above city streets. Her heart softened, aching for whatever it was that he'd seen.

"Tony..." She almost whispered his name. She waited until his eyes met hers and she was sure he was actually seeing her. "It's a porch roof. The pitch isn't that steep. I need to get the last kitten, and I can't do it with you holding my arm like that." His grip on her wrist was almost tight enough to hurt, but he eased it a bit. She kept her voice low and level. "Here, hold the hem of my dress." It would be awkward, but it was clear he wouldn't just let her go. "Ross isn't that far away. I just need to move a foot or two. Hold my dress to keep me from falling."

He frowned as she pried his fingers loose and gave him the hem of her dress, but he nodded. From his expression, there was no doubt in her mind that if the kitten moved farther away, Tony would *not* release her to go after him. She needed to act quickly. She grabbed a twig and moved it back and forth on the shingle to get Ross's attention. It worked. The kitten started stalking the twig and leaped onto it, coming close enough for her to snatch him up close to her chest. God, her hands were shaking. She managed to turn clumsily with the dress pulled tight, and came close enough to hand the last kitten to Tony.

With one move, he took the kitten, released the hem of her dress and grabbed her forearm again.

"Inside." The one-word command had been ground through his clenched teeth. It would have been easier to work her way through the open window with both arms free, but she knew that wasn't happening. With him tugging on her, she ended up tumbling through headfirst, and fell onto her knees on the mattress.

"Let me go, Tony."

He did, then sat on the bed and bowed his head as if he'd just finished a marathon. Ross gave out a worried *meow*. Olivia reached for him. Tony was clutching him more tightly than he realized. He gave up the cat, and she moved off the bed to put all six of the rascals back on the floor. They headed off to look for more trouble. She closed the window, then turned back to sit next to Tony on the bed. They stayed like that for a long time, just sitting quietly side by side.

But it wasn't a peaceful silence. Tension rolled off Tony's tight shoulders like thunder. After a while, she reached out and put her hand on his thigh. His muscles pulsed under her fingers. He was wound so tight she was afraid he'd snap in two.

"The accident you mentioned," she began softly. "You were there, weren't you? You saw it. Was it from a roof or…?"

"We were on the tenth floor."

Her breath froze. "What happened?"

To her surprise, he placed his hand over hers against his leg. As if he needed the connection before he answered.

"A crane load of steel pulled loose. The crane company swore they'd inspected everything that morning." He told the story in a flat voice, removing himself from any emotion. "There wasn't much warning, just a shudder through the building and the sound of steel cables snapping like bullets going off. When the load fell, it hit the tenth floor, where we were working. Took out a section of the floor and some cables got caught up in it. Two guys got hit by the cables. One went over the edge—my best friend, Tim."

Olivia had no words. She could imagine the scene playing out, but *he'd* seen it in real life. The thought was horrific. And far too familiar.

Her best friend, Melissa, had been driving the night of the car accident that put Olivia in a burn unit for months. Olivia had been in the front seat with Missy, while Jerod and Missy's boyfriend had been in back. The first thing Olivia saw when she'd come to, other than flames everywhere, had been Missy's face. She'd watched as the last glow of life left her friend's eyes, leaving nothing but emptiness. That lifeless stare still showed up in nightmares.

Tony took a deep breath, his shoulders rising and falling with it.

"I was just far enough away to escape without injury. At least, without visible injuries. Just terrible memories and, as you've seen, a debilitating fear of heights. Or falling. I don't know. I don't like either one, I guess." He was staring at the floor, his face still void of color. He seemed shaken to the core, and she didn't know how to help him.

"You said you didn't drink, but…would a shot of whiskey help? I have some—"

He shook his head sharply. "I've already searched for answers in a whiskey bottle. They're not there. I spent three weeks in rehab to sober up. I go to meetings, the whole works."

The heat of regret coursed through her. She'd just offered a drink to an alcoholic. "I'm sorry. That was thoughtless. How about some really strong coffee instead?"

"I should get to work…"

"That's up to you, but *I* could use a coffee, so I'm making a pot." She hesitated, realizing her hand was still sandwiched between his hand and his leg. She gently pulled herself free. "I'm sorry that happened to you. And I'm sorry I scared you just now, but I was careful and I'm okay."

She stood and headed to wrangle the kittens, but stopped at the framed-in doorway.

"Last night you said you were going back to work in the city. But how are you going to be able to…?"

He straightened, and she could see him giving himself a mental shake, and maybe a pep talk, too. "As soon as I step back out onto those girders, I'll be right back in my element again. It's where I belong. It's like getting back on the horse again after you get thrown. That's what you do, right?"

"That makes sense."

It didn't make sense at all, actually. Sure, she'd been tossed from horses before. She'd even forced herself back into the saddle afterward. But it was hardly comparable to watching a tragedy play out right in front of you hundreds of feet above the pavement. But there was something in his tone, his determined expression—and his clenched fists—that told her he needed to believe this for now. So she nodded and turned away.

"If you change your mind about coffee, it'll be in the carafe in the kitchen."

She went downstairs, and it was a long time before she heard slow, heavy footsteps above her as he got back to work. She imagined him sitting on her bed before that, staring at the floor, lost in memories. There was far more to Tony Vello than she'd thought.

Far, far more.

Chapter Seven

It was too bad Tony was terrified of heights, because it kept him from escaping the house through the same window Olivia had used. The only other alternative was going downstairs and through the front door, which would mean seeing her again. And after his humiliating panic attack when he saw her on the roof, he wasn't sure he *ever* wanted to face her again.

When he'd stepped out of his truck and saw her on the freaking *roof,* his heart had nearly stopped. All he could think was *save her.* The only problem was she hadn't wanted to be saved at all. She was too busy saving kittens. She'd put herself in danger for *cats.* No wonder his family had been so pet-averse. Pets made people do stupid things.

He'd bolted up the stairs three at a time, then turned into a brick when he got to the window. Yes, it was the porch roof—one story high. But the moment he saw the edge, and how close Olivia was to it, all he could see was the horrified expression on Tim Murphy's face in the split second before he was swept off the tenth floor. They'd both known what was going to happen. There was no way to stop it. There was just that brief moment where time stopped and he and his best friend locked eyes for the very last time.

When Olivia shoved the hissing, biting kitten at Tony, he'd snapped out of it just long enough to grab her arm. That was the one thing he hadn't had time to do ten months ago. He wouldn't let go. Not a chance. He hadn't been happy when she'd exchanged her dress hem for her arm, but she'd been too damn quick for him.

Now she knew that the man who climbed skyscrapers for a living had become terrified of heights. He'd also made it pretty clear that he had a drinking problem.

He cringed. How could he possibly look her in the eye again?

She was probably calling Bobby right now, telling him to get this broken, unstable man out of her home. The honorable thing would be for him to offer to leave. He'd proven how unworthy he was. Why make her have to confront him about it?

But when he got to the bottom of the stairs, her office was empty. She wasn't in the house—he could usually sense her energy when she was there. Had he driven her right off the property?

He heard Ginger barking outside, and then heard Olivia's voice. When Tony stepped onto the porch, he saw her leading the big gray horse toward the barn.

Olivia was laughing and talking to the horse. Or the dog. Or both. Hell, she could be talking to the birds, like some cartoon princess. After all, she'd just risked her neck to save a couple of kittens.

Ginger bounded across the yard and Tony braced for the inevitable leap on his chest. The dog's energy was endless, and it was hard not to like the goofball pup, even if Tony kept insisting he was not a dog person. He pushed Ginger off and scratched her ears.

"Change your mind about coffee?" Olivia called to him. "It's in the kitchen—help yourself." The horse was pulling on the lead, and Olivia scolded him. "Knock it off, Scout. I know you want to get back to your nice clean stall, but you need to do it at my pace."

"Do you need help?" He had no idea what help he could offer in the barn, but he had to offer. Maybe he could redeem at least a piece of his dignity.

"Actually, yeah. I tossed some hay bales down from the loft, but I haven't stacked them. I have a hard time lifting them much higher than my shoulders."

That was an unusual admission of vulnerability. He followed her into the barn, giving the spirited horse's rump a wide berth. She pointed to the bales piled haphazardly at the base of a wooden ladder that went up to the hayloft. Scout was still acting up and taking Olivia's attention, so Tony went to work, stacking the bales on top of the low pile along the wall. He finally realized she hadn't joined him.

One of the stall doors was open. "Olivia?"

"I'm in here," she answered. "Looks like Misty is getting ready to be a mama pretty soon." He walked to the doorway and watched as she ran her fingers down the mare's spine. The golden horse's backside was facing the door, her tail swishing back and forth slowly. Olivia glanced up at him and smiled. "Her bag is filling up with milk and her backside is getting soft, see?" She gently pressed on the muscles on either side of the area under her tail. Tony blinked away. It was a *horse*, but it still seemed weird to stare at her privates.

"This should all be as solid as the rest of her buttocks normally," Olivia explained. "These muscles relax before birth to make it easier for the foal to pass through." She pressed again, and he could see the muscle give way like jelly. The horse lifted a back hoof, but set it back down again without kicking. "There's a good girl, Misty," Olivia cooed. She pushed the horse to the side and gestured for Tony to look under her. "See the udder? It's not *full* full yet, but it's getting there. I think we're within days."

She patted the mare and stepped out of the stall, still smiling. "Thanks for taking care of the hay. Ready for that coffee?"

She hadn't mentioned firing him yet. "Uh...no. Thanks. Look, I just wanted to apologize for earlier..."

Olivia frowned. "For what? Oh, upstairs?" She waved her hand at him. "Don't be silly. Everyone's afraid of something, and you have a valid reason for yours."

Tony paid no attention to her words. He was looking at her arm. There was a ring of faint red circles near her wrist.

"Did I do that?" He reached out and took her forearm as gently as possible, inspecting the bruises more closely. He held her arm in his hand, tracing his fingers on the circles. Bile rose in his throat. He was an animal. A brute. A...

"Tony?" Olivia's voice was a whisper, but they were standing so close that it cut through his thoughts like a knife. "You were protecting me. I get it." Her hand went over his. "It doesn't hurt."

"I never should have grabbed you like that. I had no right…"

"You didn't want me to fall. And let's face it, I *could* have fallen. This little mark is nothing compared to what could have happened." She leaned forward and looked up into his eyes. Did she always smell like fresh air and sunflowers? Why hadn't he noticed that before? Probably because he'd never been this close to her. And her eyes—they were a brilliant blue, just like the sunny sky that morning.

Right now those wide eyes were staring up at him… *into* him somehow. He could almost feel her searching his soul. He shouldn't care, but he found himself hoping she didn't find him wanting in any way. Everything around them seemed to have hushed, as if they were enclosed in a bubble.

"Olivia…" He breathed out her name without thinking. Without any purpose, other than just needing to say it. He raised his free hand and traced his fingers along her jaw, then cupped her cheek. Her eyes went dark. Her nostrils flared and that slightest of movements sent a shock straight through him, arousing him and warming him in a way he'd never felt before. Their faces moved closer to each other, his eyes firmly fixed on her soft pink lips…right there for the taking. Parting in invitation.

"Yo! Tony! Is Liv out there with you?" Bobby's voice, coming from the driveway, drove the two of them apart as if a lightning bolt had struck the ground between them. They hadn't even heard Bobby's truck pull in. Whatever that was, it had been powerful. *Too* powerful. She was his client.

Tony stepped back again. His hippy-dippy flower child client who crawled out on roofs to save orphaned kittens. They couldn't possibly be more different. Clearly, they had chemistry, but that was just physics. Here in the real world, where Bobby Brown was walking over to greet them, he and Olivia had nothing more than a silly little spark. It wasn't anything genuine. Even if he *had* been about to kiss the woman senseless.

Olivia could feel the heat rising in her cheeks. What the hell was *that*? Tony touched her face and the world just…dropped away. What *was* that? The smart thing would have been to put space between them, but *no*. They moved closer, and Tony… He touched her face and made time stop altogether. She had no idea how long they'd stood like that. Seconds? Minutes? Hours? If Bobby hadn't shown up when he did, would they have gone further? Would Tony's hard mouth have fallen on hers? She put her fingers on her lips. What would that have been like?

"Oh, there you are." Bobby walked up, seeming blessedly oblivious to what had just happened. "I knocked on the front door and didn't hear anything, but I saw Tony's truck and I…" His voice faded as he looked between the two of them and frowned. "Is something wrong?" She broke free from the hold of Tony's heated gaze and flashed a smile at Bobby.

"Nothing's wrong at all! I just needed Tony's help stacking hay bales, and now we're headed back to the house. Right, Tony?"

"Uh…yeah. Right." He clapped Bobby on the back. "I played Old MacDonald for a little while, just to see if I had any farmer genes in me. Sadly, I don't think I do."

Bobby looked past him. "I don't know—that haystack looks pretty good to me. You might just be a farmer yet. What do you think, Liv? Is there any hope for him?"

She stared at Tony. "There's always hope, I guess. What brings you by?"

"I promised I'd check in once in a while. I was driving back from Hunter and thought I'd stop in to see the progress." He paused, noting that neither of them had moved. "The progress in the *house*. That big white thing over *there*."

Olivia snapped out of her stupor and walked out of the barn. "Of course! Come on in. I think Tony's working on the bathrooms today, right?" He turned to follow them and nodded.

"Both bathrooms are pretty much plumbed in now." Tony brushed past her and led the way to the house. "The floors are tiled. I just need to recheck all the connections and then we can slide the tubs back into place and install the hardware."

Larry had insisted on placing the tubs and faucets in place before reworking all the plumbing. It hadn't made sense to Olivia at the time, and Tony had agreed, sliding it all back out of the bathrooms so he could work. The one good thing about having no solid walls upstairs was that it was relatively easy to move stuff like that around.

"So if I stop by tomorrow with one of my guys, you'll be ready?"

"Should be, yeah." Tony paused to look back at her. "Does that work for you? If you'd rather I don't—"

He was still embarrassed about the kittens-on-the-roof episode. She stopped him before he could raise any suspicions with Bobby. Judging from that guilty look, he was about to offer to stay away. She did *not* want that, even if it might be the smartest thing for both of them, considering they'd just discovered some shocking chemistry.

"Tomorrow's great," she said quickly. "Does this mean I'll have functioning bathrooms upstairs by the weekend?" She'd been traipsing down to the single bathroom on the main floor to shower for months now, and she hadn't soaked in a tub for ages.

"They won't have four walls," Tony said "but they should have plumbing by then, yes."

Bobby turned to her with a grin when they got to the porch. "I think the plumbing is the last piece upstairs, so maybe we can drywall up there next week. I can free up a couple guys to help Tony."

The two men went upstairs while she headed back to the kitchen. It had been quite a day already. After a half hour or so, Bobby headed out, calling a goodbye to her as he left. Tony stayed upstairs for a while, but she eventually heard his footsteps coming down. She met him at the front door.

"Were you going to leave without saying goodbye?"

His cheeks went ruddy, and a blush was about the cutest thing she'd ever seen on Tony Vello.

"Sorry," he mumbled. "I'm hoping maybe we can both just…forget today ever happened, you know? The thing on the roof. The…whatever that was in the barn. Just…forget it all. Today's an aberration. We'll start with a fresh slate tomorrow." His eyebrows lowered. "I think we should keep things on a professional level. You're the boss. I'm the contractor. I'll do my job and that's all there'll be to it. Okay?"

She didn't want to forget *whatever that was in the barn*. But he was right—life would be less compli- cated if they kept their interactions professional. She didn't want him feeling embarrassed about revealing his personal story to her, so maybe this was the best approach. If they pretended to forget it happened—nei- ther of them was likely to *actually* forget—then he'd feel less vulnerable around her. She had a feeling Tony was a guy who liked to feel in control, especially of his own feelings. So she'd give him the illusion that all was forgotten.

"A clean slate sounds fine, although I still say there was nothing wrong about today." A little weird, maybe, but not wrong. Nothing that *felt* wrong, anyway. "So... good night. And tomorrow will be a new day." She couldn't resist a tease. "I'll try to keep the kittens off the roof."

Tony huffed a soft laugh, then grew more serious. "Remind me to fix that screen tomorrow." He cleared his throat. "We should have the plumbing set tomor- row. Um...good night."

He walked to his truck with his usual long strides. Everywhere he went, he seemed to do it with a pur- pose. With conviction and confidence. She thought of that *whatever* moment that happened in the barn ear- lier. There was no doubt that he'd been thinking about kissing her.

Something hummed low and soft in her belly. She couldn't help wondering if the man kissed with that same level of conviction.

Chapter Eight

Tony ran his finger along the line of caulking behind the master bathtub. He turned the faucet and piping hot water came out, going down the drain just as designed. Well, look at that. He still remembered how to plumb a bathroom. He should call his uncle—Enzo would be proud. Maybe he *should* consider going back to work with Uncle Enzo in Toms River, New Jersey. Building and remodeling expensive homes. No steel girders in sight.

He sat back on his heels. No. He needed to get back to the city. Back to Vello Brothers. Back to his life. He could do it. He *had* to do it. It was the only way to erase the nightmares.

"Oh, wow!" Olivia came in behind him. "Running water! I feel so fancy."

It had been three days since The Day They'd Erased.

Three days of strictly business conversations. She'd stayed in her office most of the time, working on her computer. Bobby and his friend Karl had come yesterday to help get the tubs, toilets and vanities in place, and he'd finished the hookups today.

"Well, I don't know how 'fancy' this open-air design is." He stood and gestured at the framed-in walls. Only the spacious shower stall was fully enclosed. He'd finished the glass block wall the day before. "But you do have two fully functional bathrooms up here now. Next week we'll start drywalling and you'll have privacy, too."

"It looks good, Tony. Thank you."

"It's what you hired me for." He didn't mean to sound brusque, but he wanted to keep the line between them very clear. Employer. Contractor. Nothing more. It was bad enough that every time he tried to sleep, he saw her sapphire eyes going soft and inviting. And every time he woke up, he was hard as a rock. He shook off the memory, afraid of embarrassing himself in front of her. "I'm glad you're pleased with it. You didn't want a jet tub up here?"

The soaking tub she'd selected was long and deep, very contemporary.

"They're such a pain to clean." She wrinkled her nose. "And I hope to put a hot tub outside someday."

"Nice." He started to pick up his tools, done for the day. Standing in her bathroom talking about bathtubs and hot tubs was crossing that line, or at least dancing on it. He was a fool to have led them into it.

"Do you want a glass of lemonade?" Olivia asked. She remembered that he'd said he liked it.

"No, I need to get going. I'm meeting Bobby and

some of the guys at the Chalet tonight for pizza and…" He grimaced. "And not-drinks."

"Have a good time with the guys. I'll be on maternity duty."

It took him a minute to catch up with what she was saying.

"Oh, the horse? Don't you call a veterinarian for that stuff?"

She shook her head and went ahead of him toward the stairs. "I only call the vet if there's trouble, and hopefully there won't be trouble. I think tonight's the night, though. Her udder is full and she's acting distracted and edgy."

"But who's going to help her…you know…"

"Give birth? She shouldn't need any help at all, but I want to be there just in case." She turned at the bottom of the stairs. "My friend Cassie's husband, Nick, gave me a security camera to put in her stall so I can check on her from my phone." She pulled her phone from her pocket and waved it. "Very hi-tech. I'll see you on Monday."

"Earth to Tony?" Bobby snapped his fingers in front of Tony's face. He'd completely zoned out of the conversation in the packed booth at the Chalet. They'd finished their pizzas and the talk had wandered to wives and kids—two things Tony didn't have. Instead, his mind kept skipping back to the thought of Olivia enjoying that big new bathtub of hers.

That particular thought had started right after their "bathing" conversation, and distracted him so much he'd left his phone sitting on the bathroom vanity at the farm. He'd have to stop by in the morning to get it.

"Sorry, man." He took a sip of his soda. Everyone else had started with beer, but no one had said a word about his choice. Bobby and Blake Randall had switched to soda themselves after dinner, as they were designated drivers. "It's been a long week, and I just realized I left my damn phone at Olivia's place. What'd I miss?"

"Blake was talking about the big charity golf tournament at the resort in a couple months. Do you golf?"

"I *have* golfed, but it's not really my game. I'm more of a soccer and rugby guy."

"So a contact-sport fan, eh? I'll try not to be offended." Quinn Walker was the golf pro at the Gallant Lake Resort and Spa, which Blake Randall owned and Nick West worked at. It was easily the largest employer in the area. "I'm a rugby fan, too. There's an amateur league over in Hudson that I've been meaning to check out, if you're interested."

"I won't be here long enough to get in any leagues. I have a job to get back to in New York." His uncle— the *ironworker* uncle, his boss—had called yesterday, inquiring on Tony's timetable for coming back to work. He'd told Uncle Rocco he still had a few weeks to go on the remodel job, and then he'd be back.

He'd promised.

"You're doing a great job with Olivia's place," Bobby said. "If you decide you want to stick around town, we should talk."

Tony shook his head again. "Thanks, but no thanks. I'm not a small-town kind of guy." That comment brought laughter from around the table. He sat back in his seat. "What's so funny?"

Shane Brannigan, a sports agent married to Tony's

new sobriety partner, Mel, was still laughing. "Those words sound very familiar to a couple of us. Right, Trent?"

Trent Michaels was an attorney, and Tony knew he was relatively new to town. He was married to Jade, the owner of the Greek bakery. He'd heard the story about their January wedding, when Jade had gone into labor with their daughter.

"Hey," Trent protested. "Just because I lived in Denver doesn't mean I was a city boy. I'm an environmentalist, remember?"

"You still didn't see yourself settling in a place like Gallant Lake," Blake Randall pointed out. "And let's be fair, neither did I when I got here. This place has a way of growing on you." He winked at Tony. "We'll believe you're leaving when you actually go. Until then, you're one of us."

A few months ago, he'd have rolled his eyes at the idea. He loved New York City. The crowds. The energy. The idea of hanging out at a townie pizza joint with a bunch of small-town guys talking about their families would have sounded like a mind-numbingly boring night to be avoided at all costs. Instead, he was enjoying himself. They were dead wrong about him staying in Gallant Lake, but he was definitely making some friends here.

"I appreciate that, but trust me, you'll see me leave eventually. Country life is not for me."

Bobby gave a soft whistle. "That's not how it looked the other day when I saw you and Olivia in the barn together. You'd just finished stacking hay, remember? And the two of you were standing mighty close…"

The other men—Blake, Quinn, Trent, Shane and

Nick—leaned in and let out an exaggerated *ooohhh* in unison. Tony didn't think Bobby had seen that much—Tony had had his back to the door—but he'd apparently seen enough.

"Jesus," Tony muttered. "This town has turned you men into a bunch of gossiping old biddies. She asked for help with the hay, and I helped. We were talking about her pregnant horse."

And thinking very much about kissing each other...

Bobby held up his hands with a laugh. "I'm just saying...it looked like a pretty intimate conversation." He noted Tony's warning glare and dropped his hands. "But I could be completely wrong."

"That horse hasn't foaled yet?" Nick West asked. "Cassie said it was due last week."

"They don't know the exact due date, but Olivia thinks it will be tonight. I guess things are...progressing. Whatever that means."

"Can she handle that alone?" Blake asked. "I mean, she has limitations..."

Tony thought about her scrambling onto the roof and couldn't help chuckling. "She seems pretty fearless."

"Being fearless and being smart are two different things," Blake answered. "My Amanda nearly got herself killed being fearless. She was trying to save our son, but still..."

Quinn nudged Tony's shoulder, perhaps noticing the way he'd gone still. "Julie says Olivia knows her limits and has a lot of common sense. She grew up on a horse farm. She'll be fine."

The conversation drifted to Trent and Jade's plans for a large reception to celebrate their wedding. The actual ceremony had been small and rushed, due to her pregnancy. They were going to have a more formal reception at the resort near the end of August. Again, Tony's thoughts drifted.

Only this time, he wasn't thinking of Olivia in the tub. He was thinking of her alone in the barn with a large horse in labor. He slid out of the booth and said his goodbyes to the men—his new friends. He *could* wait to go get his phone. He wasn't one of those guys who played video games all night or anything. But he was going to drive up to the farm and get it now. She said she'd be up. Maybe the foal had been born already and everything was fine. If not, he could…what? Help? Highly unlikely.

He drove up the hill toward the farm, anyway.

He needed to be sure she was okay.

Chapter Nine

Olivia was sitting in the barn, staring at the live video feed on her phone. She didn't want to disturb Misty until it was absolutely necessary, but the mare was clearly heading into hard labor. The horse paced in circles in the dimly lit stall, stopping occasionally to lift her tail and bite at her sides, reacting to contractions.

She hadn't received much information from the prior owners. They'd been vague and defensive about any of the questions Olivia and the veterinarian tried to ask. There was so much she didn't know.

Was this Misty's first foal, or had she given birth before? Was she a good broodmare or a testy one? They hadn't shared anything about the sire, other than she'd been pastured with a friend's quarter-horse stud,and they'd let "nature take its course." Would the foal be larger than usual? Smaller? She shifted her weight on the hay-bale seat she'd made for herself. Ginger looked up from her nap at her feet, then dropped her head down with a sigh. She seemed to be settling in for a long night, too.

Misty was back to pacing again, and she heard her give a low grunting sound. She was clearly uncomfortable. Olivia tiptoed to the stall door and peeked in. The horse didn't acknowledge her presence—just kept pacing, her tail now staying high. The foal was moving into the birth canal.

"Olivia?"

She'd been concentrating so much on the horse that Tony's low voice made her give a little cry. Misty's ears went flat back against her head at the noise. Olivia spun, her hand on her chest. She quickly shushed Tony. He'd been standing in the doorway of the barn, but now he walked toward her, speaking in a near whisper.

"Sorry, I saw the light and thought the baby might be here."

"What are you doing here?" she hissed back. "You scared ten years off my life!" Then she remembered. "Oh, I bet you're here for your phone. It's in the house—" The stall shook when Misty laid down. "Whoops…here we go…"

Luckily the mare had left her backside facing the stall door, which Olivia quietly unlatched. She kneeled to get a better view.

"Holy…" Tony kneeled beside her. "Is she giving birth?"

Olivia pointed. "Yup. See the little hooves inside that sack?"

They were still whispering, but Misty didn't look like she would have cared if they were singing. Her eyes had a distant look, and she pressed her muzzle to the floor as another wave of contractions went through her body. The front legs were out now, with the foal's head nestled against them inside the placenta, which was beginning to tear. Another push and the foal's shoulders were out. Soaking wet, the dark brown baby's nostrils were moving, taking shaky breaths. Tony's hand rested on Olivia's back.

"That's incredible," he said quietly. "It's breathing already and it's still not fully born."

Olivia nodded. "Most hooved mammals are up and ready to run in no time. In the wild, they'd be dead if they weren't." She raised her voice a bit. "Come on, Misty, don't quit yet. One more big push, máma."

As if understanding, the mare grunted and the rest of the foal came out, along with a rush of amniotic fluid and tissue. The foal lifted its head shakily, blinking and sneezing. Not a palomino like mom, but a chestnut with a white star on its forehead and, from the looks of it, four high white stockings. The foal would be flashy. Misty's eyes were closed.

"Good job, mama. Now take care of your baby. Come on." She wasn't happy that Misty wasn't already licking her foal dry. That's what stimulated the foal to keep moving and get to its feet. That meant this was probably her first. "Hand me those towels." She pointed to a box near the stall door with a pile of old, but freshly washed, bath towels in it. He handed her a few, and she moved into the stall on her knees, keeping a close eye on Misty. She was glad she'd opted for jeans tonight. "It's okay, mama. We're just going to dry off your baby while you rest." She started to vigorously, but carefully, rub the foal's neck and shoulders. From this angle she could see it was a colt. She glanced over her shoulder to Tony. "It's a boy. He looks healthy... Whoa—"

Misty heaved herself up onto her feet, then expelled the rest of the placenta before walking to the far corner. Olivia didn't like the mare's attitude, but right now something else was more pressing.

"Get a shovel and pick that up and put it in the wheelbarrow." She nodded at the placenta, tugging the colt forward and out of the warm, wet home he'd lived in for the past eleven months. "We need to make sure it's all there."

"Uh..." Tony sounded hesitant. "Okay, now you have me at a loss. Pick up *what* and put it *where*?"

Olivia was still watching Misty, who was watching the colt, who was already struggling to get his spindly legs under himself. She kept rubbing the colt, trying to get blood flowing to those new muscles.

"The placenta!" She barked the word, then took a breath and lowered her voice. The poor city guy had never experienced anything like this before. "Pick it up with the shovel before she steps on it or the baby tears it any more. I'll check it later. Sometimes the mare retains a portion and that is very bad news. It can cause an infection." She looked back at him. *Oh, boy.* His complexion was a little green. "If you're going to throw up, go do it outside. Then come back and do what I asked. Please."

He swallowed hard. "I'm good. I'll take care of it." He stood, and Misty's ears went flat back again. The horse was not happy. Olivia held one hand behind her.

"Move slow and steady. She's spooked and I don't want it to get worse."

"Spooked? By her own baby?" His voice was low and steady—he didn't sound as disbelieving as the questions implied. He brought the wheelbarrow to the stall doorway, then stepped inside with the shovel.

"It's rare, but it happens." She stood, and between her and Tony, they got the placenta into the wheelbarrow. She'd check it later. For now, she needed to keep an eye on Misty and her newborn. Tony moved the wheelbarrow out of the way and stood at the stall entrance.

"Is he trying to *stand* already? It's only been, what... ten minutes?"

"More like twenty. Takes a while for the tendons to tighten up enough to hold his weight. Give him another twenty and he'll be closer to standing." She stepped back to Tony's side, still watching Misty. "She looks freaked out, doesn't she?"

Tony huffed a soft laugh. "What I know about horses would fit in a teacup with room to spare, but, yeah... her eyes are pretty wide. She's not going to reject him, is she?"

"God, I hope not," Olivia muttered. "That's rare with horses. But I don't want to assume anything yet. This might be her first foal." She continued, basically talking to herself. "Think about it. She felt funny, then had wicked cramps, then laid down and this wiggly thing suddenly appeared in her stall. She didn't give herself a lot of time to sniff him or lick him before she stood up, and that's usually when they bond. So she's probably feeling conflicted right now—fascinated by the baby and afraid of it, too. Not enough to harm it... I hope."

"She doesn't look angry, just...cautious," Tony agreed. "So now what?"

"Now we wait." She dragged a nearby hay bale to the doorway, then sat on it, patting the other end. "We sit and watch and wait."

Tony sat next to her. She hadn't anticipated how much space the man occupied. Their shoulders and hips were brushing. He flinched as the colt made an effort to stand and splayed face-first into the sawdust. "Shouldn't we help him stand up? He's going to hurt himself."

She chuckled. "He'll be okay. Their bones are so soft at birth that they're very bouncy. He needs to stand on his own in order to strengthen those tendons." The colt made another attempt, falling over backward this time, his little legs kicking wildly before he righted himself. He took a few ragged breaths, then tried again. And again. The whole time, Misty just watched.

"Damn it," Tony muttered as the foal stumbled again, "he's having too much trouble. Something's wrong." But then, more by accident than anything, the colt ended up on his feet, swaying precariously, but... standing. "Way to go, baby horse!" Tony laughed. He flashed Olivia a grin so wide that her breath caught in her throat. The little-boy grin seemed so out of place on his usually grumpy face that all she could do was stare for a moment. Finally, she blinked and responded.

"I told you he could do it. Now we need to get him to nurse."

Misty's eyes were even wider now that the colt was teetering around on four legs. She blew out a warning huff, but didn't make a move toward him. Olivia and Tony stood slowly, and Olivia reached for the leather halter hanging on the door. She handed it to Tony.

"Put this on and hold her, okay?" He stared at the

halter as if she'd just handed him a rattlesnake. She grabbed it back. "Fine. Don't let our little mister get out. I'll put the halter on Misty, since you'd probably put it on upside down, but then *you* will have to hold her still."

"I thought you said you had to outwit a horse because you couldn't outpower it?"

"Yes, and in *this* case—" she stepped up to slide the halter over Misty's head "—you're going to convince her that you're strong enough to hold her." She snapped the lead onto the halter and gestured for him to come in. "Little mister has to nurse as soon as possible. His first drink is when he gets the important stuff, like colostrum and antibodies. I'm going to nudge him in the right direction, and you're going to make sure she stands there."

Tony was still pale, but his jaw tightened and he nodded as he wrapped his hand around Misty's halter. "I've got her."

Unfortunately, he did *not* have her. Olivia guided the unsteady foal toward the mare's udder, and Misty surged forward to keep him from touching her. She nearly ran Tony over in the process, but he managed to stay on his feet. Olivia made sure the mare was up against the wall again, then looked at Tony.

"You can hold her. Stand firm, look her straight in the eye and pretend you're a redwood."

"A redwood…"

The colt took a few hurried steps in Olivia's direction, and she hooked her arm around his chest. She blew a strand of hair from her face.

"Just keep her distracted and still. Give me the chance to get him in for a drink, okay?"

Tony's jaw worked again as he stared at her, then the mare, then the foal wriggling in her arms. "Okay. I've got her this time. Let's get this little guy his first meal."

There was something about his determination, and the fact that he was doing it for a newborn colt... It was adorable. And hot. She blinked away from his dark eyes. Of all the things she needed to be thinking about at the moment, Tony Vello's hotness was *not* one of them.

Tony watched Olivia after she turned away, not sure what that little flash was that he'd seen in her eyes. Was that a flicker of...heat? *Now?* Before he could question it, the giant horse he was supposed to be holding shoved into him, trying to walk through him like she did the last time. He planted his feet and tightened his grip on her, staring into her face, and said, "It ain't happening, Misty."

He said it like he meant it, even though there was no way he was stopping fifteen hundred pounds of horse if she really wanted to bolt. But she didn't. Misty was tense, her head high, but she stood there for now, her eyes rolled back to watch the woman holding her foal.

He hadn't seen her wearing jeans very often, but it made sense she was wearing them tonight. They were loose-fitting, but still showed plenty of denim-clad curves. Her blue knit top had long sleeves, even though it was a warm night. Her hair was pulled back in a braid. There was a smudge of dirt on her cheek. They were both dirty and sweaty. And Olivia looked hot—the sexy kind of hot.

She was playing an intimidation game with Misty, too. She'd propped her hip against the horse's side, holding her against the wall as she nudged the foal forward. The little guy was trying to latch his mouth on everything—Olivia's hand, Misty's leg. He was hungry! Finally, he took a step under his mother and found the right target.

And it was…magical. The *instant* the foal's muzzle touched her and he latched on, Misty's entire composure changed. It was as if someone melted her into mellowness, like popping a balloon. Her head dropped, her eyes softened and her body eased. Olivia noticed it, too. She turned to Tony with a big smile of relief.

"*There's* her maternal hormones kicking in." She stepped back and the foal moved tight to the mare and kept drinking, his little tail whisking around like a corkscrew. Olivia gestured for him to loosen his hold, and Misty turned to sniff and nuzzle the foal's backside. A soft chortling sound rose from her throat. And just like that, they bonded. Olivia unbuckled the halter from Misty's head and gave her a pat on the neck. "You've got this, mama."

They stepped out of the stall and closed the door, both leaning on it to admire the view. A big golden mare and a tiny chestnut foal in the soft barn light. Tony let out a long breath.

"Well, *that* was interesting."

Olivia laughed. "Understatement. Usually nature takes care of itself, but she needed a little help connecting the dots and understanding little mister was her responsibility. The instant he started to nurse, though, she got it." She turned, looking up at him with warmth in her blue-gray eyes. "I'm glad you were here. Thank you."

"I can't believe I'm saying this, but I'm glad, too. What now?"

"Now I keep an eye on them until the little guy takes his first poop, which should happen any…" She giggled. "Well, there he goes. Looks like all systems are functioning fine. Let me top off Misty's water bucket and give her some hay, and then we can go inside."

She did her tasks, then checked the gross thing he'd helped her put in the wheelbarrow. She moved it around with a stick and frowned while she inspected it, finally giving a satisfied nod. "Looks like she passed it all. I'll bury it tomorrow."

"Bury it? What is that, some superstition or…?"

She put her hand on her hip. "Are you suggesting I'm some kind of witch? What else do you suggest I do with it, throw it in the trash? It'll decompose, Tony. Welcome to life on a farm."

He followed her out of the barn and into the darkness, half laughing and half shouting as he tried to process what had happened over the past hour or so. "Tonight was more like life in another dimension of the time-space continuum for me! Babies being born, horses trying to trample me, equine afterbirth in wheelbarrows. It's all been…a lot."

She turned when she got to the porch steps, lit softly by lights on either side of the front door. She put her hand on his arm. "Steady there, city boy. Let's wash up and have a seat on the porch to decompress a little." She winked. "I still have that pitcher of lemonade."

A whiskey sounded better, but that was a no-go. He needed to get through his days without a crutch. Olivia cleaned up in the downstairs bathroom while he used the kitchen sink. She shooed him out the front door while she got their drinks, saying something about him needing the fresh air.

He inspected the wide porch swing before sitting on it. It looked and felt secure. Clearly, Larry hadn't had anything to do with it, so it was probably safe. It was easily six feet long, and deep. It was loaded with pillows over the seat cushion.

Olivia came back outside, pushing the wooden screen door open with her hip because her hands were full. Tony went to jump up, but she shook her head at him.

"I've got it. Just grab that little table there." He slid the cedar table out from the corner and she set a tray on it. Crackers, cheese, dip, napkins, cups and a pitcher of lemonade hanging from her fingers under the tray. Then she surprised him by joining him on the swing.

"I saw you looking up. The home inspector told me this thing is bolted directly through a four-by-four beam. He was able to take a look up there because there was a section of ceiling panel missing. According to him, the swing will fall apart long before the chains give out. It's my favorite perch." She filled their glasses.

He knew this was her favorite place because he'd seen her out here many times. When he arrived in the mornings, she was often on the swing with a cup of coffee. And she'd come out during the day to just sit for a few minutes, as if clearing her head in the fresh air. Of course, it was nighttime now so there wasn't much of a view, other than the stars glimmering above and a crescent moon hanging just over the tree line. It was a nice spot.

Having Olivia sitting next to him made it nicer.

"You're wearing jeans." He closed his eyes in frustration. *Smooth move.* Of all the things he could have said, those were the genius words that came out of his mouth. Olivia's eyebrows rose.

"You're very observant," she answered dryly.

"I just meant…you wear dresses a lot, even in the barn. And, you know, there's nothing wrong with that… I guess…" He just sounded smoother and smoother, didn't he? He cleared his throat. "But the jeans look good…" He rolled his head back with a groan. "I'm just going to stop talking now."

She sipped her drink, then made a sandwich of crackers surrounding a slice of cheddar. After eating that, she sat back and dabbed her lips with her napkin. She missed a crumb at the corner of her mouth, and before he knew what he was doing, he leaned forward and brushed it away with his thumb. Her lips parted, and it was all he could do not to lean even closer. She gave him a slanted grin.

"And is *this* what you're doing instead of talking?" She paused, her smile fading. "What *are* you doing, exactly? Besides providing fashion commentary."

Tony moved back, but not much. He was still close enough to smell her fresh scent, like sunshine and hay. He sat back. He was not a man attracted to sunshine *or* hay.

"Come on, you don't wear jeans much. And I noticed. That's all."

She reached for another cracker and piece of cheese, brushing against his arm as she did. "That's fair. Jeans were more practical for assisting with a birth—I figured I'd be on my knees at some point." *Did she just blush?* "But dresses are generally more comfortable when I can get away with it. Less constricting on my… scars."

His sudden horniness faded quickly. Not because she was scarred under those clothes, but because he'd forgotten. He settled back in his seat.

"Are you in pain now? Did tonight aggravate anything?"

She rolled her eyes. "Sorry I mentioned it. I'm fine. The scars pull sometimes and can be really itchy. Honestly, I've just gotten used to the looser clothing. Probably not the best look if I ever jump back in the dating pool, but that's not happening anytime soon, so I'm not looking to impress anyone."

"You don't have to work at it, believe me."

"Seriously?" Her laughter bubbled up again. "You just watched me wash off the grime of a horse's birth and you're trying to schmooze me with compliments?"

"I'm not schmoozing—I'm telling the truth. You look good to me no matter what you're doing. No matter what you're wearing." He slid across the seat so their thighs were touching. She didn't lean away. If anything, she straightened, moving to meet him. The silver flecks in her eyes were sparkling against a blue background.

Was it the late hour? Was it the adrenaline-pumping event of the foal's birth? Or was it just… Olivia? Something was pushing him closer to her. Her eyes fell to his mouth, and he was pretty sure she wanted the same thing she did. But still…never assume.

"I'd really like to kiss you right now." His voice cracked with need.

Her nostrils flared just enough for him to notice. "I think you should follow your heart, Tony."

So he did. Slowly. Gently. His lips brushed against hers…once, twice. Before he could press closer, she did it for him, sliding her arm around his neck and pulling herself up to tighten their connection. Her lips were soft under his, and parted at the touch of his tongue. And then he was inside her mouth—testing, tasting. His hand slid up her side and around to the back of her head, holding her against him. He went deeper, until he lost himself in the kiss.

He lost track of time and place, completely focused on the taste of her and the feel of her in his arms. If lightning had struck the tree ten feet from the porch, he wouldn't have cared. Wouldn't have stopped kissing Olivia. Because kissing Olivia was giving him life. Her body was pressed against his, and he vaguely realized it was because his other arm was around her waist, pulling her in.

He could feel every warm curve of her. She let out a soft moan and he felt that, too. He felt it shoot straight into his veins like a drug, filling his body with intoxicating fire. There was another sound—a growl—and he had no idea if she'd made the sound or if he had. All he knew was that she was straddling him now, and he was hard against her. And that was the reality that finally made him pull away with a groan.

"Goddamn, woman." He saw desire burning in her eyes and dropped his head to her shoulder, unable to speak while looking at her. She wanted more. So did he. But this was nuts. She was his client. They had absolutely nothing in common. Whatever they might have together physically would obviously be amazing after that kiss, but…she deserved more than some fling. "We can't do this. It's a mistake. I'm leaving in a few weeks, and…"

And I don't want to hurt you... The thought made him feel sick all over again.

Olivia's fingers moved slowly through his hair, massaging his scalp and calming his racing heart.

"I know," she whispered, her breath brushing his ear. "You're right. It would be a mistake."

He should be glad she agreed. They were on the same page. The two of them together spelled disaster. It was settled. But hearing her repeat his words felt like a cut from a dull and rusty blade. Her fingers tightened in his hair and she gently tugged his head up so she could look straight into… Straight into his soul. He felt her in there, poking around the brightest and darkest parts of his mind—seeing everything and not flinching from any of it.

"But," she started. "If this is all we have—this kiss—then…thank you." Her eyes held him frozen in place. She was still straddling his legs. Still clutching his hair. Still in complete control. "I haven't felt like that in…well, in a long time. I didn't think I'd ever feel…" She frowned, struggling for words. "So much like a woman again. Desired. Sexy. You unlocked a part of me I thought was gone forever." She leaned forward, kissing him softly before smiling against his lips. "You're a really good kisser, Tony Vello."

He started to laugh. She thought *he* was a good kisser after she'd just disassembled him and rebuilt him again with her mouth? He gently moved her to his side, willing his body to stand down.

"Woman, that was all you. I was just along for the heart-stopping ride. That was a gold-medal kiss. The kind of kiss that will become a legend in our memories. The kind of kiss that would only lead to a mess if we went further, but don't ever have any doubts about how desirable and sexy you are."

He sat up straight and cleared his throat. He glanced at his watch and shook his head. "It's after midnight. I should go."

He didn't move. All he could think about was easing her down on the swing and crawling on top of her. Touching her. Kissing her. Making love to her.

He shot to his feet then. *Damn it!*

Olivia stood, too, absently brushing the front of her shirt and stepping out of his way. He moved slowly past her. She didn't say another word until he was at the top of the porch stairs.

"Tony…" God, he loved the sound of his name on her lips. She reached out and took his hand. "Can you tell me, remind me…exactly why we're a mistake again?"

Chapter Ten

Olivia knew he was right. Of course, he was right. But for the life of her, she couldn't define *why* it was such a mistake. All she could think about was the way his kiss lit her up. Made her want him. Made her *need* him.

Tony turned, cupping her cheek in one rough hand. "We clearly have some wild chemistry going on here. But honey, you and I are bad news. For one thing, I'm leaving when the house is done, so there's no point in... more. You deserve a man who has a chance of offering a future, and I'm not that guy. I've *never* been that guy, but in this case..." He paused. "It would just be sex between two people with nothing in common other than the ability to turn each other on. Nothing more."

A flare of anger shot through her. "I know exactly what I deserve from life, Tony. And so far, I haven't gotten it. Life's funny that way. But if we decide, as two mature, consenting adults, that we want a temporary affair, no strings attached…then why can't we do that?"

His eyes were already nearly black with desire. He leaned in and kissed her. It was a good-night kiss. She knew it from the sadness in his touch. The regret in his soft sigh as he ended it and stepped away from her, holding her fingertips in his hands between them.

"One of us needs to be the responsible one, and I'm as surprised as anyone that it's me. A lot has happened tonight. We're both coming off an adrenaline high. We're tired. We're wired. We're on a romantic porch in the moonlight and we shouldn't trust moonlit decisions." He lifted her hands and kissed her knuckles softly. "Let's take a beat and think before we decide anything, okay? The weekend is here, so we won't be in each other's space for a couple days. I think that's a good thing. I don't want to hurt you."

"Then *don't* hurt me. And don't *avoid* me. We can move past this." She had no idea how, but there had to be a way. "If you decide in the daylight that you still think that kiss was a mistake, then we can set it aside and still have the same relationship, right? You show up and work on my house, I pay you and nothing has to be weird."

He gave her fingers a light squeeze before releasing them. "I'm not avoiding you. I promised Bobby I'd help him with a project at the resort this weekend. A tree came down in that storm the other night and damaged the roof of the pro shop. For the record, I *never* said the kiss was a mistake. I said that pursuing *more* would be a mistake. The kiss was…perfect. And I mean that in every sense of the word. It. Was. Perfect. No regrets, okay?"

She chewed her lower lip as she nodded. "No regrets."

* * *

On Monday, Tony arrived for work and got right to it, drywalling the exterior walls upstairs, and starting some of the interior walls, too. There'd been a stilted silence between Olivia and him at first, but she followed his lead, pretending that life-altering kiss had never happened. It wasn't easy, but she tried.

At lunchtime, she'd taken him out to the barn to see how little Flash was doing. She'd named the colt Mister Flash, not only because of his flashy coloring, but also because of his fiery attitude. He was a pistol, and Tony laughed at the way he charged around the stall, kicking at his mother. When he nursed, his little tail spun like a top. And when he got too pushy, Misty would nip him right above that spinning tail, and he'd jump.

The tension between Tony and her eased a bit after that, even though the racket he was making upstairs was making her bonkers. He was using the power screwdriver over and over and *over*. The annoyance of it all helped Olivia reach the point where she *had* stopped thinking about The Kiss.

She had her noise-canceling earbuds in, trying to cover up the screeching sound with the mellowness of her favorite Taylor Swift album as she finished a website update for a client.

After hours of noise, Tony popped his head into her office to say good night. At least, she was pretty sure that was what he'd said. Hard to be sure over the pop homage to broken hearts and revenge she'd used to drown out the ruckus. He'd waved to her after scooping up a couple of kittens for a snuggle. He was starting to do that a lot, especially with the mischievous Ross. It was adorable. She'd waved back at him, then saw his truck pulling out. The day had gone well, she thought.

The only reference to The Kiss had been when they walked back to the house from the barn. Tony told her Friday had been an "unforgettable night." She could tell from his expression that he was talking about more than the colt's birth.

Now that he was gone, she was ready to enjoy a hot bath in her new tub. She closed the kittens in the office for the night and went upstairs with Ginger at her heels. She filled the tub with steaming water, the bubbles foaming higher than the edges of the deep contemporary tub. She dropped her robe onto the floor next to the dog and stepped into the water.

It felt delicious, and relaxed not only her scars and tight muscles, but also her brain. The steamy warmth made everything—worries, plans, desire—fade into fogginess. The deep tub was a capsule that insulated her from everything other than peace and blessed relaxation. She sank into the water and leaned her head back onto the high wall of the tub. This was bliss.

She didn't hear the front door open downstairs. She didn't hear the footsteps until they were near the top of the stairs. That's when she suddenly realized she wasn't alone in the house. Ginger stood, her tail slowly wagging, as she wasn't sure she should be happy or fierce. Olivia scrambled to her feet.

"Olivia? Are you up here? Oh…" Tony was in the hallway. The hallway that didn't have solid walls yet. So he was staring straight at her, naked and wet, through the two-by-fours. She felt, more than saw, the instant when his gaze latched on to her scars. Oddly enough, she'd forgotten them. Now she felt more exposed than merely naked. Now he could see what she'd kept hidden. What made her feel ugly. Like damaged goods.

She snatched up the nearby towel and held it to her side. Less to hide her body and more to hide the wrinkled red scar that ran from her left shoulder to her thigh, wrapping partway around the front of her ribs on that side.

"I, uh…" Tony spun on his heel, turning his back to her. "Wow. Sorry. I told you I'd be back tonight to tape the drywall in the third bedroom. But I should have called out before I just walked up here." He scrubbed his hands down his face. "I really am sorry. I'll go home…"

"No." She wrapped the towel around herself. It didn't cover everything. The bloom of scar tissue showed above and below the towel. "I was just… I'm finished. Let me get dressed and you can…"

"No, I don't think I can." Was he laughing? "I'm pretty sure there's no way I could focus on smoothing drywall tape tonight. Not after seeing that."

She blinked. Was he mocking her?

"It's not *that* bad." It *was*, of course. The scars were large and ugly. She stepped out of the tub. She'd just hoped tangle of red skin wouldn't repulse him. That *she* would repulse him.

Tony turned to face her. "What do you mean?"

She shouldn't be ashamed of scars she never asked for. But shame flooded over her just the same. Her chin lifted defiantly, and she clung to what dignity she had left.

"Well, now you know why I stay covered up." She turned away, stepping between two two-by-fours into her bedroom, and walked stiffly past the bed to the closet. "Sorry you had to see that. I'll just cover up—"

She had no idea how Tony got to her side so quickly. He was just *there*. Holding her arm gently, stopping her.

"Olivia, don't ever apologize for that beautiful body of yours."

She yanked away from him, her eyes blurring with tears as she clutched the towel to keep it from falling.

"Don't patronize me. I saw you staring at the scars."

"Well…yeah. They're hard to miss…" Her face heated, but he rushed to speak before she could. "I had no idea you'd been burned *that* badly. I'm sorry you caught me staring, but all I was thinking was how much I hated that it happened to you."

She closed her eyes, her heart pounding. There was a beat of silence before she felt his fingertips brushing her bare shoulder, tracing lazy circles on her neck and under her chin, and then he lifted her head. She still kept her eyes closed, afraid to face his gaze. Afraid of what she'd see there… Desire? Or just…curiosity? Or, worse, pity.

His lips brushed hers so softly she thought she'd imagined it. Then it happened again. His arm moved around her, pulling her against his hard body as the kiss deepened.

She needed to know one thing for sure before they went any further. She pushed against his shoulder and he released her instantly, holding his hands out as he stepped back. He was eyeing her cautiously, not sure what she was going to do. That was funny, because she had no idea, either.

"I'm sorry," he said, his voice soft and low. "You're

kind of irresistible when I'm standing this close to you, but I shouldn't have—"

"The question is *why*, Tony. I don't want your sympathy. I don't want to be some pity fu—"

"Stop right there." His voice was harder now, and his hands dropped to his sides. "I don't *pity* you, and even if I did, that's not why I want to take you to bed. What kind of scum do you think I am?"

"I don't think you're scum. But..." Her shoulders fell in defeat, tears burning her eyes. "I haven't been with anyone since...the accident. And...wait." She looked up at him in surprise. "Did you say you want to take me to bed?"

The corner of his mouth lifted, and something released inside of her chest. She felt like she was breathing fully for the first time in years. The flow of oxygen made her a little dizzy. Or maybe his sexy, slanted smile was doing that.

"Taking you to bed is literally the only thing in the world I want to do." He moved closer again. "And trust me, it has nothing to do with those scars. It only has to do with you, Olivia. The way your mouth feels on mine. The way your skin feels under my fingers." His voice was coarse. Jagged, torn and oh, so rough. Goose bumps danced across her skin at the sound of it as he continued. "So yeah, I want to make love with you right now. I want it so bad I'm shaking." He held up his hand and, sure enough, it was trembling.

There was something about seeing that tiny, but persistent, tremor that made her doubts vanish. It made everything vanish but the sight of Tony Vello standing in front of her, *trembling* with desire. For *her*. She reached out and took his hand, pressing it to her chest so he could feel her galloping heartbeat. He sucked in a breath, his eyes burning with desire. She almost protested when he closed them, hiding that fire away from her.

"You're killing me, girl." He took another breath before opening his eyes again. "If we're gonna do this, well…we need to be honest with other. Friday we agreed it would be a mistake. I'm gone in a few weeks. There's no sunshine-and-picket-fence future after this."

She couldn't hold back a bubble of laughter. "No picket fence. Just sex. I get it."

His arms went around her in a flash, pulling her in for a hard, deep kiss that made her skin tingle from her scalp to her toes. *Damn.* This man knew how to kiss. He spoke against the soft skin behind her ear.

"Forget that *just-sex* nonsense. I intend for it to be much, much more than that." The tip of his tongue ran across the skin he'd just spoken against, and she let out a soft sigh and melted into his embrace. "I'm just saying whatever we do has an expiration date. You okay with that?"

His fingers were already tugging at the top of the towel. She reached for the hem of his T-shirt and yanked it up. "The only thing I'm not okay with is how many clothes you have on when I'm wearing nothing but a towel." She paused, a horrible thought crossing her mind. "I don't have any, uh, protection. Do you…?"

He lifted his head with a grin. "Do I have condoms? Don't worry, I have several. I'm always prepared." He kissed her, and she barely noticed when her towel fell to the floor. He shrugged off his shirt and dropped his shorts, kicking them away. Just like that, they were both naked.

"Sweet Jesus," Tony breathed, stepping back to admire the view. "You're beautiful."

"You're not so bad yourself." He had a T-shirt tan, but even where the sun hadn't darkened his olive skin, he was a beautiful specimen of a man. His broad, hard chest was covered with dark hair. She couldn't resist the temptation to run her fingers through it softly, sighing at the contrast of soft, curly hair and the taut muscles beneath it. He shuddered at her touch.

It was a heady feeling to know she could do that to a man. And not just any man, but the loudest, gruffest, strongest man she knew. She traced her fingers in circles and he let out a curse and grabbed her hand, pushing her back toward the bed even as he kissed her. The kiss was rough this time, and she loved it. She sunk her fingers in his hair and pulled herself up against him, kissing him back with every fiber in her body.

She hardly felt herself falling back on the bed, because he came with her without even breaking the kiss. They were frantic now, heads twisting and turning and hands moving up and down each other's body. His hand found her breast and squeezed just enough to make her arch up into him. He was between her legs, and she gasped the word *condom* at him.

"On it," he answered, twisting to the side as he put it on. Then he was over her again. "You deserve more time, more patience, more damn foreplay from me. A little wooing, even. But that may have to come later, because, well… I need to come now. In you."

"We've got all night for wooing. And I'm just as eager as you are…"

And then he filled her with one surging push. She cried out and he froze. "Liv? Am I hurting you?"

She pressed her lips to his chest. The truth was it *had* hurt. Her pelvis had been shattered in the accident, and even though it had fully healed, there were muscles still tight and aching. "Yes, a little." He went to pull out and she dug her nails into his back. "No, don't. Just…give me a minute. My hips are kind of a mess and very out of practice." He stayed still.

The next move had to be hers, and she began rocking slowly against him. The aching faded, and soon he was moving, too. He followed her lead, all while kissing and nibbling at her breasts, whispering her name and murmuring what he wanted to do to her body all night. After a certain point, the dull ache simply didn't matter anymore. They rocked together, deeper and faster. She knew the pain was there. She'd probably feel it later. But it was a small price to pay for the ecstasy building at her core, stoked by Tony and his dirty words and the thrill she felt as they drew closer and closer to the pinnacle. She bit his shoulder, trying to hang on but losing the battle. A flash of hot white light exploded behind her eyes and she cried out his name. He came right after her, holding her close as he groaned and finally collapsed his weight on her.

After a moment of nothing more than the two of them breathing deeply, hearts pounding in rhythm with each other, he turned his head to face her.

"Are you okay? Are you hurting?"

She patted his shoulder. "Stop worrying. I'm fine. I'm…blissfully fine. I am a very happy woman."

He huffed out a short laugh against her skin. "I hope you're a proud woman, too, because that was…incredible. You destroyed me, then put me back together and destroyed me all over again. I can't wait to do it again. Slower next time, but first… Let me take care of this—" he sat up to dispose of the condom "—and get my heart rate somewhere back in the don't-die range."

Then he pulled her into his arms, her head tucked into his shoulder. He was asleep in no time—she heard the moment his breathing changed. She smiled and curled up in his embrace. Yes, she ached a bit, but nothing that wasn't manageable. Nothing that wasn't totally worth it for the pleasure of making love with this man.

Nothing that would keep her from wanting to do it again.

Chapter Eleven

Tony woke with a start. He tended to do that ever since the accident, and he blinked into the darkness to get his bearings. Where was he? And why was something warm and soft sprawled across his chest?

Olivia. Heat rushed through him. Had he passed out after that incredible sex? He saw the bedside clock—it had only been an hour or so. That was a relief, because he did not want to waste one moment of this night. After all, who knew if they'd have another? They'd said no strings. No expectations. No entanglements. He ran his hand up her spine. If it was going to be one night, he couldn't spend any more of it sleeping, that was for sure. But then again, *she* was sleeping, too.

She was on top of him, one leg intertwined with his, one arm cast wide beyond him, the other bent so that her hand was next to his head on the pillow. Her head was on his chest. He'd never been much for cuddling after sex, but this was different. This was…nice.

He supposed there was no shame in needing rest after the way they'd come together and things had just exploded like that. He frowned. She'd been in some pain, though. He couldn't tell how much, and she was the one who'd set the pace after they'd paused. And that pace had been frantic for both of them. But he didn't like the idea of hurting her.

At that moment, his fingers brushed against the edge of a scar. The skin was built up there, like a ridge. And beyond that ridge, the scar tissue was tight and hard, especially compared to the rest of her body.

When he'd spotted her standing in the tub earlier, like a glorious glistening mermaid, her scars had been impossible to ignore. The skin was rose-red and so much larger than he'd expected. It covered most of her torso on the left side, and much of her left thigh. He couldn't imagine how painful it must have been. How many skin grafts she'd gone through. And she'd thought he was repulsed by it.

It was the opposite. He'd been awestruck at how strong she had to be to go through that. The scars weren't ugly to him in any way, because they were a part of *her.* And there was nothing ugly about Olivia Carson. She was tough. She was smart. He smiled in the darkness. And she was an incredible lover.

She stirred under his caress and he moved his fingers from the scar, mumbling an apology. Did it hurt to be touched there? She lifted her head, her blond waves wild around her face.

"Don't apologize. It felt nice…as long as it didn't gross you out."

He pushed her hair back so he could look straight into her eyes. "Stop it. That scars are a part of you, and I like *you* a lot. All of you. Every inch. But you have to let me know if I'm hurting you. Is it tender?"

She rested her chin on her hand on his chest and stared right back. "Not really. Not anymore. The skin gets *crazy* itchy sometimes, and it doesn't stretch very well. I have to keep it moisturized and I have exercises I do to keep it flexible." She smiled. "Massage is actually good for it, so don't be afraid to touch it."

"But you were hurting earlier, when…"

"That wasn't about the burns. I had other injuries in the accident, including a broken pelvis and torn hip ligaments. The burns went deep on my hip and thigh, and those muscles will never be quite the same. And my back isn't perfect, either. Frankly, I'm a mess."

"A beautiful mess. A sexy mess."

She laughed softly. "A broken mess."

"No. Not broken. Healed. Strong."

"Sometimes." Her stare was solemn now. "Tonight was—"

He put his fingers on her lips to stop her.

"Don't say *was*. Tonight isn't over. Not by a long shot. Hell, it's not even midnight yet." Wait. Was she giving him the boot? "Unless you want me to go?"

"I don't want you to go, Tony. I just meant that what we did…" She grinned at him. "Well, let's just say you were right. It was a lot more than *just sex*. You and I may not make sense on paper, but we're pretty awesome together in bed."

Her smile hit differently when they were skin-to-skin like this. Bodies tangled together in the afterglow of lovemaking. It was more than a smile. It was…possibilities. A door opening to something inconceivable just days ago. He'd told her there'd be no future with him. But if she kept smiling at him like that, with that sparkle in her eyes, he could easily see himself giving her anything she wanted.

To break the moment, he rolled over so she was beneath him. She was still smiling, but there was a heat there now that was more comfortable for him to deal with. Horniness, he could handle. Seeing himself in some small-town future? That would never work.

"We *were* pretty awesome," he said. "But there was one problem."

"Really? What's that?"

"It was over way too quick. It was what we both wanted and it was hotter than hell, but there's so much more I want to do with you, Olivia. And I want to do it slowly. I don't want to leave one inch of your body unkissed. Untasted. Unappreciated."

She traced her fingers down his back, brushing over the places she'd dug her nails in the first time.

"Yes, it was quick and hard and dirty. And, yes, we wanted it that way. But slow and thorough sounds very good. There's some territory on you that I'd like to spend time exploring, too. We may have to take turns."

Tony lowered himself onto her and kissed her. She wanted slow and thorough? He'd start with this kiss. Her lips were pillow-soft and velvety against his, and they gave way to him with a soft purr from her throat. She wriggled beneath him, making him instantly hard. *Stand down.* This was going to be slow, damn it, no matter what their bodies craved. He was sure their bodies would thank them later.

He kept the kiss going as his hands explored her body. Then he started exploring with his kisses, too.

Moving down her neck and across her chest. He was learning her body language already. How she melted when something felt good. How her skin blushed with warmth under his mouth when she was turned on. How she gave the slightest little hitch if something was uncomfortable. No matter how excited he was, no matter how much he was struggling to control his own urges, he could not grip her hard near her waist, on her hips or thighs, because of her scars. No clutching there. Just caresses, slow and easy.

His body was like a racehorse being held too long in the gate. But Olivia wanted it slow. And thorough. And what Olivia wanted, she got. At least from him. Always. Forever. Well…as long as they were together.

They settled into an easy rhythm, as if their bodies finally got the message that it would be worth the wait. And damn, was it ever. They spent hours taking turns exploring, tasting, devouring. They made love, and it was somehow better each time. More tender. More sensual. Whispers instead of cries. Murmured names instead of shouted ones. Touches that teased and teased before finding their targets. Instead of wanting to race, their bodies were fine with the sweet, sweet torture. Craved it, even.

When they finally collapsed in complete exhaustion from the sensory overload, he knew that Olivia Carson had just ruined him for any other woman. And that was a problem, because he was going to leave her. He had to.

Eventually.

Somehow.

Dawn was barely tinting the horizon when Olivia opened her eyes and stretched. Were there some aches in places? A few. But they were as much from unused muscles as damaged ones. It had been a long time since she'd had sex. And she'd *never* had sex like this.

If they'd had anything to drink before, she'd have wondered if it was spiked with something. But no. This was pure sexual afterglow. The wildest thing of all was she *still* wanted more of him. Even now, when she was more spent than she'd felt since the darkest days of physical rehab, she wanted more. From a man who'd already told her he didn't have more to give. Not long-term, anyway. And she'd agreed to that.

She pressed her back against his warm, hard chest. So she'd have to be satisfied with whatever she got. From whatever time they had.

"If you keep wiggling against me like that," Tony he said, his voice low and thick, "I'm going to want to go again, and I think we're out of condoms, babe."

"Sorry," she whispered, forcing herself to stay still. "You're just so nice and warm and…tempting. But I'm spent, too. And hungry. You hungry?"

"For you? Definitely." He gave a squeeze. "But yeah, I could do with some food, too." He stretched with a groan. "I make a mean omelet if you have the fixings."

"O-o-oh. A man who cooks. Lucky me." She turned to face him. "One thing those chickens are good for is lots of eggs. You make the omelets. I'll make the coffee and toast."

He started to sit up, then leaned back to kiss her tenderly. "Thank you for last night."

She was going to say something funny or sarcastic, but there was something in his tone that stopped her. He was thanking her for more than the sex. It had been far more than that, just as he'd promised. It had been… life-changing. And he seemed to feel the same way. So she kissed him back and patted his cheek softly, then sat up and reached for her robe.

He wasn't joking about making a great omelet. He made them one at a time, fluffy and folded over a filling of sausage, onion and Swiss cheese. He whistled cheerily as he cooked. She toasted some whole grain bread and made a pot of strong coffee. It wasn't even six in the morning.

Tony slid his omelet onto his plate and joined her at the table with a wide grin. She groaned and rolled her eyes. He was way too perky.

"Oh, God, you're a morning person, aren't you?"

His head tipped back as he laughed. "Guilty as charged. Is that going to be a problem?"

He wolfed down a huge piece of omelet wedged between a folded piece of toast. Olivia usually started her day with a bowl of oatmeal and coffee. Sometimes just an English muffin. This guy looked ready to eat half the kitchen. His eyes met hers. Her skin tingled. And maybe make a snack out of her, too.

"Not a problem for me, but you may have to cook your own breakfasts. I don't usually start my days with a meal like this. Are you always up this early?"

He was devouring another piece of toast and omelet. "On a working day, sure. It's easier to get into the city early, and an ironworker's days are long. A big breakfast is a requirement for that kind of labor."

"You miss it, don't you?"

He hesitated. "It's the family business. It's what I do. They're expecting me back."

"That very much did *not* answer my question."

He set down his fork. "I told you what happened. It's

hard to miss doing something after you watch someone die while doing it."

"But you're still going back."

"When I'm done here. I made a promise." He frowned at his plate for a long moment, then looked back at her. "You knew this going in, Liv."

"I know." She straightened. "Sorry. I guess I'm a little more interested in the whys today than I was last night. A little more...invested."

"What we did, what we have..." He cleared his throat. "If we go forward..."

"Do you want to go forward?"

"Without a doubt."

His answer was so fast and firm that she gasped, then let out a half laugh. "Don't even have to think about it, huh?"

That hot slanted smile returned. "About a chance to make love to you again? No, I don't need to think. Do you?" He paused. "We agreed there's no picket-fence future for us, remember?"

"I remember." She wasn't some starry-eyed innocent. She had a life. A farm. A career. Friends. She didn't need a relationship. She didn't *want* a relationship. At least, she *hadn't* wanted one. But something felt...off about just having some kind of casual fling with Tony.

"Liv?" Tony leaned forward. "It's okay if you don't want to, you know...sleep with me again. I'm a big boy. I can take it. We'll go back to a professional relationship and—"

"That's not what I want!"

He sat back in the chair, throwing his hands in the air.

"Do you not want a professional relationship or do you not want to sleep with me again? I'm confused."

He wasn't the only one. She buried her face in her hands. "I'm overthinking everything. I always used to do that…"

Wait a minute. That was the problem. She'd gone back to old habits.

"What's wrong?" Tony asked.

"Nothing. I just need to reset my brain." She stood and put their plates in the dishwasher. The sun was rising now, bathing the hillside in a soft yellow light. It was supposed to be a warm week—the first full week of summer. She refilled their coffee mugs, then nodded her head toward the door. "Let's take our coffees to the porch and get some fresh air."

Tony followed. He'd pulled on his shorts when they got up, but not his shirt. She was in a bathrobe and nothing else. And it didn't feel uncomfortable at all. If anything, it felt perfectly normal. They settled on the porch swing together, with Tony deep in one corner and Olivia leaning against him, her legs stretched out on the swing. Her scars peeked out from under her robe, and she resisted the urge to tug on the hem. She took a sip of her coffee instead.

"So," Tony began, "are you done overthinking things yet? We left that conversation hanging, and I still don't know what we're doing."

She leaned her head back against his shoulder, staring at the yard as she spoke. She was talking as much to herself as she was to him.

"Before the accident, I was always very…goal-driven. I set plans and ran after them with single-minded focus. I showed horses competitively when I was growing up. Winning was always the goal. And I did. Local championships. State champ. And I did well at nationals, too." She took another sip of coffee. "I graduated high school at the top of my class. When I was in college, I was on the dean's list every semester. Then I met Jerod and he was goal-driven too. We immediately started planning a life together. I thought I'd really made it, you know?"

Tony rubbed her arm gently. "And *after* the accident?"

She went still. Her world had shifted so much after that. Melissa was gone. Their mutual circle of friends distanced themselves from Olivia. Jerod's visits slowed until she finally gave his ring back. Then his visits stopped altogether. Everything she'd won was gone.

"After the accident, I found out that goals aren't all they're cracked up to be. Things don't always have to be defined, outlined, whatever." She turned her head to look up at him. "Which brings me back to us. I'm okay with it being temporary. Casual. I don't expect anything going forward. I don't need some imaginary end goal."

Things in life came to an end anyway. No sense thinking this would be any different.

He thought about it for a moment, then nodded, pulling her closer. "I'm glad you don't want to stop whatever this is we have going on. I just..." His eyebrows lowered. "I don't like the idea of you not expecting *anything*."

"Seriously?" She sat up. "You're the one who emphasized no picket-fence future, and now that I'm on board, you're disappointed?"

"Ugh..." He scrubbed his hands down his face and

grumbled. "Maybe now *I'm* overthinking this. Can't we care about each other without being *too* casual or *too* serious?"

"So…a relationship that's temporary, but committed?" She turned to face him, feeling a glimmer of clarity. "That works for me."

Tony grinned. "You really did need to define us, didn't you?" He reached for her, pulling her onto his lap. She didn't object. "Are you happier now that we have parameters? Temporary and committed?"

"It may not make any sense, but yes." She settled on his thighs with a rueful smile. "Apparently *new* Olivia isn't as carefree and go-with-the-flow as I thought."

"Oh, I don't know." Tony tugged at the knot on the belt of her robe until the robe fell open. "You were pretty go-with-the-flow last night." His hand slid under the robe, creating invisible sparks from his fingers against her skin. He leaned forward and kissed the base of her neck. "It would be fun to do that in the daylight, don't you think?"

She laughed, wrapping her arms around his neck. "We both have jobs to do. And you said you were out of condoms."

"It's seven thirty." He shrugged with one shoulder. "I don't usually get here for work before nine. And I found another condom in my wallet."

"I have animals to feed…"

"Right now?"

"Within the next hour, yeah."

"An hour, huh?" He kissed her neck, then nipped her skin lightly, making her gasp. "I can work with that." His kisses and nibbles traced down her chest as he pushed her robe off her shoulders. She felt brazen, out here in the open, half-naked. There wasn't a house anywhere near close enough to see her home, much less her porch. But there was something about the feel of the fresh morning air caressing her breasts—along with Tony's mouth—that had Olivia halfway to an orgasm before they left the swing.

Being topless out on the porch in daylight was one thing, but making love out here was another. Tony seemed to agree—he stood with her in his arms and took her into the house. Not up the stairs. Neither of them was patient enough for that. And the sofa was right there.

Chapter Twelve

Tony was whistling to himself as he came down the interior stairs that led from his apartment to the hallway behind Nora Peyton's coffee shop. He usually used the fire escape stairs, but a quick summer storm had blown up, so this was the driest way to get to his truck. The duffel bag in his hand held clothes and a few toiletries. He'd been spending his nights with Olivia for nearly a week now, and the bag he'd quickly filled on Tuesday hadn't been enough.

"Well, well, well." Nora was standing in the hallway. That was the downside of using these stairs—he was visible to anyone in the back room of the café. "If it isn't my tenant, Tony. It's still pouring out there, so you may as well come up front and have a coffee."

He hoped she hadn't noticed the duffel, which he now set out of sight on the stairs. Nora's coffee was the only thing he'd been missing—she really knew how to run that big Italian espresso machine she had. He hadn't had much sleep this week, which was a small price to pay for making love to Olivia nightly. A cup of coffee with a double shot of espresso would give him enough juice to actually get something accomplished at the house.

Nora's cousin, Amanda Randall, was sitting at a table not far from the counter. A couple of older guys were playing cribbage by the window. He'd learned that John and Steve were regulars here. He gave Nora his order and joined Amanda, who had waved him over.

"Look, Nora!" she exclaimed. "It's Tony! Weren't we just talking about him?"

Lovely. Maybe stopping here hadn't been such a great idea after all.

Nora walked over with his coffee and sat at the table. "Yup." She nodded. "I was beginning to think you'd found a coffee shop you liked better than mine."

Amanda snorted. "Or a better place to sleep."

"Oh, I think you might be on to something there." Nora stirred her own coffee. "I haven't seen his truck in the back lot for four or five nights now. I wonder where he's staying these days?"

"And who he's staying wi—"

"Alright, ladies." Tony stopped their game. "I guess the stories are true. There are no secrets in a small town."

"That is true," Nora agreed. "But that did not answer our questions."

"You weren't asking me questions. You were talking to each other, remember?" There was no malice in their curiosity, but that didn't mean he had to feed it. "And yes, I've been staying…elsewhere. Exactly where, or with whom, isn't something a gentleman discusses without the other person present."

Both their mouths dropped open in unison. Nora started laughing.

"Well, *damn*. I'm impressed. Disappointed at the lack of information, but impressed."

Amanda stared at him, her eyes narrowing. He stared right back without flinching. She was the first to blink. Growing up in the Vello family had toughened him. He didn't intimidate easily.

"You *are good*," she laughed. "But this is not the way things are done in small towns, mister." She leaned in. She was blond, like Olivia, but more petite. Where Olivia was quiet, Amanda was outgoing and perpetually on the move. Even now, her foot was tapping the floor. "It's quiet here. We live through other people's adventures. And our friends live through *our* adventures. So spilling the details is just…neighborly here."

Tony leaned in. His uncle had raised him to be a hardscrabble negotiator. Whoever blinked first, lost. And he still wasn't blinking. "Olivia may choose to kiss and tell, but *I* will not. And I am *not* your neighbor. I'm just a guy passing through."

Amanda sat back, looking far too pleased with herself. "You just let us know it *is* Olivia you've been with—which we knew, of course. *And* you said *kiss and tell*, which tells us you two have been kissing, which we *hoped* was true but now it's confirmed."

Damn. He'd been away from New York for too long. He was losing his edge. Or these women were just that good. He pointed at each of them.

"Where are you from originally?"

"Atlanta," Nora answered with a soft Southern drawl.

Amanda shrugged. "Born in the Midwest, but I lived in Manhattan before I came here. Why?"

"That means neither of *you* are small-town people, either!" He took a long sip of coffee, thankful for the jolt of extra caffeine. "So don't try to con me with your folksy routine."

Amanda laughed so loudly that John and Steve looked up from their cribbage game. John was glowering. She leaned back in her chair and lifted her coffee mug in a mock toast.

"Touché. We're former city girls. So take pity on us for being in this small town and spill something. *Anything.* Such as…how serious is it with you and Olivia?"

He shook his head. "You'll have to ask her." Their expressions made him feel like he'd just kicked their puppy. He let out a long, heavy sigh. He should have used the outside exit from the loft. "Look, I like Olivia. Very much. But as far as getting serious, that can't happen. I'm leaving, and she knows that."

Nora and Amanda looked at each other, and he had the feeling they were having a silent conversation. And it somehow did not feel like it was favorable for him. Nora pursed her lips.

"You haven't stayed here all week. I saw your packed duffel bag, so you're not planning on staying here for the next week, either. That sounds pretty serious to me."

He threw up his hands. "Tell me again why this is your business?"

"We care about Olivia," Nora answered.

"We care about you, too," Amanda added.

Nora didn't look as enthusiastic about the other woman's claim. "I know you're both consenting adults. I just don't want her—" she hesitated "—or you to end up hurt."

"I don't want that, either. Trust me, we've been very open with each other about this."

"Why do you keep saying you have to leave?" Amanda asked.

"Uh...because that's where my life is. My job. My home. My family."

"Then why are you *here* if your life is *there*?"

That was a really good question. The obvious answer was Olivia. But there was something else about this place. Yes, it was a small town, but it was a lively one. There was always something happening at the resort, or some little weekend festival downtown. Next week was Old Home Days, which was a celebration of the town's history...and an excuse for the local businesses to have sidewalk sales. There was going to be a parade and everything. Maybe Olivia would like to watch it.

Tony frowned at his coffee mug. He was changing. This town—and that woman—had changed him. Or were at least working on it. Old Tony would have scoffed at the idea of taking his girl to a townie parade. New Tony was looking forward to asking her.

But the new Tony wasn't real.

"Oh, I think you stumped him with that one, Amanda." Nora stood as customers came into the café. "Maybe the answer he wants to give doesn't feel quite right anymore." She patted his shoulder as she walked by. "He might be seeing a life for him *here*. By the way, I have someone asking about the apartment, so there won't be any penalty if you decide to break that monthly lease and live somewhere else."

He was still thinking about the conversation when he drove back to the farm. If Nora had a tenant lined up, should he just move to the farm? Was there a life for him here? Or was he just hiding from the inevitable?

Olivia called his name from the barn when he got out of the truck, so he headed in that direction. She probably wanted help with the wheelbarrow. She usually cleaned stalls in the morning. He walked through the big doors and stopped.

Scout was outside his stall, tied to one of the barn posts. There was a saddle on his back. Tony had never seen the horse saddled before. Olivia must be going riding. Just then, Olivia led Misty out of her stall, with Flash doing his usual laps around his mom. For every step Misty took, Flash took twenty. And today, every time he passed her, he nipped at the stirrups of the saddle she had on. Both horses had saddles on.

Wait a minute...

Olivia, wearing jeans and a knit top, laughed at his expression.

"That's right, cowboy. We're going for a ride together."

Olivia didn't think she'd ever seen the color drain from someone's face as quickly as what she was seeing right now. Tony's jaw dropped, then he stepped back, as if he wanted to run. His head went sharply back and forth.

"No way. Scout tries to bite me at least once every time I take him out of his stall, and now you want me to *sit* on him? No thank you."

She started to laugh, then realized he was still backing away.

"Tony, stop. I'm not going to force you to ride if you really don't want to, but I think you'll like it. Scout is very well-trained, and he can't bite you if you're riding him." She crossed her fingers behind her back because that wasn't completely true. But Scout had always been a perfect gentleman whenever she'd ridden him. "Wait…is this because you don't like heights? You're afraid of falling?"

Tony rolled his eyes. "It's *not* that. But falling is a concern. So is getting bucked off. Hitting a tree. Making a general fool of myself."

She smiled. That last one sounded the most plausible. Tony had a lot of pride—he didn't like not being in control of a situation.

"We're just going to go around the two pastures. I want to check the fence, and it's easier to ride than walk."

"What about Flash?" The colt had taken a break from running around to nurse.

"He'll follow wherever his mom goes, and we'll be inside the pastures most of the time. We'll just walk slowly. You'll be fine. Scout is a really good horse. It'll be like riding with autopilot switched on."

Tony walked over to Scout. The gray horse didn't help matters by flattening his ears and shaking his head at Tony. "This does not look like a horse who wants to be ridden. Especially by me. And I've never ridden a horse before in my *life*."

"His attitude will change as soon as I get the bridle on him." She hoped. "Why don't you hold Misty, and I'll finish getting him ready. It'll be fun, I promise."

"I can think of a lot of things more fun to do than this." He looked completely unconvinced and tense. She reached out and grasped his fingertips, giving a squeeze.

"If you go riding with me, maybe we can do one of those fun things afterward."

Now she had his attention. "Are you suggesting an afternoon in bed if I get on this beast? Can I make requests?"

She leaned in for a kiss, and he obliged as he took Misty's reins from her. "You men are so predictable. You'll do anything for a little roll in the sheets."

"Hey, I didn't say anything about *little*. I said an *afternoon*. Don't renege on me now!"

She slid the bit in Scout's mouth and led him out of the barn. Tony followed with Misty, then they switched horses. She'd only ridden Misty a few times when she'd first arrived, and didn't trust her with a novice like Tony. Plus the mare was bound to be distracted with her baby running around.

It took a few minutes to get Tony to figure out how to get on Scout and how to hold the reins. Scout jumped a little, so Olivia had to give a quick riding lesson, including not digging his heels into Scout's ribs to keep his seat. That was a good way to *lose* his seat. As soon as Tony moved his legs away from his sides, Scout settled right down into the good trail horse she knew.

Both pasture gates were open, and they went through the first one and walked the horses along the fence line. She was looking for rails that may have been knocked down by tree limbs or anything else that might need repair. At first, Tony was stiff and terrified on Scout, but the horse's easy walking gait got him to relax eventually. They stopped near the top of the hill so Flash could grab a snack, nursing from his mom.

"Wow—what a view." Tony looked out over the valley and the lake shining blue below. "What's that?" He pointed at the two stone towers just visible near the water, with their conical roofs.

"That's Halcyon. It's literally a castle that's next to the resort. It's where Blake and Amanda Randall live."

"Blake and Amanda live in a *castle*? Here in the middle of nowhere? It must have cost a fortune to build."

She'd been to the historic castle several times for dinner with the Randalls and their children, teenager Zach and young Madeleine. Somehow they'd made the large mansion feel like a warm family home.

"They didn't build it—it's over a hundred years old. But I'm sure they spent a lot renovating it. It's an amazing place." She watched Flash move away from Misty, off to explore. "In fact, it's how they met. She's an interior designer, and Blake hired her to make it a home. Then it ended up being *her* home, too."

It occurred to her that their story wasn't that different. She'd hired Tony, and now he was unofficially living at the farm. She could tell from his expression that he was thinking the same thing. They'd carefully avoided discussing long-term plans, though. She knew he was still thinking about his job and family in Staten Island. He talked to them regularly. She tried not to stoke the flame of hope growing inside of her. Hope for a future that looked a lot like this—the two of them on horseback on the hill, appreciating the place where they lived.

His gaze went from her hair, which was falling free today, to the long-sleeved top and jeans.

"You're not dressed like a prairie woman today."

"Excuse me?"

He grimaced, shifting his weight in the saddle. "That sounded bad. I meant…you look great. But you look great in dresses, too. And I know you like them for the looser fit. It's just…why do you cover up so much? It's eighty degrees and you're in long sleeves."

Olivia nudged Misty with her heel to start moving back down the hill.

"I do wear the dresses for comfort. I may not need that much looseness anymore, now that the skin grafts are healed. But I got used to it." She pulled up on the reins so Flash didn't tangle in them as he dashed right in front of Misty. "And I wear sleeves because people don't need to see those scars. It's for their own protection."

Tony had Scout right next to her, and he reached out to take her hand. "Sounds like it's more for *your* protection. They're a part of who you are, and making yourself uncomfortable just to cover them up doesn't make sense to me."

She pulled her hand away. His words were logical, but she'd made up her mind after the accident that no one would see the burns unless she wanted them to. A few friends and Tony.

"I don't want strangers staring at me. I hate it, in fact. I don't know what's worse, being gawked at in silence, or the questions some people ask. 'Oh, what happened? Does it hurt? Can't you get plastic surgery to cover it up?'"

That last one was a real question a woman had asked

when she was walking out of the physical-therapy center in Maryland early in her recovery process. She'd been trying to embrace her scars then, like Tony was suggesting, and was made to feel ugly and incomplete somehow. That was the day she began covering herself. She told Tony the story as they rode the perimeter of the second pasture. He was silent for a while when the story ended.

"I can see where comments like that would hurt," he finally said, his voice low and gentle. "But it feels like you're punishing yourself for other people's issues."

She blew out a long breath. "That's pretty much what my therapist said. Maybe I'm hiding, or maybe it's just where I'm comfortable. For now, I have no intention of changing." She gave him a sideways glance. "Even if I end up looking like a prairie woman."

"Ha!" Tony shook his head. "Trust me, you're the world's sexiest prairie woman. You're not going to let me forget that one, are you?"

"Not right away, no."

They rode to the barn. Fortunately they'd only found a couple of loose boards, and Tony said he'd fix them that week. He groaned and stretched after dismounting.

"Holy hell, we didn't ride that long but I'm still sore in places I didn't know could be sore." He gave Scout a pat on the neck. "But you were right—he's a good horse to put up with a greenhorn like me."

She led Misty and Flash inside. "Maybe you should take a soak in the tub before you think about anything else." She slid the saddle and bridle off Misty, then took care of Scout and gave them each a flake of hay. Tony grabbed her on the way to the house, swinging her around in a circle, then kissing her hard.

"The only way I'm going in that tub is if you come in with me."

"I think that could be arranged."

They walked to the house hand in hand. Ginger was waiting for them from her shady spot on the porch. The chickens were cackling and scratching in the grass nearby. The sun was warm and the hillside was lush and green. Olivia looked around and felt a warmth blooming inside of her.

This was the life. And she didn't want it to end.

Chapter Thirteen

Any thoughts Tony had about Gallant Lake being a sleepy town were dispelled at the Old Home Days festival. The fun started Friday night, with a kayak race from the resort to the docks in front of the gazebo in town. Nick West won it handily. His wife, Cassie, was waiting to greet him, bouncing their son on her hip. The celebration party was lively at the Chalet, and Tony found himself acting as designated driver for, well… everyone. He took Matt Danzer home to the A-frame near the ski lodge he owned with his pregnant wife, Jillie. On the way back to town, he dropped attorney Trent Michaels at his home. His wife, Jade, was in the rocking chair on the front patio when they arrived, their infant daughter, Daphne, asleep on her shoulder.

Next stop was to drop Nate Thomas at the waterfront home he shared with his wife, Brittany, and their son, little Nate. And the last stop was at the home of Blake Randall, where Tony finally got to see the historic castle Halcyon up close, where it was even more impressive.

Blake invited him in, but Tony knew Olivia would be wondering where he was. He didn't want her worrying. Blake tapped the hood of the truck twice in farewell, and Tony drove off after one last incredulous look at the mansion. Not the kind of place one expected to see in what he'd thought was the *boondocks*.

The guys he'd met here were hardworking family men who liked to have fun, but never forgot their responsibilities. Even the police chief, Dan Adams, had stopped by the bar tonight, although he joined Tony in drinking root beer. He'd taken a few of the others home—Nick, Asher Peyton and the golf pro, Quinn Walker.

Olivia was on the porch swing with Ginger when he pulled up and parked. Like the other men, he was coming home to the woman he cared for most in the world. There was no doubt he was falling hard for her.

She stood, and the light from inside the house shone behind her. It highlighted the outline of her curves beneath the yellow cotton dress she wore over a soft white scoop-neck shirt. With her golden hair, it had the effect of making her look like a goddess. Tony's knees went weak. Who was he kidding when he told himself he was falling for her? He'd fallen. All the way to the point of no return. He was in love with her.

Olivia came with him to the parade the next day. At first she'd said no, and he knew she was thinking about covering her scars. And thinking about being together in public. It's not like they were a secret, but a public outing together was a big step. It made them more than *casual*. They hadn't felt anything close to casual for the past few weeks, though. There was just the one thing they hadn't discussed—what would happen once the work on her house was finished.

But that morning, Olivia told him she wanted to go to the parade after all. She said a lot of the clients she'd designed websites and marketing plans for would be participating, so it was "good business."

Tony looked at her now, laughing as a bunch of clowns rode by on bicycles as part of the parade, and he knew she wasn't thinking about business. She was having fun. She was pressed up against his side, grinning up at him as she pointed to one of the bigger clowns on the smallest bike. She said he looked like Tony riding Scout.

Tony was emphatic in his denial, which just made her laugh more. The sound, so pure and uninhibited, shifted something inside of him. He looked up the street, where festive banners blew in the breeze, tied to every old-style lamppost. The sky was bright blue above, with a few scattered, picture-perfect cotton clouds. The scene was an American postcard.

"Tony?" Olivia asked. "You okay?"

He smiled into her sapphire eyes.

"I love you."

He didn't blurt the words out—he said them calmly and confidently, because he meant it. And she didn't seem shocked by them. Her eyes lit up, and her smile deepened until dimples appeared.

"I love you, too."

"I'm glad."

And that was that. No talk of what might be next. Just two people at a parade, falling in love. She rested her head on his chest, and he kissed the top of her head. When he opened his eyes, the world was still going on as normal. The high-school marching band was going by, playing an energetic arrangement of *Uptown Funk*. Well…the world was as normal as it could be in Gallant Lake.

The sidewalks were crowded with people. He was surprised to realize he knew so many of them. The guys from last night. Their wives and children. They waved as they walked by, saying hello and looking at him and Olivia with knowing smiles.

He *belonged* here. It was unbelievable and yet more believable than any other thought he'd ever had. He'd stumbled on this town by accident. Found this woman through a temporary job. And now he saw a *future* here.

The only problem? He still had a life in Staten Island to deal with.

Olivia was in love with Tony Vello. More incredibly, Tony Vello loved *her*. She hummed happily as she hurried down the sidewalk. The town was much quieter today than it had been over the weekend during Old Home Days.

Tony's sidewalk declaration of love had surprised her, but only in its timing. She'd known he was falling as hard as she was. She just hadn't been sure he was willing to admit it, even to himself. But that night, he'd shared not just that he loved *her*, but that he was feeling at home in *Gallant Lake*.

Things were good. Life was good. It had been a

long time since she'd felt that way. Tony had brought joy back into her world. And hope. He was smiling more. He was more relaxed. They'd gone horseback riding again this morning, and Tony had laughed that he couldn't call himself a cowboy until "they" got some cows.

He said it as if "they" might be a thing for more than just a few more weeks. She sidestepped around a woman pushing a stroller, nodding hello as she passed. She wanted to believe in that future, especially now that they'd declared their love for each other.

Maybe it was just her good mood, but the sun seemed especially bright on this warm July afternoon. It was as if the whole universe was feeling her happiness. The only thing missing was a cartoon bluebird landing on her shoulder to sing a song.

"Olivia!" Nora pushed open the door to the coffee shop as Olivia walked by. "I have someone here you'll want to meet."

"A potential client?" She checked her watch. She still had plenty of time to get to the bakery and home for dinner. She wanted to surprise Tony with his favorite cream-filled pastry for dessert—Jade's famous Greek *bougatsa*.

"Nope." Nora held the door open for her. "Tony's cousins are here. I saw them upstairs knocking on his door, but we all know he hasn't been spending any nights there lately." Nora winked. "Don't worry, I didn't tell them that. But I saw you going by and thought you might want to talk to them or call Tony or something."

Tony had been talking about how much he missed his family. She knew he talked to them and texted, but he hadn't been home in a couple of months now. He was avoiding them, still upset about his new fear of heights. It wasn't healthy. She'd told him he needed to face them, and now they were here.

She almost laughed when she saw the two men. There was no doubt the dark-haired, dark-eyed pair at the counter were Tony's relatives. The one on the right could be a twin.

She introduced herself to Luca and Paulie Vello. Luca, the one who looked the most like Tony, was jovial and easygoing. Paulie was shorter and stockier, like a sparkplug. He seemed more reserved than Luca. They explained they'd driven up as a surprise for Tony, and that's when she realized she could bring more than just a fancy dessert to tonight's dinner as a treat for Tony.

Chapter Fourteen

"I'm just saying I want to consider more paint colors before we make a final choice," Olivia argued. "So I picked up more samples and taped them to the wall. Maybe the living room should be bright blue instead of soft yellow. I could go bold, you know?"

Tony thought she'd settled on all her paint choices. It wasn't like her to be indecisive when it came to the house. But he set the pork roast on the stove top and turned off the oven. It needed to cool, anyway, so he had time to indulge her. It felt like he'd already seen a dozen color options for the living room. Olivia wanted him to look at more, though, so he obediently followed her with a bemused chuckle.

"Baby, you're already plenty bold." He reached out to pinch her backside. She squealed and jumped, swatting his hand away in the doorway to the living room.

"Behave yourself, and go look at the colors."

"Yes, ma'am."

He stepped into the living room and came to a sudden halt, blinking to make sure he wasn't imagining things. Luca and Paulie were standing in front of the sofa with big proud grins on their faces.

Luca shook his finger at him. "Didn't my pop teach you *anything*? You never pinch the customer's ass!"

It took three strides for Tony to reach his cousins and wrap them in a tight embrace. He was overwhelmed with emotion at seeing family again, and he closed his eyes tightly to contain the tears burning there. He pounded Luca's back.

"What the hell are you doing here, man?" Tony sniffed and finally pulled back, holding Luca's shoulders and staring at him with a laugh. "Damn, I'm glad to see you, but…how? Why?" He had a chilling thought. "Is everything okay at home? Nonna…?"

"Everyone's fine, man. But Nonna would sure like to see her favorite grandson."

"Please," Tony scoffed. "We all know Paulie here is her angelic favorite." Tony hooked his arm around Paulie's neck, who protested when Tony rubbed his knuckles into his hair. He finally got himself free.

"Screw you, Anthony!" Paulie flipped up a middle finger. "I didn't drive all the way up here for abuse!"

"Why *did* you drive up here?"

Luca folded his arms on his chest. "Because *you* don't seem interested in making the drive home, dude. How long have you been away? Half a year now?"

Tony shook his head. "Nice try. It's been two months. Well…almost three. You seem to have survived just fine without me." He patted his cousin's stomach. "Looks like you've been eating my meals while I was gone."

Luca swatted his hand away and tossed a few curses at him, then grinned. "My belt's still on the same hole, but *your* waistline looks like you've been eating well out here on the farm. Jeez, there's a sentence I never thought I'd be saying to you."

Tony looked back, realizing he'd forgotten where they were and who was in the room with them. Olivia was watching with interest. She laughed when he held his hands out in a gesture of *what the hell?*

"I ran into them at the coffee shop. They said they were here to surprise you, so I figured I'd help them." She shrugged. "Surprise?"

"That's why you called and said you wanted to cook a roast instead of grilling steaks—so we'd have enough food." He shook his head. "You haven't seen these two brutes eat. We're doomed."

She ignored Luca and Paulie's protests, and winked at Tony. "They warned me that might be the case, so I picked up some extra sides at the store. A potato salad, baked beans plus our dessert—Jade's *bougatsa* pastry *and* a couple pounds of cookies. We'll be fine."

Luca put his arm on Tony's shoulders. "And we picked up a couple six-packs, so…"

Tony stepped back. "Those are for you two, not us."

"You're *still* not drinking?" Luca asked. "I thought you just needed to dry out for a little while?"

Paulie slapped his hand to his face. "Really, Luca?"

This was one reason why he'd been avoiding home. Home was where men and women ended a long day of hard work with a cold brewski. Or two or three.

"I've dried out for good, guys. Is that going to be a problem?"

There was a quick beat of tense silence before Luca shrugged and shook his head. "Not a problem at all. Hand to God. We're just glad to see you, man. We were hoping to talk you into coming home, but..." Luca looked at Olivia in the doorway. "I'm beginning to see why you're in no hurry."

Tony stared at Olivia, too. She was becoming his whole world. But his *old* world had just arrived, ready to drag him home. His chest felt heavy.

Olivia giggled, having no idea of the turmoil he was feeling. "I think you've struck him mute, fellas. That pork roast is starting to cool, so why don't you come sit and catch up over a meal."

The evening started exactly how Olivia had hoped, with the guys laughing and telling tales on each other. It was like having three Tonys in the house—big, handsome men with big voices and big personalities. She spent most of her time just listening in amazement to their stories of hijinks far above the streets of New York. Practical jokes they'd pulled on each other. Near misses they could laugh about now. No one mentioned the accident that *hadn't* been a near miss.

She saw a subtle change in Tony as the night went on. He'd mellowed over the past few weeks, settling into a slower, quieter, Gallant Lake pace of life. But with Luca and Paulie here, he got louder. Tougher. His Staten Island accent got deeper. The men teased each other mercilessly, calling each other names and cursing as they tried to one-up one another. It was all done with affection, but the level of testosterone in her house was climbing by the minute.

It was a side of Tony she hadn't seen in a while, and she couldn't decide how she felt about it. Was this the *real* Tony? Or was he just trying to match his cousins's macho attitudes to avoid being roasted by them? Last week he was talking about what it would be like to *stay* in Gallant Lake. Tonight he was joining the guys in making fun of the little town.

All the annoying tourists. The lack of restaurant options. The lack of a nightlife. How everyone wore denim and flannel and baseball caps. Olivia stayed quiet and let the boys-being-boys thing go on, but the ease with which Tony stepped back into what she assumed was his old persona hurt a little. She understood what peer pressure could do, but he was sitting at *her* table saying this stuff.

And then he left with them. They were clapping each other's backs and laughing as they headed out to their trucks. It made sense—she didn't have room for them all and he *did still* have his own apartment in town, although he said he'd given Nora notice. It would seem strange to send his family to the apartment while he stayed behind. Especially since he'd seemed to skirt around the topic of their relationship all evening.

Luca and Paulie had seen him pinch her when he'd walked into the living room. His cousin had teased him about understanding why he'd spent so much time remodeling her house. Tony hadn't rushed to say "oh, yeah, we're dating" or anything like that. He hadn't said much about them at all.

It's not as if he'd treated her *badly*. He'd helped her serve dinner and helped clean up. Under the table, his knee had been up against hers all through the meal. He'd snuck a hot kiss in the kitchen when he apologized for going back to the apartment with *his boys*.

"They drove up here to see me, so I can't just send them back to the apartment without me. You understand, right?"

"Of course," she'd answered brightly. "You'll probably be up all night talking. I can make pancakes for the gang in the morning if you want to come back here."

He'd agreed, then gave her one more swift kiss before answering Luca's shouts and heading out with them. She was happy for him to have time with his family.

But she couldn't shake the feeling that something had shifted now that his former life had barged into their little world here in Gallant Lake. That he might decide to head back to the city after all, despite his recent hints that he might stay here.

Tony might be like everyone else in her life—willing to walk away.

"What did my Dad tell you about mixing business and pleasure, Tony?" Luca pulled three cans of soda out of the fridge and shared them with Paulie and Tony. "I mean, I get it. She's pretty. She's nice. She's available. And she's a fun little distraction from you getting back to where you belong. But there's no way in hell you'd rather live on some farm in the boonies than in Staten Island. Carla's been asking about you, so why not come home and let *her* distract you while you get back to work?"

Carla was an old flame Tony had had an on-and-off relationship with through the years. If they were both

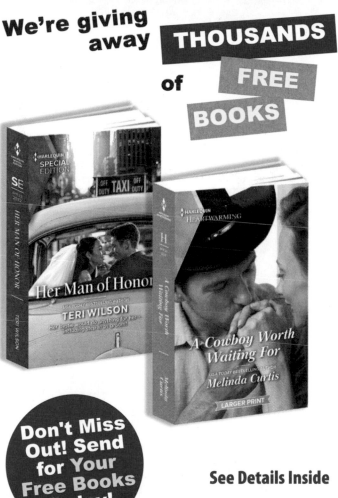

Get up to 4
FREE FABULOUS BOOKS
You Love!

To thank you for being a loyal reader we'd like to send you up to 4 FREE BOOKS, absolutely free when you try the Harlequin Reader Service.

Just write "YES" on the Loyal Reader Voucher and we'll send you 2 free books from each series you choose and a Free Mystery Gift, altogether worth over $20.

Try **Harlequin® Special Edition** and get 2 books featuring comfort and strength in the support of loved ones and enjoying the journey no matter what life throws your way.

Try **Harlequin® Heartwarming™ Larger-Print** and get 2 books featuring uplifting stories where the bonds of friendship, family and community unite.

Or **TRY BOTH and get 2 books from each series!**

Your free books are completely free, even the shipping! If you continue with your subscription, you can look forward to curated monthly shipments of brand-new books from your selected series, always at a discount off the cover price! Plus you can cancel any time.

So don't miss out, return your Loyal Readers Voucher today to get your Free books.

Pam Powers

LOYAL READER
FREE BOOKS VOUCHER

▼ DETACH AND MAIL CARD TODAY!

YES! I Love Reading, please send me up to 4 FREE BOOKS and a Free Mystery Gift from the series I select.

Just write in "YES" on the dotted line below then return this card today and we'll send your free books & gift asap!

➡ ⎯ YES ⎯ ⬅

Which do you prefer?

| ☐ **Harlequin® Special Edition** 235/335 HDL GRAH | ☐ **Harlequin Heartwarming® Larger-Print** 161/ 361 IDL GRAH | ☐ **BOTH** 235/335 & 161/361 IDL GRA5 |

FIRST NAME | LAST NAME

ADDRESS

APT.# | CITY

STATE/PROV. | ZIP/POSTAL CODE

EMAIL ☐ Please check this box if you would like to receive newsletters and promotional emails from Harlequin Enterprises ULC and its affiliates. You can unsubscribe anytime.

SE/HW-622-LR_MMM22

free and lonely, they hooked up occasionally. She liked hitting the nightclubs and having a fun time. Carla was a good person, but she was more friend than lover. Besides, Olivia had ruined him for other women.

"We could use you on the job, man." Paulie sat at the kitchen island next to him. "It's been a bit of a scramble the past few months without you as team supervisor."

Tony shook his head. "Your dad could promote anyone to my position, including you."

"How can Dad promote someone to a job you still have? He's expecting you to come back." Luca joined them, pulling up a barstool. "We *all* expect you back. In fact, we expected you back over a month ago, after your little rehab stint. What's really going on with you?"

Tony stared at his can of soda, turning it back and forth on the granite countertop, watching the rings of condensation bead up.

"Well, for one thing, don't *ever* let me hear you refer to Olivia Carson as a *fun little distraction* again. She's not some side piece, she's..." He struggled with how much he wanted to reveal. "She's important to me, guys. Really effing important. Respect that and respect her."

"Wait," Paulie said. "Are the two of you *serious*? How would that work? You'd come up here on weekends or something?"

"I don't know. Obviously, it's new for both of us." A part-time relationship would never be enough for him, and he didn't think Olivia would be wild about it, either.

"Would she move to the city?" Luca asked.

"No way. She loves the farm, and she does animal

rescues there. She has two…no, *three* horses and I don't
see her giving them up."

"Well, then you've got a problem, because your life
is in the city. Your job. Your family. Your…history.
And I don't see you giving *that* up."

"The only thing I'd be giving up would be the job.
My family would still be my family…" He fixed Luca
with a hard look. "Right?"

"Well…yeah, but…" Luca sat back with a sigh. "It's
not just any job. It's the family business. Granddad
built it for his boys, and Dad kept it going for all of
us after your parents died. You can't just walk away."

Tony's eyebrows rose. "I'm pretty sure I *can*, but I
haven't made any decisions yet."

Luca looked annoyed, his voice suddenly hard. "Are
you *walking* away or running?"

"Excuse me?"

"Ever since the accident you've gone into hiding.
First you hid in booze, then rehab and now with the
pretty blond farm lady." Luca held up one hand. "I'm
not disrespecting her, but it's time to get back to your
life. The accident was hard on all of us. And on the
business. Did you know Dad lost three contracts after
that? We're lucky to have picked up the Context Building job in Jersey City, and we only got that because
the other contractor went bankrupt in the middle of
the job."

Tony stared straight ahead, trying to wrap his head
around this news.

"How did I not know any of this?"

"I think we've covered that," Paulie answered. "You
drank yourself into a stupor, then Nonna made you go
get clean, and you never came home."

He shook his head. It wasn't that simple.

"I've been on the phone with you, Uncle Rocco, Nonna—everybody—multiple times since I've been gone. No one said a word about any of this."

Paulie patted his shoulder. "No one wanted to stress you out while you were trying to…get better. But, yeah, it's been tough. It's like we lost *you* the same day we lost Tim. And now we see you sitting here and you seem to be…you. But you're *here*. You're not home. Look, I want you to be okay. Everyone does, including Luca."

Luca hesitated, still agitated, then nodded. "Of course."

Tony hadn't wanted a drink this bad in a long time. He closed his eyes and counted backward from five. Then ten. Then fifteen. It was a centering trick his counselor had taught him to stop his brain from spiraling.

"Tony?" Paulie squeezed his shoulder. "What is it?"

"I'm not quite *me* yet, guys. That's why I didn't come home after rehab. I don't think I can go back on the girders."

"You grew up on those girders," Luca scoffed. "Of course, you can."

He thought of the day he saw Olivia out on the porch roof. Just the memory was enough to make his skin clammy.

"I'm afraid of heights."

Luca started to laugh, but stopped when he met Tony's eyes. His jaw dropped.

"Seriously?"

"I couldn't even go out on the porch roof at the farm. I had a panic attack! How the hell am I supposed to walk the girders?"

A tense silence settled on the apartment. Shame burned through him, but they had to find out eventually. Paulie cleared his throat.

"Because of the accident?"

"I saw my best friend go over the edge, Paulie. Tim was looking right at me, and I couldn't get to him." Tony closed his eyes again, trying to push away that memory. "I got over my drinking, but I don't think I can get over that. Which makes me useless on a jobsite."

"So *that's* why you're hanging around here in Bumpkinville?" Luca asked.

"It's why I stopped here, but I'm *staying* because..." He stopped himself before admitting he was staying for love. He didn't want to deal with the hazing he'd get.

"Because of Mother Earth up there on the farm?"

"Careful, Luca. I mean it." He took a steadying breath. "I started a job, and I need to finish it."

"Looked pretty finished to me."

"Not quite. I need to do some trim work and paint the rooms, install a few more lights, then get the furniture settled in place."

"How is it a contractor's job to move furniture?" Luca demanded. "It sounds like you're dragging this out, man. Complete the job and get your ass home, where you belong. The longer you wait, the harder it will be. I bet as soon as you get back on the job, you'll get your mojo back."

Paulie wasn't convinced. "This is more about the farmer than the farmhouse, isn't it? Are you and her getting serious?"

Luca scoffed. "Of course not. Tony's the biggest

player in Staten Island. He's not going to fall for some mousy—"

"One more time, Luca, and we're gonna have a problem," Tony said, cutting him off angrily.

"Oh, shit. You *are* falling for her, aren't you?" Luca sat back, stunned. "Tony, there's no way this is going to work. She's nowhere near your type." He shook his head. "That settles it. You need to come home before you make a huge mistake and end up getting her pregnant or something."

Tony's breath caught in his chest at the image of Olivia carrying his child. Stomach rounded and her glowing. A little girl toddling around the yard, chasing chickens and laughing while Olivia chased her. It was idyllic. And Luca was right. It was completely out of character for Tony.

Could he really change his whole life so quickly? Would he be happy in Gallant Lake for the rest of his life? Or would he eventually get restless and end up hurting the one person he cared about most? The farm felt like heaven—*Olivia* felt like heaven. For now. But was it realistic?

Or was his cousin right? Was he just hiding in *this* life to avoid the world where he truly belonged? Hell, the only reason he was *in* Gallant Lake was because he'd taken an exit off the highway to avoid a traffic jam. There was nothing poetic about that. Nothing that fit some fairy-tale narrative of being destined to grow old here…with Olivia.

Luca continued, his voice lowering. "I'm not saying Olivia isn't great. Like I said, she's pretty and funny and nice. She obviously cares about you. I get why you're tempted to try out this…lifestyle. But you need to figure out *why* you want to do that. Is it because you think you belong here or because you think you *don't* belong in the city?"

Well. Damn. Setting aside his feelings for Olivia... why *was* he in Gallant Lake? And would he still want to be here a year from now? Ten years from now?

Paulie drained his soda and stood. "Decisions don't need to be made tonight. Point me to a bed, because all this heavy talk has worn me out."

Luca claimed the sofa, Paulie went to the guest room and Tony headed up to the loft. His mind was still spinning with questions and newly planted doubts. Would it be fair to Olivia for him to stay here? What if he got restless down the road? What if his head finally cleared and he missed his old life in the city?

Olivia told him she felt like everyone walked away from her eventually. He didn't want to be the one to break her heart again. If he was going to do this, the sooner, the better. Before they got too deep.

The only problem was he was already about as deep as a man could get.

Chapter Fifteen

Nora joined Olivia, Julie and Amanda at a window table in the Gallant Brew. The morning crowd had slowed, and Nora's employee, Cathy, could handle the coffee counter for now.

"So," Nora began, "you don't seem happy about Tony's family showing up last week. Did they not get along?"

"Oh, they got along just fine. With each other."

Amanda set down her mug. "Were they rude to you?"

"No-o-o. Not rude." She thought about the men's visit. "Luca and Paulie are good guys. But they obviously don't understand what Tony is doing in Gallant Lake. It's clear they want him to come home. They said the business needs him."

"Wait." Julie leaned forward. "He didn't agree, did he? I thought he said he was staying here? That he was moving into your place?"

Nora nodded. "He told me he'd be out of the loft at

the end of the month. I assumed he was going to the farm, but…?"

"That's what we'd talked about." Olivia stared out the window. It was another bright, sunny summer day, but it felt eerily like winter at the edges of her heart. "He barely made eye contact with me when they all came for breakfast the next morning. They kept talking about the building they were working on and how Tony's uncle needed him working on the floor decking and how the work crew missed him. And Tony seemed to be listening. A lot."

That calm center Tony had been starting to build upon vanished once his cousins showed up. Maybe it was natural for him to fall back on what seemed to be his normal family role with them. And his family just happened to be one of those big, noisy Italian clans that thrived on trying to top each other with wild tales.

But she couldn't shake the feeling he already had one foot out the door. She didn't know what had happened after they all headed to his apartment that night, but he was obviously preoccupied and uncomfortable that next morning at breakfast. It was Paulie who'd carried most of the conversation, asking about the farm, the horses, the chickens. He'd asked about her work, and seemed to perk up when she said she worked from home.

"So you could pull up stakes and work from anywhere?"

"Yes," she'd answered. "But I'm not going to. I've got the perfect office right here, thanks to your cousin."

Rather than respond to her compliment, Tony had looked even more troubled.

"Hold on." Nora's hand brushed her arm, making

her jump. "Do you think he's going back to his old job in New York?"

"I didn't. But now... I don't know. He's been acting almost guilty since they left."

Julie frowned. "That doesn't make sense. He and Bobby were talking about him coming on as a partner and starting his own contracting crew in addition to Bobby's, so they could take on more work."

That was news to Olivia. Tony told her he'd had lunch with Bobby, but not that they'd talked about any sort of partnership. If he was going to partner with Bobby, then he'd *have* to stay in Gallant Lake. But that *if* was a giant question mark. Julie was still talking.

"There's one way to know for sure. *Talk* to the man and ask him what's going on."

Amanda agreed. "It's funny how many problems can be avoided with a little communication. Has he talked to them since they left?"

"He hasn't said much about it, but I know he has. I think he's been texting with them, too." She started to chuckle. "When they were here, they offered to stay to help him finish the work on my place, which would have freed him up more quickly to go home."

"But he didn't take them up on it?" Nora asked. "That's a good sign, right?"

Nora had a point. Tony had been quick to turn down the offer. But he was almost done with the re-model, anyway, so maybe it didn't mean that much. She dropped her head into her hands.

"I don't know. All that's left is trim work and paint-ing. It's not like he needs help for that."

"I don't imagine he needs help with anything," Amanda said. "Remodeling a house must come pretty easy to a guy used to building skyscrapers. I mean, it is quite a comedown…" Amanda's eyes went wide and she looked around the table. Nora and Julie were glaring at her. "And I'm not helping, am I?" She waved her hand in front of her face. "Forget what I said. Tony seems very happy, and you two have something really special together. I don't see him walking away from that."

"It's been done before." She and Jared were planning their wedding before the accident happened. And he'd found a way to walk away from that. From her.

"We've all had our bad apples," Nora said. "Tony's never struck me as one of those. But I stand by what Amanda said. Communication solves a lot of issues. Go talk to him about what he's thinking now that his cousins put the pressure on. See where his head's at. Then you'll know if you need to worry and what to worry about. Right now, you're just guessing and fretting."

Nora was right, as usual. The older woman—late forties?—had a tendency to dispense the best and most compassionate advice.

Julie sipped her coffee, looking at Olivia over the brim. "You should also be prepared. What will you do if he *does* go back? It's not like he'd be going a thousand miles away. It's a two-hour drive."

"It's not the driving distance," Olivia answered. "It's the…culture difference. We'd be in two totally different worlds. And he *likes* that world. How long would he be happy coming back to a sleepy farm in the Catskills? I don't think I could compete. And I don't want to."

"Like I said…" Nora said in a singsong voice.

"I know." Olivia smiled. "Communicate first, worry later."

It was sound advice. But her worrying genes ran deep.

* * *

Tony was bringing Misty and Flash into the barn when he saw Olivia's truck pull in. The colt was prancing and leaping around his mother as they went through the barn doors, then he bolted ahead into their stall and waited. Poor little guy was probably ready for a nap after charging around the pasture for the past hour. It was fun to watch him getting stronger and faster every day. Olivia had been teaching him to lead with a tiny, foal-sized halter, but Tony figured he'd stay close enough to his mom to get to the pasture and back while free.

A month ago he would never have imagined himself leading horses around, cleaning stalls, or falling in love with the woman now chasing chickens away from the driveway with a laugh.

Are you here because you belong here or because you think you don't belong in the city?

His cousin's words had been rattling around in his head for a week. Was it possible his desire to stay was just a tangled way of avoiding his old life and new phobias? Flash came charging back out of the stall and did circles around Tony and Misty again, as if hurrying them along.

"Well, look at you, wrangling horses all by yourself," Olivia said as she walked to the barn. "Little mister is feeling his oats, I see."

"I swear he gets more full of himself every day." Tony led Misty into the stall and the colt bounded in after them, giving a kick out toward Tony's leg as he did. Luckily, he missed this time. He'd connected the other day and those little hooves were sharp. Olivia held the gate closed before Flash could get out again.

She opened it for Tony after he removed Misty's halter, then latched it behind him as he turned to her. "I saw the storm clouds rolling in, and figured you'd want them inside."

"Thanks. They said the rain wouldn't get here until later, but I guess they were wrong. Let's go in the house before it starts." They tossed a flake of hay into each stall for the horses, then went to the house. Fat raindrops started falling, and the chickens scattered as Tony and Olivia broke into a jog.

"I really need to get a coop for these birds," Olivia said when they reached the shelter of the porch. "The guy at the feed store says people have spotted coyotes up on this hill, and the Blakemans down the road lost a few chickens to them just last week." She swept her hair back over her shoulder. "Plus, it's a pain to search for eggs everywhere in the mornings."

"Show me what you need," Tony said. "I can throw something together for you before…" He caught himself. "Before, um, I finish the house. You know, while all my tools are here."

Olivia opened the door, shooing away Chandler and Monica so they couldn't escape. Ross leaped toward Tony's leg. Ginger bolted inside, scattering the kittens. They were growing like weeds. Phoebe had already gone to live with Julie and Quinn. Monica and Chandler were promised to new homes. They'd all be gone soon. Tony couldn't help thinking the house would be quiet without the mischiefmakers darting out from behind every corner all day long. He bent over to grab Ross, who'd just done exactly that. He knew the kitten wanted to climb his leg, but he'd gotten too big and his claws were too long for that to happen without lots of pain—and blood—on Tony's part.

He held the smoky gray kitten in front of his face. "How many times do I have to tell you I am not a tree? No more leg climbing, little dude."

Olivia laughed. "I tried to warn you…"

"I know. It was cute when they were the size of cotton balls. I had no idea how sharp those claws would get." Tony turned the kitten to face her. "Look at him!" Tony turned the kitten to face her. "How do I say no to that face?"Olivia took Ross from him, shaking her head with a smile as she spoke to the kitten. "Rossie, you need to stop taking advantage of Uncle Tony. Under that crusty exterior, he's a big old softie and he'll let you get away with things you shouldn't be doing."

He's a big old softie…

No one had ever called him that in Staten Island. A *softie.* Is that how she saw him? More importantly, is that who he wanted to be? Olivia was still cooing to the kitten.

"He saved mister Flash from getting rained on. He's talking about building a chicken coop. And he loves you little guys as much as I do…"

Her voice trailed off when she looked at Tony. "What's wrong?

"Nothing." He coughed and cleared his throat. "I should get back to work."

She didn't look convinced. "What's today's project?"

"I'm putting the second coat of paint on both guest rooms, and I might start the hallway. All the trim is painted, so the end is in sight."

Those last words hung in the air so heavily he could

almost see them shimmering in the air. Olivia's expression told him she felt the weight of them, too.

"What happens then?" she asked. "When we get to *the end*?"

They both knew what they were talking about, and it wasn't paint. He had no idea how to answer. She moved closer, resting her hand on his arm.

"Tony?"

He knew what he needed to say, but as he stared into her eyes, he couldn't force out the words. She let out a long breath, then closed her eyes and nodded sadly.

"You're going back to New York, aren't you?"

"Well…at some point I need to. I have to at least touch base with my family and see what's going on with the company. The guys told me my uncle's been struggling, and I had no idea. I owe them…" He paused, then rushed to reassure her when her eyes began to glisten with unshed tears. "I'm not going anywhere until the work on the house is done. And I'm not saying I'm going to stay in Staten Island. But I *do* have a life there to consider—my town house, the job, my family. I need to deal with all of that."

"And…" She hesitated, then gathered herself to continue. "And what about your life *here*? How are you going to deal with that?"

He took a step back, jamming his fingers through his hair. "Damn it, Liv—I don't *know*! I love what we have together, but… My cousin asked me if I was using you and the farm to hide from my so-called real life. I denied it, but… What if I wake up in six months and realize I don't belong here? What if I suddenly start missing everything about who I used to be?" He reached for her, but she waved him off, making his chest tighten in pain. "I love you, but I don't want to end up hurting you down the road if I discover I'm here for the wrong reasons."

A sad smile flickered across her face before quickly disappearing. "If you really loved me, you wouldn't have to keep adding the word *but* every time you say it."

Son of a... He felt light-headed. She was right.

"Okay." He met her wide eyes. "This conversation just got heavy in a hurry. Let's sit and talk it out, okay? On the porch?" He'd glanced out the screen door, and the mini storm had slowed to a gentle rain. If only the same could happen to the storm in his heart.

"Yes, we need to talk. Let me grab some water. I'll meet you out there."

"I can help—"

"I don't need your help." Her answer was swift and sharp. She was angry. No...she was hurt. Exactly what he'd wanted to avoid. He held up his hands in surrender.

"Got it. I'll be outside." She started to turn away, but he stopped her with his hand on her arm. "Liv... this doesn't have to be the end. Let's not go into it as if we're ending things. That's not what I want."

She stared back for a long time, then nodded. "It's not what I want, either." She headed for the kitchen, and he could see from her heavy footsteps and sloped shoulders that it was exactly what she expected.

Chapter Sixteen

Olivia stayed in the kitchen longer than she needed to, just staring out at the window at the hill behind the barn. The rain was misty now, blurring everything into a watercolor image of green and brown and gray. The gray matched her mood.

She *knew* it. She knew something had changed for Tony when his cousins showed up. Before that, she'd been worried about the way he avoided any talk of his world in Staten Island. Now she was worried that he *wasn't* avoiding it. Luca and Paulie had opened the door, and Tony had strolled right through it without looking back. Without her.

She gave herself a mental shake and grabbed two bottles of water from the fridge. The past few weeks had been idyllic. And now they were over.

Tony was staring off down the hill when she joined

him on the porch. His somber expression said he knew it was over, too. Gallant Lake was always supposed to be a temporary stopover for him. The problem for both of them was that love was permanent.

He looked up when the screen door closed behind her. His gentle smile broke her heart. He reached for a water, then slid over on the swing and raised his free arm to welcome her at his side. She obliged, unable to resist the pull of his warmth. Once she was settled in, he brushed her hair with his lips.

"I love the way you smell, babe." He nuzzled her hair. "I love the way you feel in my arms. I love everything about you."

"But…" She couldn't resist poking.

"No *buts*." He sighed against her. "Well…maybe there are. But that doesn't change how I feel. You need to know that."

"You're leaving." She didn't frame it as a question.

"You know I need to go clean things up there. You were encouraging it a couple weeks ago."

"But that's not what you're doing." She hesitated, unable to ignore the hope that still flickered. "Is it?"

Tony rested his head on hers. It was heavy, but not as heavy as her heart felt.

"Liv…"

She pushed away from him, needing to see his eyes.

"Do you remember the first day we met? When you told me to *just spit it out*, because if we couldn't communicate there was no point?" His expression was troubled, but he nodded in silence. "Well, we need to do that now. No protecting each other. Just…spit it out."

"This is all pretty raw for me, Liv. I'm still processing it, but…yeah. I need to deal with that life I've been hiding from. And, yes, you told me so, but it took my cousins to make me see it." He stared at the floor, his eyes dark and distant. "Here's the thing. Luca asked me if I was hiding here in Gallant Lake, looking for reasons to keep from going back, and I realized that's exactly what I've been doing. Maybe that's a well-duh admission—it seems pretty obvious when I say it out loud."

Olivia frowned. "Are you saying you were grasping at straws to stay here and I was a convenient excuse?"

"No! I mean…not like that…"

There was no humor in her answering laugh. "That was *not* a reassuring response."

He grimaced, then turned to face her. "The thing is, I won't *know* the answer until I go back there, Liv. And I need to know. *You* need to know. Neither one of us can go forward if I can't face this. The guys said the company's struggling. My uncle's stressed out. They lost contracts after the accident. They need me, at least for a while."

"A while? So you're going back to stay."

The words crossed her lips like vinegar.

"No!" Tony took her hands in his. "That's not the plan." That wasn't exactly a denial. "But I have to help them get back on their feet. Make sure they have someone who can do my job before I leave. I owe them that much. And…it's only two hours away. You could come there. We could…"

She started shaking her head before her thoughts were fully formed.

"No. If I'm there it will just…confuse things. Besides, I'm not the one who's mixed up about where they belong. I belong *here*. I think you do, too, but I can't make that decision for you."

Her nerves began to settle as she realized not only *was* this going to happen, but…it also *needed* to happen. Whether it broke her heart or not. He was right to return. She gave his fingers a squeeze. "You should go back. Now."

His eyes went wide. "Now? No, I have to finish painting and—"

"I'm perfectly capable of painting walls, and I have friends who would be over the moon if I actually asked them for help. All the heavy work is done here." *Including me falling in love with you.* "Go figure your shit out, Tony. You won't be any good here—or anywhere—until you do."

"I don't want to leave you, babe. You need to know that." His forehead furrowed. "And I don't need to leave before this is finished."

"This is already finished." The words fell heavily between them.

"Olivia, I love you. I don't want—"

A wave of anger and hurt propelled Olivia to her feet.

"You're the one who told me you need to go. And now that I agree, you're turning it around and arguing with me." Her hands gestured wildly, finally waving toward his truck. "Just *go* already. Don't gaslight me with the I'll-be-back nonsense. The last guy who said that to me never did come back, so the least you can do is be honest. Tell me you're leaving, and stop trying to make me feel *good* about it." She clenched her hands tightly, adrenaline pumping through her, creating a volcano of emotion.

"Of all people, I *understand* why you have to go back. I understand that you've been hiding. *I* was hiding here at first, too—avoiding everyone. Even now…" She gestured toward her long skirt. "I hide my scars. I get it. You think you love me—" He opened his mouth to object, but she didn't let him. "—but you're not sure. No, don't deny that. If you were sure, you wouldn't need to test us like this. If a few words from your cousin make you question your love for me, make you seriously think you might wake up someday and realize I was just a distraction and you won't be able to stay… How is that supposed to make me feel, Tony? How grateful am I supposed to be for a love that may or may not be real, that you may or may not come back for, that you may or may not believe in? I'm all in with us, and you're—you're…"

A sob caught in her throat, ending the torrent of words. Panic clawed at her, but pride held it back.

Tony stood. He started to reach for her, then thought better of it when he read her face.

"If you really want me to go now, I will." His voice was solemn. Steady. As if her hysteria had settled him somehow. "I don't know how to explain that I *know* I love you. The thing I don't know is… I don't know if it's enough to keep me *here*, until I go back *there*. A better man might not need to test himself like that, but I'm *not* a better man." He paused for a long moment. The only sound was the soft whisper of rain beyond the porch, and their slow, heavy breathing.

"Olivia, I need to go face my fears down. I *need* it. I can't go through the rest of my life not knowing if I'm strong enough. It would be bad for me, and damn it, it would be bad for *you*. I said I'm not a better man. The thing is…" He finally reached out to take her shoulders and pull her closer. Not into an embrace, but close enough for them to look deeply into each other's eyes. To feel each other's pain. "The thing is, I *want* to be a better man. For you. *You* make me want that, Olivia. And there's only one way it happens."

There was a moment after Olivia's final skin-graft surgery when her physical therapist told her she had a choice to make. She could give up and accept the life she had, with a drastic lack of mobility in order to avoid the pain of rehabilitation. Or she could fight for every inch of life she could grasp. She could push herself beyond her limits. She could face the pain in the moment for the promise of a better tomorrow.

This was one of those moments.

She didn't want him staying with her if he wasn't sure.

And the only way he'd be sure was to leave.

Tony had seen the exact instant Olivia knew he was right. Her eyes softened. Her chin quivered just a little. And her shoulders sagged in surrender under his fingers. He'd wrapped her in his arms, and rested his head on hers. They'd stood like that, in silence, for a long time. She'd pulled away first, smiling when he'd clung to her for an extra second. He'd almost changed his mind right then, but they'd both known what had to happen.

A horn blared behind him, snapping his attention back to navigating the traffic on I-95. It was midday on a Thursday, but the traffic was always bumper-to-bumper near the Newark airport. He didn't want to miss the Staten Island exit. He maneuvered across four lanes of traffic as he passed the airport and took the exit over the bridge to the island.

The houses in his Rossville neighborhood were bumper-to-bumper, too. Neighbors could almost shake hands from one window to another. The town houses were nestled in the center of the community. He parked his truck and stared at unit forty-five.

It was surreal that he'd been gone from his home for three months. Nothing had changed. Same nondescript beige siding. Same curtains hanging inside the same windows.

The pot of flowers and another hanging basket near the door were new. Probably courtesy of Paulie's new romantic interest. It seemed that James, a cardiac nurse, had pretty much moved in during Tony's absence. If James was willing to do that officially, and contribute to the expenses, maybe Paulie would be able to buy Tony out of his half of the mortgage.

Nothing major had changed inside. The cleanliness and a few little splashes of colorful accents indicated the recent influence of someone who wasn't a construction worker. Tony's suite was still monochrome—gray walls, gray carpet, gray bedspread. He'd read somewhere that gray was a hot design trend at the time, so he'd gone all in with it.

As he stood there, duffel in his hand, he felt a fresh hit of missing Olivia. The hits came in waves, often out of nowhere. At any moment, he might suddenly imagine her face or, in this case, her voice.

She'd hate this room.

This place is lifeless. Where's the warmth? Where's the personality? You need some art on the walls. Bo-ring.

A soft scratching in the pet carrier he'd set on the

bed helped snap him out of it. Ross was overdue for a litterbox break.

Olivia had handed the soot-gray kitten to Tony this morning when he'd stopped for one last, heart-wrenching goodbye.

"What?" he'd asked. "Ross needs a last goodbye, too?"

"No." She'd shaken her head with a soft smile. "Ross needs a home, and you need a kitten."

"I'm pretty sure I do *not* need a kitten."

"Says the man holding said kitten under his chin and nuzzling him." She was right, damn it. "From the day you accused Ross of being a sewer rat, he's been your shadow. Take him with you. If you decide to stay there, at least you'll have a cat as a reminder of your farm days."

"I'm not going to stay—"

"I said *if.*"

"I don't need a cat to remind me of this." He'd looked around the yard, frowning at the chickens wandering around. He'd planned on building a chicken coop for them. "All I have to do is think of you, and I do that every hour of the day. That won't change on Staten Island."

A shadow touched her smile before she'd straightened. "Take Ross, anyway. I'll feel better knowing he's taking care of you."

That was the argument that sealed the deal. If it would make her feel better, he had no choice. He poured litter into the litterbox Olivia had sent with him, then released the kitten from the carrier. Ross immediately began to explore the room, treading carefully across the bed before lowering himself, *Spider-Man-*

style, down the bedspread to the floor. Tony sat on the edge of the bed and watched absently, wondering what the hell he was doing here. He could be home with...

He bit back a curse. *This* was home. He owned it, or at least half of it. So why was he thinking of an old farmhouse in the Catskills as home?

Because that's where Olivia was.

Chapter Seventeen

His grandmother wept when he walked into his aunt and uncle's place in Tottenville, on the southeast corner of Staten Island. The big brick house, built in the 1960s, occupied most of the double lot. An in-ground swimming pool took up the backyard, even though the house was only a few blocks from the beach. And, yes, there was a statue of the Madonna in the front garden.

"Tony!" Nonna scrambled up from her recliner. "Finally, you come home! Come hug me, my big beautiful boy!"

She was in her eighties now. A little slow to get moving sometimes, but once she was underway, watch out. And if you got in her way, you might get her heavy cane with the tripod base against your shins. She was the tiniest and toughest woman he knew. He obliged her with a long embrace.

When his parents died in a car crash, he'd been an angry kid, hell-bent on getting in trouble. Uncle Rocco and Aunt Mary became his legal guardians, but it was Nonna Vello who'd kept him *out* of trouble with a mix of tenderness, pasta and discipline. To this day, if she'd grabbed at his ear, he would have ducked to avoid having it pinched and twisted. But instead, she clung to him, whispering in his ear.

"My boy. I knew you'd find your way back to us. No more gettin' drunk?" He shook his head against her. She held him out at arm's length and stared hard. "You're different. I want to hear about that later."

"Don't go making a fuss over him, Nonna," Paulie objected. "He brought a *cat* home with him."

Their grandmother frowned. "A *cat*? Why, do you have mice?"

Tony gave his cousin a thanks-a-lot glare over his shoulder before answering. "It's an orphaned kitten. He needed a home. What's the big deal?"

His Aunt Mary walked in just then, folding him into another long hug. "The big deal is Vellos don't do pets, Tony. A guard dog, maybe. But cats? They get into everything and if you don't have mice, what's the point of all that bother?"

He couldn't help smiling at the familiar rhythm of the accent he hadn't heard in a while. And the volume, as if the whole house was in on the conversation. The way certain words were practically shouted for emphasis. The way she pronounced *bother* as *bah-thah*. He gave her a quick kiss on her forehead.

"Well, *this* Vello does pets, Aunt Mary. He's funny and he makes me happy."

Before she could answer, clearly unconvinced, his uncle joined them.

"Oh, well, as long as Anthony is happy, then I guess we can all just relax and not worry about anything." He was laughing, but Tony could see a glint of accusation—or was it hurt—in the man's eyes. "Nice to see you can still find Staten Island on a map."

They clasped hands and did a one-armed man-hug with the obligatory back pound. The only indication of emotion on his uncle's part was the way the hug lasted just a fraction longer than usual before he stepped back with a cough.

"So you back for good or what?" Rocco asked. "Luca tells me you found yourself a girl up in the mountains."

As much as he tried to push it aside, the perpetual slide show of Olivia images spun through his mind. On the porch swing. On horseback. In the kitchen. In bed...

It was his turn to cough now—man code for holding back messy emotions. "I met a woman, yeah. A client." He knew he couldn't get away with that story with his family. "Who became more than a client."

Nonna perked up. "And you like this girl? Paulie says she's pretty. Is she Italian?"

He chuckled. "She's not a girl, Nonna. She's a grown woman and I like her very much. She's not Italian, but she can cook a halfway decent lasagna."

Nonna sniffed. "Only halfway decent? What do you like about her, then?"

Every little thing. Every inch of her. Her laugh. Her eyes. Her touch.

"She makes me happy."

His grandmother paused a beat before turning away. "I thought that's why you got the cat."

Touché. "She's the one who gave me the cat."

Aunt Mary was ushering everyone to the dining room, where the table was set and groaning with food. Nonna turned, her eyebrows sliding higher. "So more than just happy in the sheets then? She cares about you. So where is she? Why didn't she come with you?"

He felt his cheeks heat up. Leave it to his grandmother to cut straight to the point. "She has a home and a job and animals to take care of."

"And these animals are more important to her than you?"

"Maybe not, but she can't leave them to starve."

They took their usual seats, with Nonna at one end of the table and Tony to her right. Rocco and Mary were at the other end, and Paulie took a seat near them. James was working the weekend shift at the hospital. The youngest cousin, Joey, had just arrived with his wife, Helen, and the three littlest Vellos—Joey Jr., Nicholas and baby Sophia. Luca rushed through the door five minutes after they started. Each arrival amped up the volume—a mix of laughter and hardcore razzing between the men. Most of that verbal abuse was aimed at Tony for being away so long, and he took it all with a grin and rolled eyes.

As the eventual quiet of people enjoying a good meal—baked ziti with meatballs, a full ham and all the sides—settled over the table, Nonna picked the conversation back up with him.

"Are we gonna meet this girl of yours?"

He gave up on getting his grandmother to call Olivia

anything but a girl. All females below her generation were girls and that was that.

"I don't know, Nonna. It depends on how things go with me back here. It's not that far distance-wise, but it's a whole different world to her."

"Different world?" She sniffed again. "It's Staten Island, not Mars. Was she raised by wolves or something?"

He choked on his ziti, taking a drink of his water to clear his throat. "No, she grew up in Maryland. She was an equestrian."

"O-o-o-h-h." Nonna made the two-letter word sound like a song. "Too good for us, then."

"Of course not!" His voice sharpened, and then he saw the glint of humor in his grandmother's eyes. She was poking at him. Testing him. His voice softened. "You'd love her, I promise."

"Not if I never meet her." She hesitated, the spark of verbal warfare fading from her eyes. "If I'd love her, does that mean *you* love her, Anthony?"

He licked his lips, then took another sip of water. Aunt Mary had set a wineglass near his plate, but he had no intention of using it. No more hiding. Not in booze. Not in silence.

"Yes," he answered. "I love her."

He wasn't sure what to expect in his grandmother's reaction, but he never anticipated her taking her linen napkin and swatting him with it. Twice. Hard.

"Then what the hell are you doing here alone?" she demanded. "I raised you better than that, didn't I?"

He held his hand up to deflect her third swing with the napkin. "Jesus! Nonna, stop!" All conversation at the table hushed. Everyone was watching, wide-eyed. "What are you hitting me for?"

"Where is she?" she demanded. "This girl...what's her name?"

"Her name's Olivia, and I told you she's on her farm up in Gallant Lake."

"And you're here because...?"

He looked around the table, slack-jawed. "Because I live here? Because I work here? Because my family's here? Come on, Nonna." A little good-natured ribbing he could take, but it was beginning to feel like he had a flamethrower aimed at him tonight.

Her eyes narrowed in accusation. "You didn't care about *living* here, *working* here, *family's* here for the past three months, so why now?"

His mouth fell open again, and stayed there until his sister-in-law reached over and gently closed it with her fingertips. Helen's face was one of the few not getting obvious satisfaction from him being accosted at the table.

"What matters, Nonna," Helen began, "is that he *is* here. Let's not chase him away at his first meal with us, okay?"

Tony shook his head. He stared down at his grandmother. "*You*, of all people, know why I left."

The old woman sat back in her chair with a *harrumph*. "I know why you left—I *sent* you there, remember? But it was supposed to be three *weeks*, not three months."

Tony carefully set his fork and knife on the edge of his plate. "Okay, so we're gonna do this now. Fine." He looked around the table again. "I didn't know if I wanted to come back to the job. Wasn't sure I could. Not after…"

His grandmother's hand rested on his forearm. "What happened to Timothy was horrible, God rest his soul." Everyone made the sign of the cross."That day changed all our lives, and yours the most. We almost lost you." She leaned forward, looking up at his face with her wise, dark eyes. "So what makes you think you *can* do the job now?"

He swallowed hard. "I'm *not* sure I can." His uncle straightened, and Tony looked Rocco straight in the eye. "I just know I have to try, and I can't put it off any longer."

Rocco stared back, then his shoulders dropped a little. "And if you can't do the job?"

"Then I'll help you find and train a replacement. I won't leave you in the lurch again. I'm sorry I flaked on you, Rocco. But you should have told me the company was struggling."

Rocco's face turned scarlet. "Struggling? Who the fu—" He looked at his young grandchildren and took a breath. "Who told you that bullsh—" He closed his eyes with a grimace, and Tony couldn't help smiling. Rocco's language was more suited to a construction site than a table with children at it. "Who told you that?"

Luca shifted in his seat. "I might have suggested it…"

"Wait a minute." Tony's voice rose. "Are you saying it's not true? I left everything…"

Luca leaned across the table. "If you left it, it wasn't that important, was it? I wanted you to see where you belonged, Tony, and you belong *here*."

Tony started to rise from his chair, seeing red.

"That's enough," Joey said firmly. It was funny how the youngest of the cousins had ended up being the quietest and most levelheaded. Maybe it was because he was the only one *not* walking steel girders, or because he was the first to marry and start a family. He'd gone to school to get an accounting degree, and managed the office and bookkeeping for the family business. Joey folded his napkin by his plate, patted Joey Jr. on the head, then addressed the table.

"The company *did* hit a rough patch after the accident. Financially, because we lost some contracts. Emotionally, because we *all* had to deal with losing someone we cared about. We had to get through the lawsuits and settlements." His voice dropped. "And we all had to watch Tony try to drink himself to death."

Tony winced. Joey wasn't wrong. The memories of that day had been relentless at first, and the only way he'd been able to dull their impact was to drink himself into a stupor. Joey eyed Luca next.

"We all missed Tony, but it is not *our* place to decide where he belongs or what's important to him." He paused. "And the company's back on solid ground now. We're getting jobs again. Planning things has been tough not knowing if Tony was coming back or if we should replace him. But we're still doing business without him."

He faced Tony. "But I don't think you're here for what you think *we* need. You're here for what *you* need."

Tony's jaw worked back and forth. He nodded. "Maybe. The only problem is I don't know *what* I need." He gave Luca a hard look. "As far as what's important to me…well, you have no idea. And you really don't want to be interfering in my life again. Got it?"

Luca slumped back in his chair. "Fine."

"I think it's time for pies!" Aunt Mary jumped up from her chair, and Helen got up to help. "I made apple, lemon, rhubarb and chocolate. We'll put them on the sideboard and you can serve yourselves. Who wants coffee?"

The tension eased around the table as conversation moved back to jokes, food and gossip. But nothing eased inside of Tony. If the company didn't need him, then one of the things that brought him home no longer mattered. But tomorrow morning he was scheduled to work on the Jersey building. They were putting the floor decking on the twelfth floor. He couldn't leave until he knew he could walk out onto that deck and do his job.

If you left it, it couldn't have been that important…

Luca had it all wrong. Tony had come home because the woman he'd left behind in Gallant Lake *was* that important. Important enough that he needed to feel worthy of the love waiting for him there.

Olivia had a house full of people. She hadn't been in a crowd like this since…well, it had been a long time. Certainly never in Gallant Lake.

Not only that, but the houseful of people were also here to *help* her. And she'd *asked* them for that help. She brushed a strand of hair from her face and smiled. Tony would be proud.

He'd be especially proud of her attire today. A dress wasn't practical for painting, but instead of jeans on a hot day, she'd put on a pair of shorts. One of her scars extended ten inches below the hem. And her top's scooped neck and short sleeves revealed another good portion of scarred skin.

She'd had a near panic attack that morning when she'd looked in the mirror. Her skin had tightened at the thought of everyone seeing what she'd been hiding for two years. Some of her friends had seen it, of course. But the guys who were here, all the husbands, hadn't seen the scars. They'd have questions, even if their wives tried to shush them.

There'd been a soft thermal top hanging on the back of the bedroom door, and she'd had it in her hand twice before she'd tossed it into the closet and headed downstairs. Tony was off facing his fears. It was time she did the same.

She was in the kitchen now, washing paint from her hands. Everyone insisted that she stay inside painting with one crew, while the others worked outside. She had no idea what needed so much work out there, but the police chief, Dan, had insisted they were just cleaning up a few things.

"Liv, do we have more bottled water in the fridge? The cooler just has soda." Mel Brannigan walked into the kitchen. "Jillie spent a little too much time in the sun painting the chicken—" Mel stopped, then laughed. "Wow, I guess I've been in the sun too long. I'm not even making sense.Poor Jillie is out-to-here pregnant, and I promise she's not painting any chickens. Anyway, she just needs to sit in the shade and have some water…do you have any?"

Jillie Danzer and her husband, Matt, owned the ski lodge on the far side of Gallant Lake. Olivia didn't know them that well, but she knew Jillie was eight months pregnant. She and Matt had shown up this morning with the others, ready to help any way they could. It was apparently the Gallant Lake way.

Olivia took some bottles of water out of the refrigerator. "Here's an armful to replenish the cooler on the porch." Mel started to turn, but Olivia stopped her. "Hey... I want to thank you for everything you did for Tony. You know, finding a support group for him, being there for him when he was just a stranger. It meant a lot to him. And to me."

"It's what people in recovery do for each other. I fought the same demons he did." Mel paused. "Have you heard from him?"

"Mostly by text. He got home and settled in, and he's back to work." He'd called twice. Once right after his arrival and again a week ago, but the conversations had been stilted and awkward. There was so much uncertainty between them...and *within* each of them. Other than those two calls, it had been texts in the two weeks since he'd left. He'd sent a few pictures of Ross getting into mischief in the town house. She shrugged at Mel. "He said this is something he has to do, like it's a test or something."

Mel nodded. "There are times in recovery where you don't trust yourself. Where you think one wrong step will prove all the bad things you've thought about yourself. You think you don't *deserve* to be a better person. I didn't truly start believing in my recovery until I revisited the fashion district in Manhattan and put myself in that world again. I ran into a very bad influence, and..." Mel's eyes were distant now, her voice low. "I could have blown everything that night. But I didn't." Her violet eyes met Olivia's. "That was the night I knew I was going to be okay. Tony may need one of those moments to believe in himself."

"I just wish he could have had that moment here, with me."

"*Here* isn't where his ghosts are." Mel turned to the door again. "Don't give up on him."

Olivia stared out the kitchen window, which looked up the hill at the pastures. All three horses were together in the south pasture. Now that Flash was older, Misty was finally tolerating Scout's presence again, as long as he didn't get too close. The old gelding got the message, but the tiny colt didn't. He was scampering around Scout while he grazed, minding his own business. Misty watched, then went back to eating. Olivia smiled, talking to her reflection in the glass.

"Sometimes you have to let things go to see if they're really yours."

"True," a voice said behind her. "But sometimes they're thick-headed and you have to go and *show* them they're yours."

It was Amanda. Julie, Nora and Cassie were right behind her. Nora pushed through the group and washed her hands at the sink. "The work crew is getting hungry. I think we'd better fire up the grill and get those steaks cooking."

Olivia nodded, stepping out of the way. She'd made the mistake of mentioning at lunch with Julie and Amanda last week that she needed a little help finishing the painting and getting the house back in order. The next thing she knew, there was an entire work party being planned, with husbands and friends and... And it was pretty incredible.

Nora had declared herself in charge of organizing

dinner, and Olivia learned the older woman was very good at running things. She and her husband, Asher, had met in Gallant Lake when his son and her daughter fell in love and started a family. They were expecting their third grandchild this fall.

Olivia turned to Amanda. "What did you mean by *go show them*?"

Nora shook her head at her cousin. "Amanda, it's not our place to—"

"She *asked*," Amanda pointed out.

"Yeah, she *asked* after you dropped a vague opinion bomb on her."

Amanda waved off Nora. "Look, Asher made the big gesture to win you back. In my case, *I* had to make the big gesture and chase after Blake to show him how much I loved him." She turned to the other women, then frowned. "Julie, you and Quinn sort of figured things out together. And Cassie, you were going to leave Nick, but you didn't. And now you have your baby girl. Ugh! This isn't helping…"

Shane Brannigan came into the kitchen, painting trays in hand. He stopped abruptly when he saw all the women gathered.

"I was looking for Mel, but clearly she isn't here and I am way outnumbered. Where do you want us cleaning up supplies, Olivia?"

She pointed toward the mudroom beyond the kitchen, which was also the laundry room. "There's a utility sink in there."

Amanda jumped forward to stop him. "Wait! *You* made a grand gesture for Mel, didn't you? To win her back after you…left." Amanda's voice fell. "Oh. You were the one who left."

Shane shrugged with a grin. "Guilty as charged. I thought I knew what I wanted—that big corner office in LA I'd always dreamed of. Turns out what I wanted was Mel, right back here in little old Gallant Lake." Shane turned to Olivia. "I needed to figure that out on my own. Tony will, too. Just give him time."

"Or…" Amanda wasn't giving up. "Go after him."

"Oh, my God," Nora laughed, pushing Amanda toward the back door. "You're relentless! Leave the woman alone and go fire up the grill."

"But—but Tony stayed in the love shack. And you were at Halcyon together. That's a double dose of Gallant Lake magic."

Olivia had heard the stories about the rumored romance-loving spirit of Halcyon. It was too ridiculous to take seriously. But the other reference…

"Love shack? Are you talking about the farm?"

"No! Nora's *apartment* is a love shack, sweetie." Amanda took a platter of hamburger patties out of the refrigerator. "Let's see… Nora and Asher, of course. And Cathy and Carl before that. Then Mel stayed there and fell in love with Shane. Cassie stayed there and fell in love with Nick. Jade and Trent fell in love while she was living in the loft last winter. And now Tony was there, and you fell in love. The place has serious romance juju!"

"Neither Quinn nor I stayed in the loft," Julie pointed out, "and look at us, happy as clams together! Same with Matt and Jillie. Dan and Mack. Nate and Brittany. I love your love of romance, Amanda, but you see stardust everywhere you look."

"Well, maybe the stardust is *everywhere* in this town. All I'm saying is I think you and Tony are beau-

tiful together. And if you think so, too, don't be afraid
to go after the guy and tell him!"

And with that, Amanda was out the back door.

"Did someone give that girl an energy drink or
something?" Nora asked with a laugh. "She is definitely on a roll today. Olivia, I'll admit that apartment
of mine has been attached to a lot of love stories, but
not *all* the love stories. Besides, I've also had tenants
who just live there quietly and move on." She set her
hand on Olivia's arm. "Don't rely on magic. Listen to
your heart when it comes to Tony."

Cassie stacked paper plates, plastic cups and uten-
sils on a tray. "I agree. Follow your heart. Love will
find its way if it's meant to be." She laughed. "Oh,
my God, I sound like one of those sappy social-media
memes, don't I?"

Olivia took a large bowl of salad greens from the
refrigerator and put it on the counter she could add
vinaigrette. "Tony's only been gone two weeks, ladies. If I go chasing after him now, I'll look pathetic."

Julie nodded toward Olivia's shoulder and the exposed scars she'd completely forgotten about. No one
had said a word all day. "It seems like you've decided
to stop worrying about what other people think. And
I mean that as a compliment."

Olivia didn't see the new addition to the farm
until she stepped outside with the salad a few minutes later. An assortment of tables and folding chairs
had been set up under the huge oak tree next to the
house. Beyond the tree, next to the barn, was a brand-
new chicken coop. It was square, like the house, and
painted white—that explained why Mel had said Jillie
was painting chickens.

The coop was up on legs so the chickens could find shade underneath, and it was inside a wire enclosure that provided plenty of space for the chickens to wander, with a gate that matched the screen door on the house. Around the outside of the coop were nesting boxes the birds could access from inside, but Olivia would be able to open the hinged tops from the outside to gather eggs. The whole thing was as adorable as it was practical.

"Tony gave us very specific instructions when he heard we were coming over." Nate Thomas walked over to join her as she checked it out. She'd texted Tony about the work party, but he'd barely responded other than wishing her luck with it. "We just followed his blueprints, with Bobby taking the lead, of course." He nodded to where Bobby was moving something into place around the bottom of the enclosure.

Olivia's knees went weak. It was a section of white picket fence.

Nate followed her eyes and chuckled. "Crazy, right? Tony was very emphatic that we had to put a picket fence around the outside, in addition to the chicken wire. Something about it being a better barrier against predators. Bobby offered to build something even more solid, but Tony insisted it *had* to be picket fencing."

Tears burned her eyes.

There's no sunshine-and-picket-fence future…

Except…maybe there was.

Chapter Eighteen

Tony called Olivia as soon as Bobby sent his text, which read:

B: Mission Accomplished

She answered on the first ring. Her laughter was tinged with suspicion.

"What does this mean, Tony?"

He played innocent. "I don't know what you're talking about."

"Don't give me that, Vello. What are you up to?"

"I just suggested that picket fencing might look nice around the chicken coop."

"I hear you did more than *suggest*."

"Eh...maybe."

"What does *that* mean?"

"Come to the city, Liv." He didn't even phrase it as

an invitation. He blurted it out like an order. That's
how much he wanted her with him.

"Um…*what*?"

"Come to Staten Island."

"Why?"

Tony was sitting on the front steps of his aunt and
uncle's house. It wasn't quite as hot here as it was over
at his town house. Their house was close enough to the
beach that there was at least a slight breeze. But not
enough to cool his nerves. This call was…everything.
He scrubbed his hand down his face.

"I have a lot to tell you. Too much for a phone call.
And… I really need you to come." Nonna had insisted
on meeting Olivia before she'd approve his plans. And
if he was going to upend his life, Nonna's approval
was important. Because the rest of the family hadn't
seemed very enthusiastic about it so far.

Olivia let out a sigh. "You know I can't just *leave*. I
have animals to care for. I have a job. A farm."

"I'm not saying come here for a month. Drive down
next Friday, and you can drive back Sunday if you have
to. You have friends who can feed the horses, and the
rest of your menagerie."

"I guess so. I honestly have more friends than I realized."

Her voice was soft. He could tell she was outside,
and could hear the hubbub of conversation in the background. Bobby told him the Gallant Lake women had
rounded up a large work party, just waiting for Olivia
to actually *ask* for the help. When she did, they went
into high gear, giving him the perfect opportunity to
get the chicken coop built for her.

"Did you have fun today? Did they get everything

done?" It hurt him to think she'd ever felt she didn't have friends.

"Yes to both. Everything's done, and the furniture's back in place. There are even a few pictures hanging on the walls...and I have a chicken coop. The dinner crew is almost done grilling."

"Good. Before they leave, line someone up to feed the animals so you can come to New York next weekend."

"Tony, I'd really like to know *why* I'm coming there."

"Because I miss you." Christ, he missed her so damn much. "Because I have to have you in my arms again, even if only for one night. Because we need to talk, and not on a phone call."

"That doesn't sound good. Can't you just say it now?" Her voice was resigned. She was expecting the worst. He wanted her to see his world. Meet his people. It was important for her to know where he came from—not just from his stories, but for her to *see* it. Experience it.

"This is important to you—me coming there."

"It really is important. And not in a bad way. I... I want you to meet my family." He could hear someone—Blake?—calling in the background that dinner was ready. Tony wanted to be there, but coming home had been the right thing to do. "Liv?"

"I thought you wanted to talk?"

"That, too. Please."

There was a long pause. "Okay. Friday afternoon." She sounded like she was setting an appointment to face her doom. He couldn't let her think it would be that bad.

"You can't blame my family for wanting to know more about the woman who kept me away for so long. The woman I've been pining for since I got here."

"So this really is a meet-the-family kind of visit?" If anything, she sounded even more reluctant.

"It's a very nice family, I promise. Although some say we're an acquired taste."

He finally got a soft laugh from her. "Fine. Meet the family. Got it. But we agreed that a long distance or part-time thing wouldn't work for us. I won't be making regular booty calls to Staten Island."

"We'll see if you still feel that way after you've had my aunt's *bistecca fiorentina* with risotto pomodoro," he laughed. "You might want to be here *every* weekend, booty call or not."

Olivia didn't answer right away.

"Tony... I can't—"

"I was teasing." He'd pushed too hard. "Sorry. I promise I won't ask you for a long-distance relationship of any kind. Just—just say you'll be here on Friday, and we'll talk things out face-to-face. I have so much to tell you."

"I swear, if I didn't want to see you so badly, I'd say *no way*. But I guess I owe you the benefit of the doubt after seeing this charming chicken coop. And we do need to talk. Send me the address and I'll see you Friday."

Tony was sliding the phone in his pocket when Paulie came up the sidewalk. "Did she say yes?"

He nodded. This week was going to take forever to pass. "Friday dinner right here."

"So your plan is still to go? Even though you're not afraid of heights anymore?"

It was true—his fear had pretty much evaporated on his first day back on the job. He'd had a full-blown panic attack when he got to the top floor, sweating right through his shirt before he'd even picked up a power tool. But his cousins had stayed close. Luca pushed him to get to work as quickly as possible, which helped. The rhythm of the job was so familiar that his nerves had slowly faded.

He still couldn't walk the heights without thinking of Tim, but at least he could function. It just didn't feel like he belonged there anymore.

Paulie patted his shoulder as he stepped past him."I'll stay at James's Friday night so you can have the town house to yourselves. We can start packing up his stuff."

Tony stood and followed Paulie into the house. "When's he moving into the townhouse?"

"His lease is up in September, but we hope to have everything sorted before then. And since we're moving up into your suite, we need you gone first. Preferably in time to be able to paint—James hates all that gray. Says it reminds him of the hospital."

"Don't worry. I hope to be gone in a couple weeks." He waved at his aunt and grandmother in the living room. "If she says yes."

"After meeting *this familia*?" Paulie said with a laugh. "She'll probably run for the hills. Or should I say *back* to the hills?"

Joey's oldest kids went running past them, yelling something about jumping in the pool. Mary called after them not to touch that water unless an adult was out there, then she got up and followed, just to be safe.

Nonna came over for a hug, swatting Paulie in the

process. "Shuddup, you, about this family. We are wonderful, and even better together, right, Tony?"

He returned the hug, patting her on the shoulder. He winced as Joey Jr. started yelling angrily about some injustice. "We're definitely *louder* together."

She ignored that comment. "Is she coming?"

He stared down into her warm brown eyes. "Yes."

"And you talked to your uncle?"

"Yes, but we may need to continue the discussion. He's not happy."

Nonna shook her head sharply. "I told you *I'll* handle Rocco once I meet this girl of yours."

"She'll be here Friday."

He was pretty sure this was a good idea. Not *completely* sure, because with his family you could *never* be sure. But if they didn't chase Olivia away with her hair on fire, he might just have a chance to change his life, and hers, forever.

Olivia was going to throttle Tony when he arrived... if he *ever* arrived. The plan had been to meet at his place, but she'd been in the middle of navigating way too many lanes of traffic when his text came through. She let the car's system read it aloud.

"Job running late. Go to my uncle's house. I'll meet you there. Sending address."

She muttered a few curses as a tractor trailer tried to push her out of her lane—the lane the GPS insisted she needed to stay in to get off this hellscape. She jammed on her brakes and managed to hold her spot, ignoring a horn blaring behind her.

Tony wanted her to meet his family *alone*? It was bad enough she didn't know why he'd convinced her to come here, but this made her even more uncomfortable. She didn't seem to have a lot of choice in the matter. Another text came through.

"They're harmless. They know you're coming and will welcome you. I'll be there ASAP."

And that's how she came to be sitting in his aunt's large living room, on a gold brocade sofa with Mary Vello and Tony's grandmother, Sophia Vello, who insisted Olivia call her "Nonna.". His cousin, Joey Vello, was outside watching his children in the pool while his wife, Helen, sat in the high back chair across from Olivia.

She was surrounded by Vellos, and they all had stories to tell about Tony as a boy and Tony as a teen and how they built their business and how his their ancestors had come to America via Ellis Island.

All the names and stories were beginning to blur together, but she didn't realize that was just a ploy to lull her into numbness before they turned the interrogation on *her.*

Where did you grow up?
What was it like on a horse farm?
Where's your family from?
You have pretty hair—is it natural?
Why did you leave Maryland for the Catskills?
Aren't you lonely there?

The questions came at her fast and furious. Her anxiety level grew, mainly because she wasn't at all sure why she was here or what they'd been told. Was Tony hoping to convince her to move to Staten Island? She could tell that's what his aunt expected, with the way she went on and on about how great life was there. Oh, and did Olivia notice the house for sale down the street? She was tap dancing her way through the questions when she realized the one thing they *weren't* asking. And they had ample reason to.

Tony had faced his fears by going back to walking the girders. She'd faced hers by not hiding her scars. It had gone well at the picnic, and she decided to surprise him today by wearing a sundress that revealed a good portion of the scars on her back and shoulder. If she thought about it too much, she could almost feel her skin contracting, begging to be hidden. But the Vellos hadn't said a word. When she saw Tony's grandmother glance at it for the third or fourth time, Olivia smiled and put her hand on the old woman's hands.

"I can tell you want to ask. I was in a car accident a few years ago and was badly burned. A drunk driver hit our car head-on. My best friend was killed."

Sophia took one hand and placed it over Olivia's. "I'm so sorry, my dear girl. Tony told us a little, but not that you'd lost a friend. That's what you share with each other, isn't it? He lost his friend, Timothy."

They'd had more to share than loss, but it was something that got them to open up to each other. She nodded. Sophia leaned back to look at the scar more closely now that she had permission.

"He said you always keep it covered, but not today."

Tony had been telling his family a *lot* of things about her. And his grandmother had no problem being direct—it was easy to see where Tony got that from. But Olivia wasn't going to bare her soul to people she'd just met. She met Sophia's curious gaze straight on.

"No, it's not covered today."

The old woman stared for a moment, then nodded with a small smile.

"Good."

Before Olivia could ask what she meant, a tall, slender man came through the door and greeted everyone. His black hair was twisted into short, tight dreads. His skin was almost as dark as his eyes. He was heartstoppingly handsome. He held out his hand to Olivia and she stood to greet him.

"You must be Olivia." He smiled warmly. "I'm James. You've met Paulie, right?" She nodded and he continued. "Paulie and I are—"

"Jimmie and Paulie are together!" Sophia announced, pronouncing it *tah-geth-ah*. "They're *gay*!"

James winced slightly, although there was no malice in Sophia's words. She'd announced it the same way she'd announce "it's Christmas!"

Olivia couldn't hold back a short laugh. "I gathered that. Nice to meet you."

James didn't roll his eyes at Sophia, but she could tell he wanted to as he shook her hand. "It's *James*, and, yes, Paulie and I are a couple." His eyes danced with humor. "Nonna here is very proud of us." His voice dropped so only she could hear. "You'd think we invented gayness."

She liked James right away. He wasn't as intense as the Vello clan, and he smoothly pulled her away from the others and into the kitchen, where it was peacefully silent. She let out a long sigh, leaning against the counter.

James snorted. "They're a lot when you're new to the family. I told Paulie I felt like an exhibition at the fair, where people get to stare and poke at you. But they're really good people."

"I get that impression, too. It's just that I've been

on my own for a while and yeah…it's a lot. Especially without Tony here. He got held up at work."

James opened a beer and offered one to her, but she declined and grabbed a soda instead. He tapped the top of his bottle against hers in a toast. "Trust me, that was on purpose."

"You think Tony intentionally sent me into the lion's den alone?"

The thought didn't sit well with her.

"Not at all," he quickly replied. "But I definitely think Uncle Rocco was told to keep Tony busy today. They did the same thing with me and Paulie. I was here for over an hour before he showed up. The Vello women like to size up anyone looking to join the family, and they want to do it without interference."

She thought about all the questions tossed her way. "It *did* feel a little like an interview. The thing is, Tony and I aren't actually together at the moment. I think he brought me here to convince me how great life in Staten Island with the Vellos is, but… I already have a home."

"In the mountains. He told Paulie and I all about it last weekend. Horses and chickens and dogs. Oh, hey—" James brightened "—I want to thank you for sending the kitten home with Tony. I've been trying to talk Paulie into getting a cat or dog when I move in, and he was *not* having it. But I think little Ross is changing his mind. That cat has so much personality!"

"Well, I still have a couple of his siblings at home. I could send one down to keep him company." She hesitated. "You're moving into the town house? Won't that be a little crowded—three guys and two cats?"

He hesitated. She couldn't read the expression that

flitted across his face, and she had the feeling he didn't want her to. Then he flashed a bright smile.

"The more, the merrier, right?"

She wondered if Tony's plan was to have *her* move in, too, which would make for a *very* crowded two-bedroom town house. Not that it would ever happen.

There was a sudden burst of noise from the front of the house, followed by deep male laughter and then greetings from the women. Olivia heard Tony's voice and, without a second thought, rushed past James and down the hall. Regardless of what problems and decisions they had ahead of them, she needed to be in Tony's arms. He must have had the same thought, because his arms opened wide as soon as he saw her.

She rushed into his embrace, shocked at how much she needed to feel his warmth and his familiar solid chest against her cheek. She closed her eyes when he rested his head on hers.

He was sweaty. He was dirty. And he was hers. For the first time, she realized that moving *could* be a possibility. Not that she wanted to leave the farm, but the thought of losing Tony felt like a far worse pain.

Neither of them spoke. The hubbub around them began to quiet, and still they stood there. Finally, Tony traced his fingertip across the scar on the back of her shoulder, tugging on the narrow strap of her sundress.

"I like this." She knew he was referring to more than the dress.

"I thought you might. You're not the only one who can face their fears."

"Mmm-hmm. They're not so scary once you stare them down, are they?"

She shook her head against him, filled with a frustrating mix of emotions she wasn't proud of. She'd *wanted* him to be able to conquer his fears. She was *proud* of him. She just didn't know what it meant for their relationship.

When she didn't answer his question, he put his fingers under her chin and gently tipped up her head so he could look into her eyes. Her breath caught in her chest, enraptured by the heat and the love she saw shining in the mahogany depths. His voice, low enough so only she could hear, rumbled all the way to her heart, lighting a growing flame of hope.

"You and I are gonna be okay, babe."

Chapter Nineteen

He watched as her eyes went soft. The troubled lines on her forehead eased, and her body relaxed against his. By the end of the weekend, he hoped to have her fully convinced. He left her only long enough to get cleaned up and grab a fresh polo shirt before dinner.

The meal was the usual Vello chaos, with everyone yelling over everyone else as platters loaded with food went back and forth across the table. The only one who was quieter than usual was his grandmother. Aunt Mary started to clear the dinner dishes, and Olivia jumped up to help, following her into the kitchen.

"You feel okay, Nonna?" he asked quietly.

"I feel fine, Anthony. Why?"

This weekend had been designed to win his family's buy-in to his plan. Was it possible Nonna didn't like Olivia for some reason? That would be awkward.

Now that he'd held Olivia in his arms again, it wouldn't change anything. But he still wanted Nonna's support.

"Do you not like Olivia?"

She drew back in surprise. "Not like her? What's not to like? She's pretty, she's smart, she's strong and for some reason, she loves a lunkhead like you."

"Wait…are you *mad* at me? What'd I do?"

The old woman waved her hand in disgust. "I'm ashamed of you, Anthony." *Uh-oh.* She'd used his given name twice in the last minute. That couldn't be good.

"*Ashamed* is a strong word. Why are you ashamed, Nonna?"

It wasn't until then that he realized the table had grown silent, with all eyes on his grandmother and him.

"Why am I ashamed? Because I raised you better than this! You find a girl…" She paused, then corrected herself. "You find a *woman* who is everything you need and deserve and she *loves* you. So what do you do? You *leave* her! *Mannaggia!* I thought you were an intelligent man. Instead, you're nothing but a foolish boy, Anthony. I can see you love her, so why did you do that?" She whipped her napkin at him, making him flinch backward. "Why are you here and not with her?"

"Stop doing that!" he protested. "Of course, I love her. That's why I asked her to come. I wanted *you* to love her so you'd understand…"

"Understand that you're going back to the mountains with her?" Nonna demanded.

Tony looked up at the wide-eyed faces of the family he loved. Behind his uncle, who was slightly less enthralled than everyone else, stood Olivia. She was in the kitchen doorway, one of Mary's chocolate pies in her hands, staring at him. Waiting on his answer. He slowly smiled at her, feeling his entire future falling into place.

"Yes, Nonna. I'm going back to the mountains with her," he said firmly. "If she'll have me."

Helen hopped up and rescued the pie from Olivia's now-shaking hands. The love of his life, the holder of his heart, the woman who saved him. Her eyes never left his face. He stood, and it was as if they were the only ones in the room. No one else, not even the people he'd loved his entire life, mattered right now. It was just Tony and Olivia.

"You didn't bring me here to convince me to stay?" she asked. When he shook his head, her shoulders eased. "Thank God." As if suddenly realizing how that might sound to their audience, she rushed to apologize. "No offense! You're all wonderful and I can see where Tony got all of his charm from, but this is not..."

"It's not your home. I get it." Luca spoke up, surprising Tony. Luca had been the angriest when he'd laid out his plan to pull out of the business and sell his share to Luca, Paulie and Joey. He'd accused Tony of turning his back on his family legacy. But now... Now he sounded like he really did understand. Especially when he looked up at Tony. "It's not *your* home anymore, either, is it?"

"I don't know how to explain it, but...no. My home has a big front porch in the Catskills, with horses in the pasture and a dog at my feet and the woman I love by my side." He ran his fingers through his hair, staring at Olivia. "This isn't exactly where or how I planned to say this, but... I tried to slide into my old world.

My old role. The fear of heights went away, but it still doesn't work for me here. I want to come back to Gallant Lake. I want to come back to you."

Olivia blinked a few times, biting her lip to control her emotions. "I feel like I'm breaking up a family or something."

"You're not." Uncle Rocco wiped his mouth with his napkin, then tossed it onto the table. "Tony was moving away from his life here before he met you. He got lost because he didn't have any place to go *to* until now. You're his place."

She looked back to Tony. "I'm your place?"

"You are."

The corners of her mouth pinched inward as she tried to hold back a smile, but she finally surrendered to it. Her eyes brightened and she came around the table and slid her arms around his waist. "Well, then. I think you should come home to your place, Tony."

His mouth captured hers and they kissed long and hard, ignoring the catcalls of his family. Finally, Paulie called out to them.

"Before you go to this mystical so-called *place* together, can we *please* have our pie?"

Olivia laughed against his mouth and they reluctantly pulled apart, although they remained standing with their arms around each other's waists. Nonna reached for Olivia's free hand, and Olivia bent closer to hear what she had to say.

"You'll be good for my Anthony. I can tell."

Olivia looked over her shoulder at him and smiled. "He's pretty good for me, too, Sophia."

"Phfft! I told you to call me Nonna. You're going to be a Vello."

Everyone shouted *whoa!* at the same time, including Olivia.

"Nonna," Tony cautioned, "let's not get ahead of ourselves." He kissed Olivia's forehead quickly, then stared into her eyes as he spoke to his grandmother. "That's definitely the plan, but let *us* set the timing, okay?"

"Just be smarter about it than you've been over the past few weeks. You need to keep this woman, Tony!"

He pulled Olivia closer.

"I intend to."

Olivia was having the best dream. It was dark and warm. Tony was there, whispering something hot and sweet into her ear. They were naked and exhausted from a night of lovemaking that had every muscle in her body aching in the sweetest way.

She wanted to stay here *forever*. If only Dream Tony would stop that annoying whispering. She tried to push him away. She explained that she needed to get a little more sleep. But he kept whispering. And then he started to tickle her ribs. And she realized she wasn't dreaming.

"No!" she squealed, giggling. "What are you doing? It's still dark out. I'm tired!"

"Oh, wah, wah, wah. Stop your whining and get up." Tony yanked back the sheet, smacking her bare behind lightly.

"Get up?" She was awake now, her eyes open. "You mean get out of bed? Why?"

"Because I woke you up nicely?" He kissed her shoulder. "Because I have a surprise for you?" He kissed her again. "Because you love me? Take your pick, sleeping beauty, but get up."

"Hey, I can't help it if you wore me out!" She sat up, blinking into the darkness. Then she squealed again when Ross clawed his way up the side of the bed and bounced toward her, full of kitten playfulness. "Oh, my God, is the whole world awake at this hour in Staten Island?"

Tony tossed a sweatshirt at her. "No. That's the whole point. Come on, Liv. We've got somewhere to be."

"But the sun's not up."

"Again…that's the point."

"Why do I need a sweatshirt?"

"Because the sun's not up. Trust me, you'll want it where we're going."

He stood at the foot of the bed, shirtless, with the gray kitten in his arms and a slanted grin on his face. As usual, a shock of long, dark hair fell across his forehead. He was the hottest thing she'd ever seen, and he was *hers*.

They'd come back to the town house after the raucous dinner with his family last night. Paulie went to James's home, so they had the place to themselves. And they'd taken full advantage of that, not making it past the living-room sofa when they came through the door. Then they'd moved upstairs to Tony's astonishingly gray room, and brought their own spice to the space. Against the wall. On the dresser. And, eventually, in bed.

And *then* they'd talked…for hours. He'd explained

how he knew almost as soon as he'd arrived home that he wasn't going to stay. He'd just had to work out how to extricate himself from the company, his mortgage and the family with as little impact on them as possible. It was still going to take some time running back and forth, but he'd be able to come back to Gallant Lake within a week or so, and he'd be there for good.

That was when he'd looked at her and gave her a one-shouldered shrug. "Of course, I don't have my apartment there anymore, so I don't have a place to move back to."

She'd playfully pretended to think about it. "Oh, that *is* a problem. I mean, I *do* have a couple of spare bedrooms, so I suppose you could stay at the farm for a while…"

He'd laughed. "Well, I guess a spare room is better than the hayloft, but I can think of a room I'd rather sleep in. Yours. And for the record, I want to be there for more than *a while*." She'd assured him that was what she wanted, too.

He explained he'd have to come back to the city to help his uncle occasionally until they got a replacement for him on a long-term basis. And he and Bobby were already working out a partnership in Gallant Lake for home construction.

"Come on, princess. We need to get moving." Tony set her duffel on the bed. "Did you bring any clothes suitable for a jobsite?"

When she stared back in silence, he laughed. "You really are an angry kitten in the morning, aren't you? I thought you might need something. Helen loaned me a pair of her jeans—they should fit."

She tugged on the jeans and a top. Her driving flats would have to do for sturdy shoes, since she'd left her boots on the farm. She pulled the oversized sweatshirt over it all.

"This isn't exactly the kind of New York fashion I'd envisioned wearing."

"You'll be the prettiest girl there, I promise."

They went out to his truck in the dark and he drove north. As they crossed the bridge toward Manhattan, he glanced her way.

"This isn't actually *our* worksite we're going to. A friend of mine is letting us into a building his company is putting up. It has more of what I want to show you."

Tony parked the truck at the base of an enormous, but skeletal, building that stretched up into the still-dark sky. His friend Lincoln had unlocked the gate to the site, and the burly man tossed Tony a wad of keys when they got out of the car.

"Wear your hard hats," Lincoln said gruffly. "You know the way. You only got an hour, so don't do no mile-high nonsense up there."

"Got it, Lincoln. You know why I'm here."

The other man turned, grinning from under his hoodie. "I know you got me prime seats for the ballgame tomorrow, and *that's* why you're here." He chuckled. "Just get yourselves outta here on time, because the best seats in the universe aren't worth me losing my job for this."

Tony knew the developer, so none them would be in that much trouble. He still didn't want his friend catching any flak for letting them trespass for an hour.

"Don't worry. You're the best, Linc!"

Tony handed Olivia a hard hat and put his own on as they started toward the building. Or, more accurately, the *partial* building. The bottom third of it had outer walls and windows, but above that it was just steel and floors. The construction elevator was on the outside of the building—it was large, orange and made of slatted metal, like a cage.

"Hope you're not afraid of heights," he said as he pressed the button to start the noisy, vibrating ride to the sixty-fourth floor. She was looking out the plastic window as the city fell below them. Manhattan was coming awake before the sun, as usual. Cars and delivery vans were scurrying up and down the streets. Office and apartment lights were coming on. He felt the little zip of adrenaline he always got at the sight. He'd been a part of this city his whole life.

His arms were around Olivia's waist, her back to his chest. She tensed, and he frowned.

"Wait...you're *not* afraid of heights, are you?"

She glanced up at him. "Normal heights don't bother me, but this rickety elevator rattling its way toward the clouds is freaking me out a little."

"There's nothing rickety about this thing. We could put twenty workers in here and they'd all be safe. But I don't think I ever paid attention to how noisy it is when there's just two of us."

"And how are *you* doing?" she asked. "I know you said you got your ironworker mojo back pretty quickly, but...does it bother you at all?"

He thought about it. The building his uncle was constructing now was only fifteen stories, but that didn't make it any less deadly if you went off the girders to the ground below. After a rough start on his first day on the job, he'd felt almost like himself again by the end of the shift. Except it was a lonely, hollow version of himself. He wasn't complete without Olivia.

He smiled down at her, adjusting her hard hat when it started to slip. "I'm okay. It's like riding a bike, right?"

She let out a little squeal when the elevator jerked to a stop.

"It's not like any bicycle *I've* been on, but…sure."

He slid the metal door open and took her hand, leading her onto the floor and away from the ledge and the open sides of what would become an eighty-story, office-and-apartment building. He turned on his flashlight and quickly ran through the safety rules.

No, they weren't supposed to be there. Yes, it was safe, as long as she stuck with him and they stayed near the center of the structure, far from the open outer walls. Yes, she had to keep her hardhat on.

Luckily, there wasn't much wind this morning. Strong winds up this high could rattle the calmest nerves. The permanent elevators would eventually be in the center of the narrow skyscraper, and there was a picnic basket waiting next to the framed-in elevator shafts.

Olivia started to laugh. "Are we seriously having a picnic in the dark?"

He took her shoulders and turned her toward the eastern horizon, which was beginning to glow a soft orangey pink.

"It won't be dark for long. There's coffee and bagels in the basket." He'd had to give Lincoln an extra fifty bucks to cover his parking at the ball game in order to get him to set up the bagel picnic in the predawn hours. If Tony had planned on staying in New York, he'd never hear the end of Linc's teasing for being a "big lovey-dovey marshmallow." Good thing he had no intention of staying.

They sat on the eastern side of the elevators and watched the sun come up through the surrounding buildings, sipping coffee and munching on bagels.

"This is incredible," Olivia said. "You always see sunrise pictures from the mountains or the beach, but this is just as breathtaking. And listening to the city come alive below us is like hearing a symphony warm up before a performance. It's magical."

He draped his arm over her shoulder. "Sunrise has always been my favorite time to be up here. All the windows shine like copper and you can feel the energy rising. It's what I love about this city—the energy, the unexpected beauty, the…" A series of angry car horns blared. Rush hour started early, even on a Saturday. He chuckled. "The *noise*, the people, the attitude of the whole damn place. Up here a man can feel like he's the king of the world."

"You're going to miss this." She frowned. "Are you really ready to walk away from this life to move to a farm?"

He paused, working to put his feelings into words. "I'd originally planned on keeping you on pins and needles about my decision until we got up here this morning, but I didn't want to cause you any more pain. Besides—" he squeezed her shoulders "—the minute I saw you yesterday, there was no way in hell I could even *pretend* I might not commit myself to you…to *us*. And to not make love to you like we did last night? Uh-uh. That was worth spoiling any surprise."

"So why *are* we here?" she asked softly, pressing against him. "Just to show me the sunrise that you're going to miss after you move to Gallant Lake?"

"That's the thing, Liv. I *won't* miss it. Or at least I won't regret losing it. I love all of this, but it doesn't begin to compare with how much I love *you*. That's what I wanted you to see. I know you think it's hard for me to walk away from this life. Even *I* thought it might be impossible. But when I got back here, I realized that this is nice. And familiar. And sometimes even incredible." He turned to face her, cupping the side of her face with his hand. "But it is *nothing* compared to loving you. That sunrise? *Nothing* compared to seeing myself in your eyes. The adrenaline rush of Manhattan waking up? *Nothing* compared to making love to you. The satisfaction from this line of work? *Nothing* compared to seeing you on that porch swing with a book in your lap and a mug of coffee in your hand, smiling up at me. *That's* the only thrill I want, Olivia. The thrill of being loved by a woman like you."

His lips brushed hers. They were both trembling, and not from the morning chill. This moment was big. This moment was them saying *yes* to the future. He kissed her tenderly, then lifted his head so he could look into her eyes.

"Some morning real soon," he whispered, "we're going to wake up early and watch the sunrise in the Catskills. And I'll drop to one knee next to that old porch swing and ask you to marry me. That's the only life I want, Olivia. A life with you."

He caught a tear on her cheek with his thumb. She smiled, and the trembling was gone. She was as sure of this moment as he was. She reached up and touched his cheek with her fingers. It was a touch that healed every remaining wound on his heart.

"Don't wait too long for that morning, Anthony Vello." She was whispering now. "I'll be waiting to say *yes*."

* * * * *

SPECIAL EXCERPT FROM

H HARLEQUIN

SPECIAL
EDITION

*Returning to her picturesque coastal town was
the best move Layla Williams ever made. But now
her restaurant is in trouble. Help comes from an
unexpected source: the boy Layla left behind.
Wall Street wizard turned EMT Shane Kavanaugh
could transform Layla's homecoming into another
chance for them both. If they're ready to put their
hearts on the line.*

*Read on for a sneak preview of
Anna James's Special Edition debut,
A Taste of Home,
the first book in the
Sisterhood of Chocolate & Wine miniseries.*

Chapter One

New Suffolk, Massachusetts

Layla pushed the swinging door that led to La Cabane de La Mer's kitchen and stepped inside. The sounds of simmering pots and sizzling grills filled the air. She smiled and sucked in a deep satisfying breath.

She moved to the first prep station. A petite young blonde with a pixie haircut stood bent over the metal counter chopping potatoes. "Hi, Lucie." Her *chef de partie* was the only kitchen staff who had agreed to stay on when Layla had purchased her grandfather's restaurant nine months ago, after he and Nonny retired to Florida. She'd needed to hire three line cooks to replace those on her grandfather's staff who'd thought _ her crazy when she'd announced she'd turn his place _ into an upscale French bistro. So what if New Suffolk wasn't Paris? She'd make it work.

Antoine's smug image floated into her brain. *Lying, cheating bastard.* He thought she couldn't make it without him? *Hah!* She might not have her three Michelin stars yet, but she would. She'd turned his restaurant into one of the top places in Paris. She'd do the same here.

"Would you like to taste the lyonnaise potatoes?"

She gave herself a mental shake and concentrated on the task at hand. "Yes, please." Layla scooped up a thin slice covered with caramelized onion with her disposable tasting fork. She inserted it into her mouth. The potatoes were cooked to the correct consistency. Not too soft, not too crunchy. "Perfect."

Pitching the fork in the trash as she passed by, she wandered to the next prep table. "Hi, Luis."

Her *poissonnier* mumbled something she couldn't make out as he presented tonight's special.

Layla swallowed to clear her dry throat. Had she made the wrong decision in hiring Luis? She would have preferred to hire another female prep cook to replace Gabrielle when she'd moved away last month, but with his impeccable references, Luis had been the most qualified candidate who'd applied for the position.

Yes, he could be gruff at times, and a bit temperamental. Still, it wasn't like he wouldn't take direction from her.

Not like Pierre.

Her blood boiled every time she thought about how her ex, Antoine, had insisted she hire the arrogant sous-chef, and refused to allow her to fire his condescending ass when he kept going over her head every time he disagreed with her.

Stop it. Not all male cooks had a problem working for a woman. After all, Luis couldn't be a better fish cook. He really got her menu, and everyone on the team liked him. She shouldn't look for trouble where none existed.

Grabbing another disposable fork from her pocket, she scooped up a bite. "The sole meunière is delicious."

She gave a satisfied nod and turned her attention to her sous-chef. "You're in charge of the kitchen, Olivia. I'll be in my office if anyone needs me." She needed to meet with Zara to review the restaurant finances. Her sister had insisted they discuss some supplier invoice matters now that couldn't wait until their scheduled meeting in three days.

Layla exited the kitchen and strode down the hall to her office. She opened her laptop and logged into the reoccurring Zoom meeting. Her sister's face appeared on screen. "Hey, Zara. How are things in Manhattan?"

Thank goodness Zara had agreed to stay on as well after she'd purchased the restaurant. With five years' experience managing Gramps's place, her knowledge was invaluable.

"How are you feeling?" They'd skipped last week's review because Zara had come down with a stomach bug. This was the second time in as many months Zara had caught a nasty virus that had left her bedridden.

Layla scrutinized her sister's image. Truth be told, she didn't appear one hundred percent recovered. Not if her washed-out pallor was anything to go by.

"Let's get started." Zara's weary expression tore at Layla's heart.

"You know, we can reschedule if you're still not well."

Zara didn't respond. Instead she shared her screen and pulled up a QuickBooks entry. "Here's the information from last week."

Layla scanned the invoices sitting on her desk and compared them to the entries in Zara's file. "I don't see the butcher payment. Can you go to the next page, please? Maybe it's just in the wrong place."

The color drained from Zara's face. She looked as if she might get sick.

Layla sucked in a quick breath, concern overtaking her irritation—after all, she'd stepped away from dinner service for this meeting! But her sister's well-being had to come first. "Okay. Enough is enough. You need to go back to bed and get over whatever bug you've got. We'll finish this when you're feeling better."

Zara dragged a hand through her long brown hair. "Layla, I—"

"Don't argue, Zara. Just get some rest and feel better soon." Layla waved and ended the call.

She sighed and added the two remaining invoices to the pile in the corner of her desk along with a sticky note reminding her to confirm the payments when she and Zara met next.

Damn. Zara had never voiced her concerns. She couldn't imagine what Zara might want to discuss when the invoices appeared to be in order. Hopefully, she'd be feeling better soon and they could talk about whatever was on her mind.

Shrugging, Layla rose from her chair and exited her office, walking the opposite way down the long hall. She stepped into the conservatory of the colonial mansion, now a spacious dining room, with to-die-for views of the Atlantic Ocean.

Three couples sat at intimate tables for two. She glanced at her watch. Seven at night. She would have expected more people on a Friday evening. No matter. Layla straightened her whites and readjusted the toque atop her head. Smiling, she approached the first table. It was time to meet and greet.

"Frank, Kim. It's so nice to see you." She wouldn't have expected the Bay Beach Club members—New Suffolk's version of a country club that catered to the affluent visitors who summered in the little beach town—to be in town at this time of year.

"Layla." Kim smiled. "We just had to stop in while we're in town for a little getaway from the city. We so enjoyed coming here last season."

"Yes," Frank agreed. "My coq au vin was delicious." He pointed to his empty plate.

"And you have one of Frank's favorite wines." Kim pointed to the almost empty bottle of Louis Jadot Eche-zeaux Grand Cru.

"You're on par with some of the finest bistros in Paris," Frank added.

A rush of pride flooded her chest. "Thank you. I'm glad you enjoyed your meals. Enjoy the rest of your weekend."

"We will. We'll be back again before we head back to the city," Kim said.

Layla wanted to pump her fists in the air and do her happy dance. She wouldn't, of course. Instead, she pinned a polite smile in place and gave a nod of her head. "I look forward to seeing you."

Layla moved to a couple seated by the window.

"Good evening. I'm the executive chef, Layla Williams. Thank you for dining with us tonight."

"Hello. I'm Winnie and this is my husband, Tom."

"Is this your first visit to La Cabane de La Mer?" She didn't recognize the fiftysomething-year-old couple.

"Yes," Tom said.

"My clients at the Mermaid talked about this place all last summer, so we thought we'd try out your place," Winnie added.

The spa at the beach club. "A fellow New Suffolk business owner. I'm glad you came for dinner tonight." Layla made a mental note to return the favor once the club opened for the season. "How were your meals?"

Tom opened his mouth to speak, but his wife cut him off.

"Excellent, but a bit pricey for beef stew if you ask me. The diner down the street serves a similar dish for a lot less."

Layla shuddered, but her smile never faltered. Of course her elegant boeuf bourguignon was more expensive. Her dish couldn't compare to something served in the local greasy spoon. And probably labeled "pot roast" to boot, she thought.

"Now, darling." The man reached across the table and patted his wife's hand. "It's our anniversary. This is a special occasion. You don't need to worry about the cost tonight."

"Happy anniversary." She gave a discreet wave and motioned for the server to come to the table. "Please enjoy dessert and a glass of champagne, on the house." She always treated customers when they came in for special occasions. It was just good business.

"Thank you." Winnie's eyes lit up with excitement.

"You're welcome. Enjoy the rest of your evening."
Layla moved on to the next table, but she couldn't banish Winnie's remarks from her mind.

After speaking with the last couple, she returned to the kitchen, nodded to the line cooks and walked into the back room to take inventory for the next day's menu. She scrubbed her hands over her face. What was wrong with her tonight?

There's nothing wrong. She gave herself a mental shake and yanked open the cooler with more force than she'd planned. The door ricocheted off the outside wall and came flying toward her. She jumped out of the way to avoid being hit.

Layla stepped inside the cooler. She'd already cured the duck legs for the cassoulet. At least no one would compare that traditional dish to anything made in the local diner.

Stop it. The diners tonight had liked her food. No, they'd *loved* her dishes. So, why complain about the cost? This town needed an upscale restaurant. Right?

They could patronize Gino's. It might not be in New Suffolk, but it was only five miles from here. Her shoulders sagged. The Italian food was superb and the prices... *Even better. Enough.* She needed to stop this madness. People liked La Cabane de La Mer. She was proud of what she'd built over the last nine months. With a little more time her place would be even more successful.

Layla double-checked the rest of the ingredients she'd need and exited the cooler.

Emily walked in as Layla returned to the kitchen. She grabbed a salad from the cooler.

"How's it going out there?" Layla asked. "Any more customers come in in the last hour?"

Emily nodded. "Table three would like to speak with you." She let out a little chuckle.

Layla arched a brow. "What's so funny?"

"It's Mrs. Clement."

Oh, Lord. The elderly woman who always tried to fix her up with her nephew every time she came in. "No problem. I'll go and speak with her now." She'd politely decline to meet Mr. Wonderful—this according to his besotted aunt—just like she'd done all the times before. She wasn't interested in a relationship. Not with Mrs. Clement's nephew. Not with any man.

Her hands clenched into tight fists. She wouldn't allow any man to make a fool of her ever again.

Layla would focus her energy on what mattered most—her restaurant.

She straightened her shoulders. Holding her head high, she marched back into the dining room.

"Hey, Wall Street. That was pretty good work you did tonight—for a newbie."

"Hah, hah, Cruz." Shane Kavanaugh snorted as the ambulance rolled to a stop in the New Suffolk regional community medical building. "I left New York six months ago. I'm an EMT." Step one of his life plan—complete. Step two… He couldn't wait to start paramedic classes in the fall.

Duncan Cruz rested his hands on the steering wheel and faced Shane. "Gotta say, it's a heck of a career change."

Shane viewed the switch as refocusing on his original goal—a career in the medical field—something he'd wanted to do from the time he was six years old and his father, Victor, first got sick. Dad would have preferred he join Turner Kavanaugh Construction, the company his father had started with his best friend more than thirty years ago—but Shane was sure Dad would be proud of him for being true to himself—even if he hadn't lived long enough to see the man he'd become. Above all else, Victor had wanted his kids to be happy.

New York had never made him happy. He'd tried like hell for a long time to believe it would, but he couldn't fool himself any longer.

The money was great. He couldn't deny that. He'd been like a kid in a candy store buying every treat he could find in the beginning. Having cash to spare had been a powerful draw for a guy who… Well, while he couldn't classify his family as poor—not by any stretch of the imagination—but growing up, there definitely hadn't been money in the Kavanaugh home for frivolous things.

What was the old saying? *Money can't buy you happiness.* Yes, that was it. Whoever came up with that saying was spot-on.

"Let's just say the city life's not for me." He missed walking down Main Street and greeting his fellow neighbors by name. Missed the sense of community that came with small-town living.

"You're a small-town boy through and through, huh?" Cruz let out a roar of laughter.

Absolutely. "Hey. I like it here in New Suffolk."

Life in Massachusetts suited Shane just fine. Always had. He never needed to pretend to be something—someone—he wasn't. He was good enough—as is. He'd finally realized that.

Duncan pulled the keys from the ignition. "Hey, wanna go down to Donahue's and shoot some pool after we restock the ambulance?"

He nodded. "Yeah, sure. Sounds good. Loser buys the first round."

Duncan grinned. "I guess you'll be buying then."

Shane shot him a disparaging glance. "We'll see about that." He jumped out of the ambulance and strode to the stockroom.

Thirty minutes later Shane drove his F-150 up to Donahue's Irish Pub. As always, the place was rocking on a Saturday night. He hoped they wouldn't have to wait too long for a pool table. He pulled into a spot in the back of the lot and hopped out of the truck.

Snow fluttered from the clear night sky as he exited the driver's seat. The first day of spring might officially arrive in twenty days, but it felt as if the warmer weather would never get here. Shane zipped his bomber jacket, shoved his hands in his coat pockets and picked up his pace as he strode toward the entrance.

Loud music accosted him as he stepped inside. A group of local musicians rocked out on the stage in the back of the room. The song ended and the singer announced the band would take a thirty-minute break. Shane strode down the short narrow hall that led to the bar area.

He scanned the room. A woman standing near the front entrance caught his attention. Shane studied her as she moved in his direction.

Tall and thin with long dark curly hair, her hips swayed ever so slightly as she moved through the throng of people. She wasn't Hollywood gorgeous, but he found her quiet beauty attractive nonetheless. Who was she?

She disappeared from his view.

Shane searched the crowd for a few minutes but couldn't find her anywhere.

"Excuse me," a female said.

He jerked his attention toward the voice. His mystery woman stood in front of him. Tonight was his lucky night.

"Could you please move?" The woman offered a winsome smile. "I need to leave." She pointed to the door behind him. "I can't get by."

"Oh, I'm sorry." He grinned and stepped aside.

"Thank you." Her gaze connected with his and she stiffened. "Shane."

How did she know his name? He scrutinized her face, then recognition slowly hit him.

Holy hell.

"Layla?" *No way.* The Layla Williams he remembered had shoulder-length light brown hair. Not long, dark, silky curls and certainly not the sexy curves this woman sported.

"Yes. It's me." Her gaze darted around the space.

"It's been a while." At least a few years.

"Yes," she agreed.

Why wouldn't she look at him? "How are you doing?" he asked.

"Fine. Um… You?" came her clipped reply.

Nothing had changed over the years. The rich Manhattan socialite still wanted nothing to do with a townie. Would she be as standoffish if she viewed his bank statement? Most women found him—his portfolio, he mentally corrected—quite attractive.

His wealth may have secured admittance into New York's upper echelon, Melinda *had* married him, after all, but admittance and acceptance were two different animals. He'd learned that the hard way.

"I'm surprised to see you." He couldn't hide the disdain in his voice.

"I'm…hanging out with some friends."

Here? Shane's jaw almost hit the ground. Donahue's wasn't a dive, but… He'd never have guessed a Williams would enter such an establishment. They'd frequented the Bay Beach Club during those years they'd summered here. He ought to know. He'd waited on her and her family often enough over the years.

"At least I was. I'm heading over to my restaurant now."

He'd heard she'd purchased her grandfather's place when he retired.

"I opened La Cabane de La Mer last summer." A look of pride flashed across her expression.

She'd have been better off sticking with a name for her restaurant that sounded less uptight, pretentious. Something with wider appeal, in his opinion. "How is your restaurant doing?" He'd noticed fewer cars in the parking lot when he passed by on the way home each day. Then again, many of the businesses in town suffered from a turndown in commerce during the winter months, when tourism tended to slow in the coastal towns.

Layla flashed a wide smile that stole the breath from him. The way it lit up the room, and transformed her face from…well, she'd always been beautiful, but the warmth and joy radiating from her now jolted through him like a bolt of lightning.

"It's great." She glanced at her watch. "But I have to go."

Same old Layla. A bitter smile crossed his face. "Of course." He gestured for her to pass by.

As she walked by him, murmuring a distracted "Bye," and disappeared outside, it was as though he'd imagined the transformation of a few moments ago. An odd feeling of disappointment shot through him before he shrugged it off and continued down the hall.

Shane walked into the bar and peered around. Several patrons sat in the high-back chairs along the length of the long glossy wood bar to his right. He spotted Levi Turner at the far end. Walking over, he clapped his friend on the shoulder. "Hey, man. What's up? How did you get out of the house tonight? I thought you have Noah on Saturday nights."

Levi turned sideways in the chair and faced him. "I usually do, but he's with his mother tonight. I'm supposed to meet Cooper here for a beer, but he's late."

"How is your little brother?" Shane waved at the bartender and he came toward him.

"I'm fine." Cooper Turner walked over and grabbed the seat next to Levi. "Sorry I'm late."

"No problem." Levi slid a pint toward his brother. "It might be a little warm now."

Cooper snorted.

"What can I get you, Shane?" the bartender asked.

"I'll take the New Suffolk IPA, Ben."

"Me, too," Cooper added and shoved the warm glass of beer aside.

Ben nodded, grabbed a couple of frosted glasses and headed to the tap a few feet away.

Shane scanned the room but couldn't find Duncan

anywhere. They'd left the EMS building at the same time. He must have stopped somewhere along the way.

He directed his attention to Levi and Cooper. "So—"

Someone slammed into him from behind. Shane whirled around and caught an older man before he landed on the ground.

"Sorry 'bout that," the man grumbled.

Shane stared into the man's vacant gaze. Something about his weathered features seemed familiar.

"Another bourbon, Ben," the man called.

"Not a chance. You've had enough, Gary. You're shut off."

"Gary Rawlins?" Shane's gaze widened.

Gary jerked his blurry gaze to him, and snarled, "Yeah. What of it?"

No wonder the man had looked familiar. This was his best friend's father. He held out his hand. "Shane Kavanaugh."

Gary did a double take and a small smile crossed his once handsome face. "Well, I'll be damned." He pumped Shane's hand. "Haven't seen you in years." He wobbled, but straightened himself before he fell. Clapping Shane on the shoulder, he said, "Mind ordering me a bourbon?"

Shane's mouth fell open. "How about I call you a cab instead?"

Ben returned, and set full mugs down in front of him and Cooper. "Already done. The cab will be here any minute."

"I'm not ready to go home," Gary objected.

"Okay, but you know the rules." Ben pointed to the door. "You're banned from this place if you don't leave when I tell you."

Gary groused some more as he made his way to the exit.

"Sorry about that," Ben gestured to Gary's retreating form.

"No problem." Shane waved off Ben's concern. "Does this happen often?" Jax's father tended to indulge on certain occasions, but he'd never seem him this bad before.

"Often enough." Levi snorted.

Ben shook his head. "We've had an arrangement with the cab company for years."

"Ever since Jax left town," Cooper added. "You ever see him when you lived in Manhattan?"

"Sometimes." Shane nodded. "When he was around, which wasn't much."

"Who would have thought one of New Suffolk's own would make it big?" Levi said.

"Rachel and I went to one of his shows last year, when his photos were featured at a gallery in Boston," Cooper added.

"Hey, look who just walked in." Cooper pointed to three women who stood by the front entrance.

"Who are they?" Shane asked.

"The middle one with the blond hair is big brother's fiancée," Levi scoffed.

Cooper elbowed Levi in the side. "Would you just stop already?" To Shane he said, "Her name is Isabelle."

Shane's eyes widened. "Nick is engaged? When did this happen?"

"Yesterday." Levi snorted and shook his head. "Worse—"

Cooper cut in before Levi could continue. "Not all marriages end up in the toilet. You just need to meet the right person." He jerked his head to Shane, a back-me-up-here expression on his face.

"Don't look at me for confirmation." He wouldn't be making his way down the aisle again. Not in this lifetime. *That's for sure.*

"Oh, come on." Cooper rolled his eyes skyward. "Don't tell me you're a card-carrying member of the He Man Woman Haters club, like my brother here." Cooper gestured to Levi.

Levi snorted. "I'd say the answer to that is no, given he was checking out a hot little number not more than five minutes ago."

"What are you talking about?" he asked.

Levi leaned back in his chair and shot a challenging glance in his direction. "You're going to deny you were checking out Layla Williams?"

Shane opened his mouth but Levi jumped in before he could say anything.

"I saw you when you came in. I waved, but you obviously didn't see me." Levi arched a brow and flashed a smug smile. "You were otherwise engaged."

"Didn't you used to have a wicked crush on her when we were kids?" Cooper asked.

Levi smirked. "Oh yeah. I forgot about that. You had it bad for her."

"I don't know what you're talking about." *Lie much?* Because yeah, he'd just told a whopper. Yes, he'd fallen hook, line and sinker for Layla all those years ago. That fourteen-year-old boy had been naive enough to believe their backgrounds wouldn't matter. *Yeah, right.* Lifting his mug to his mouth, he swallowed a gulp of his beer.

"Not much has changed, has it?" Levi nudged him

in the ribs. "She wouldn't give you the time of day back then and it looked like tonight was no different."

"Whatever." He gave a dismissive gesture. Shane could care less. He might find Layla attractive, but he sure as hell wasn't interested in pursuing her. He'd had his fill of Manhattan socialites, enough to last the rest of this lifetime and into the next. "I'm focused on my career right now. I'm not looking for a relationship."

"Amen to that." Levi lifted his mug and clinked it with his.

"Oh, come on," Cooper insisted.

He shook his head. Love wouldn't last. It never did. He ought to know.

When it ended... His gut twisted. *Never again.*

The reward wasn't worth any amount of risk.

Chapter Two

Layla woke on Sunday morning to the bright light blazing into her bedroom. She jumped out of bed and walked to the window. Sunshine glowed in a cloudless blue sky. A few people meandered along Main Street, even at this early hour.

Although she enjoyed this view of the town green from her place above the Coffee Palace, she missed the serenity of waking to the sounds of surf crashing on shore and the waves rolling in from the sea. Layla wished she could have continued to live in the second-story apartment above La Cabane de La Mer. Lord knew the space would have been more than enough for her, and she could have saved the monthly rent she paid to live here, but the private lender she'd used to secure the loan required to finance the restaurant renovations wouldn't allow it.

She glanced around the room. For now, the gray Ikea modular couch and black lacquer rectangle table would suit her fine. Not to mention the perks of living above a fabulous coffee shop and the friendship she'd found with Elle, the woman who lived across the hall, and Abby, the coffee shop owner.

Layla turned from her view and headed down the short hall to the bathroom. After a quick shower and dressing in warm clothes, she descended the exterior back staircase and walked around to the front of the building once she reached the parking lot. She walked inside and stepped up to the counter.

"Good morning, Layla. Oh, my. Do I have something to tell you. Things got quite interesting after you left Donahue's last night." Abby tucked a lock of titian hair behind her ear. She shuffled to the display case containing a selection of confections.

How lucky was she to have been inducted into the sisterhood? For the first time in her life, she had steadfast female friends she could rely on. Although truth be told, she was still getting used to the gal pal thing. Her sister was the outgoing one of the two of them. Zara loved to party and be surrounded by swarms of people, while she'd always preferred to be with Gramps in his kitchen.

Gramps never thought she was weird because she'd rather cook than go hang out at the mall or get her nails done. He never shoved her in front of a boy she'd crushed on and laughed when she'd almost lost her lunch trying to talk to him.

While she might have outgrown the nausea, her cautious, wary side still made frequent appearances—but she was working on that thanks to these wonderful, supportive, funny, loving women.

Layla grinned. "Do tell."

"You know who," Abby pointed to the back room, "finally plucked up the courage to ask that cute guy she'd been drooling over, for the last few weeks, to dance."

"By you know who, she means me." Elle sashayed in from the kitchen. Her long blond hair was piled on the top of her head in a haphazard bun. The hairstyle added a good four inches to Elle's petite stature.

"So…" Layla grinned, enjoying the comradery. "What happened after you danced?"

Abby let out a low whistle. "Just the dancing was pretty hot. The two of them were stuck together like Velcro. And that kiss…" She fanned herself.

"Get your mind out of the gutter." Elle's cheeks flamed.

"Someone had a good night. That's all I'm sayin'," Abby retorted. "Anything to eat today?" she asked Layla.

Layla studied the trays of sweets. "I can't decide which one I want. Surprise me."

Wax paper in hand, Abby reached inside the display case and plucked a figure-eight Danish from one of the trays on the top shelf. "Cherries and cheese okay?"

She nodded. "Sounds yummy."

"Excuse me." A short woman with a chin-length brown bob appeared.

Elle glanced over her shoulder. "Oh, hey. This is Mia. She just started here today."

Something about the woman seemed vaguely familiar, but Layla couldn't place a finger on what. "Hi,

Mia." Layla extended her hand over the counter. "Have we met before?"

Mia cocked her head to the side and scrutinized Layla's face. "I was just wondering the same thing."

"Maybe you two have bumped into each other here." Abby moved to the coffeepot and filled a large to-go cup. She added cream and sugar and handed it to Layla. "She and her three girls come in on the weekends along with Mia's mom, Jane Kavanaugh."

Shane. She remembered their brief exchange at Donahue's the other night. Yep. She couldn't have made a bigger fool of herself if she'd tried. The minute she'd recognized him... Can you say shy fourteen-year-old with a schoolgirl crush complete with sweaty palms and a topsy-turvy stomach? At least she hadn't lost her lunch. *Thank You, God, for small mercies.*

She'd annoyed him, for sure. *No news there.* He'd always found her irritating. *Poor little rich girl.* Oh, he'd never called her that to her face, but she knew damn well he believed it, according to some of the other locals who'd worked at the Bay Beach Club those years her family summered in New Suffolk.

"Layla?" Elle's voice cut into her thoughts.

"Sorry. I remember now," she said to Mia. "Your mom introduced us here at the Coffee Palace a few months ago—right before Christmas. The five of you had stopped in for a treat after taking your daughters to see Santa at the community center. It's nice to see you again."

Recognition dawned in Mia's gaze. "Right. It's nice to see you, too."

The bell above the door chimed. A tall man entered the shop.

"Shane." Mia's eyes widened. "What are you doing here?"

Layla whirled around. Lord, it was as if her thoughts had conjured him.

Shane swaggered over to where they stood. His big grin sent a tingle down her spine and made her insides go soft and mushy.

What was wrong with her this morning? So what if Shane had a great smile? He meant nothing to her.

"Ladies." He gave a brief nod of his head. "I'm here to support my big sister."

"By all means." Abby stepped aside and motioned for Mia to replace her at the counter.

"Hi, Shane." Layla's words came out in a rush.

He jerked his attention to her. "Layla. Hello." He gave her a polite smile.

A smile was good. So much better than the frown he always wore around her all those summers ago. "It's nice to see you again." Layla sucked in a deep breath. She wouldn't freeze up again. "I mean I haven't seen you in years and now it's been twice in two days." She gave a nervous laugh.

"Right." He eyed her as if she were delusional.

First, she couldn't string two words together, and now she couldn't stop talking. *Bumbling fool.*

Shane turned his attention to his sister. "I'll take a large black coffee, one of those giant cookies with M&M's and an apple fritter."

"Hungry much?" Mia aimed a smirk at her brother.

"Ha, ha. The second pastry is for Mom. She's outside." He jerked his head toward the entrance. "I ran into her in the parking lot, but she got a call. I said I'd order for her."

The chime sounded again and Jane Kavanaugh stepped in. "Good morning, everyone."

"Hi, Jane," Abby and Elle said at the same time.

"Hello." Layla smiled. Would Shane's mother remember her?

"Layla." Jane gave her a hug. "It's so nice to see you again."

Shane frowned. "You two know each other?"

"Of course we do. I've known Layla for years. I used to see her all the time when she visited her grandparents."

Layla prayed Jane had never suspected the truth about those occasions—that she'd arranged to run into Jane on purpose—so she could find out how Shane was doing and what he was up to.

Yes, she'd crushed on Shane something fierce in those days. Heat crept up her neck and Layla suspected her cheeks had turned red.

That was a long time ago.

"Do you want something to drink, Mom?" Mia asked. "Shane only ordered one coffee."

"No. I've got a mug in my car." Abby rang up the order while Mia filled a cup and placed each sweet in a paper bag.

Jane picked up her order. "I'm off to run a few errands."

"Bye," Layla called.

"Me, too." Shane grabbed his bag and cup and turned to the door.

"Have a great day." Layla winced when he just stared at her. She breathed a sigh of relief when he exited the shop. "I've got to get going, too. Take care." Coffee and Danish in hand, Layla headed toward the exit.

"Wait a minute," Elle called. "I almost forgot. Are you in for tonight?"

Layla turned to face the women. Their weekly Sunday night poker game. Those cutthroat women took the game seriously. Layla couldn't blame them. Not with such high stakes at risk. Reese's Peanut Butter Cups Miniatures, Hershey's Nuggets, and the occasional fun-size Hershey Bars thrown in for good measure. "Heck, yeah. I can't wait."

"How about you?" Elle turned her attention to Abby.

"Absolutely. And cousin or not, you get none of my winnings," Abby replied to Elle.

Layla cocked her head and jutted her chin. "You think you're going to win, do you? We'll see about that."

Abby crooked a smug smile. "Yes, we will."

"What about you, Mia? Care to join us for a little fun?" Elle asked.

"Are you sure? I wouldn't want to intrude."

"Positive," Abby responded. "The more the merrier."

"I agree," Layla added.

Mia smiled. "I'd love to. Let me see if I can get my mother to watch the girls for me. I'll give her a call during my break and let you know."

"Great." Elle gave a little wave and strode to the back room. Mia followed.

"See you later," Layla called over her shoulder as she walked to the exit.

Layla stepped outside. The blazing sun glinted off the white snow covering the town green. She sipped her coffee, passing the new boutique that had opened right after Thanksgiving, the local courthouse and the police station as she made her way through town.

She turned right when she reached the public beach access. The peaceful tranquility of the waves crashing on shore calmed her mind and body. Who cared if most of the sand was covered with a foot of snow? Not her. She proceeded down the boardwalk and trudged through the gleaming white snow toward the ocean. High tide had washed away some of Mother Nature's white blanket, leaving a strip of sand visible about two feet from the water's edge.

Sipping her coffee, she meandered along the narrow path taking care to avoid the water to her right and the snow to her left.

The pavilion came into view. A lone man stood inside; his elbows propped up on the railing. He stared out at the waves crashing on shore.

Shane. Layla recognized him as she approached. She studied him from this vantage point. Dressed in jeans and a hooded sweatshirt, he cut an imposing figure.

High cheekbones, a rugged square cut jaw. He'd always been handsome, although her fourteen-year-old self wouldn't have used that term to describe his tall, lanky frame, his wavy brown hair that was just a little too shaggy to be considered clean-cut, and those mesmerizing sapphire-blue eyes. *Don't forget his smile.* It had made her innocent heart slam in her chest. If she were honest, it still did.

Shane spotted her. His piercing gaze bore down on her, scrutinizing, assessing.

Something flashed between them. Intense, fiery, it threatened to consume her.

She blinked. Shane was gone when her eyes fluttered open.

Her mind whirled, a chaotic swirl of emotion. What had just happened between them?

Shane glanced at his watch. Ten more minutes and he'd need to leave for work. He munched the last of his cookie as he stared out at the sea and breathed in the crisp clean air.

A man raced along the beach chasing after two young children who laughed and played in the snow. It reminded him of the walks he used to take with his dad when he was a kid. They'd stop at the Coffee Palace, where Dad would get a coffee and he'd get a cookie. They'd walk along the beach and end up here, at one of the tables in the pavilion. Shane would tell him about his week at school and Dad would tell him about whose house they were renovating or building and how much he looked forward to Shane joining the family business one day.

Shane smiled into the wind. Despite what he'd told his father about wanting to work in the hospital so he could make people better, like the people who'd made Dad better—at least they had in the beginning—he'd taught him how to wield a hammer and by the time Shane reached his early teens, he'd accompany his father on small jobs.

He caught sight of someone else approaching in his peripheral vision. Layla. Shane shook his head. Leave it to her to come along and disrupt his thoughts.

Shane blew out a breath as she continued walking. He studied her face now that she was closer. How could he have forgotten who she was? She still looked like the girl he'd met in her grandfather's kitchen all those years ago.

His mind drifted back to that day.

"Boys, would you like some lemonade?" Mrs. Williams stepped over the short stack of two-by-four planks on the floor as she entered the bedroom in the upstairs apartment above the restaurant.

Shane glanced over at her as he held a piece of Sheetrock in place while his father tacked the gypsum board to the new frame they'd just made.

"I've got fresh-baked cookies, too," Mrs. Williams added. *"They're right out of the oven."*

"You guys go ahead," Dad said to him and Levi. *"Take a break. Just be back in fifteen minutes."*

"Follow me," Mrs. Williams said.

They walked into the living room. Shane marveled at the paintings that hung in gold frames on the walls and the decorative...what had his father called the large vases that sat atop the glossy wood tables? Urns. Yeah, that's what they were. He'd never seen anything so fancy in his life.

"It's this way, boys." Mrs. Williams walked into the kitchen.

Shane's mouth fell open when he spotted the young girl about his age standing with a tray of chocolate-chip cookies in her hand. Her hair was tied back in a ponytail and freckles dotted her nose. His stomach flip-flopped all over the place. She had to be the prettiest girl he'd ever seen.

"Boys, this is my granddaughter. Layla, this is Mr. Turner's son Levi." She pointed to her right. *"And Mr. Kavanaugh's son Shane."* She gestured left to him. *"They're helping with the renovations to the bedroom we're redoing for you and your sister to stay in when you come here for visits."*

"Hey." Levi grabbed two cookies from the plate on the counter and a glass of lemonade.

"Hi." Shane smiled. He couldn't take his gaze off her.

"These are really good," Levi mumbled.

"See, I told you, Layla," Mrs. Williams said.

"You made the cookies?" he asked.

Layla nodded.

Shane reached for one and bit into the gooey treat. "They're awesome."

Layla's cheeks turned bright red, but she smiled at him.

A rush of warmth flooded through him. His pulse went through the roof.

He smiled back.

Shane blinked. Why was he wasting time on memories that didn't matter anymore? He returned his focus to the surf.

Layla's gaze connected with his.

Something zipped between them, powerful and strong; his heart pounded even faster for a moment.

Shane inhaled a lungful of air and blew it out slowly as he tried to steady his erratic breathing. Why was he allowing her to affect him this way? Like Levi had said yesterday, she hadn't given him the time of day back then and nothing had changed as far as he could see.

It's nice to see you again. Her words flashed into his mind and the genuine smile on her face...

There went his traitorous heart again.

Shane banished the *what-ifs* banging around in his head. He'd already learned the hard way; girls like her brought nothing but heartache.

Shane strode into the empty locker room at the regional medical building and Duncan followed.

"I can't wait to get home and put up my feet for a couple of hours. It's been a long day." Duncan grabbed his jacket from his locker and shrugged it on.

Shane nodded. "You got that right." Three trips to the hospital over the last eight hours had kept them busy.

"See you later." Duncan exited the locker room.

Shane finished changing into his street clothes. After packing his uniform into his duffel bag, he slung the strap over his shoulder and headed toward the exit to the parking lot.

He spotted a light on in Mark Burke's office as he made his way down the dimly lit hall. What was the EMS director doing here on a Sunday evening? Shane started to knock but held back when he heard voices.

"I'm well aware of the limited town budget," Mark said.

"You keep saying that," someone else responded.

Shane stopped and listened. The voice sounded familiar, but he couldn't connect the voice with a face.

"We can't afford to lose anyone, Lionel."

Was that Mayor White? Had to be. There wasn't another Lionel in New Suffolk as far as he knew.

"We're already operating the EMS at minimum staffing levels. If we lose even one person, we can't properly serve the community," Mark added.

"We may not have a choice. You know the EMS budget relies heavily on donations and other revenues generated," the mayor said.

"We've got the gala fundraiser coming up in roughly six weeks," Mark responded. "I'm sure we'll be able to raise the funds we need."

"You'd better hope so," Lionel said.

Shane sucked in a breath. Would Mark really have

to cut personnel if the upcoming gala couldn't generate enough money? Damn. He could be one of those people. *Last in, first out.* That's the way it usually worked—in the business world. How many times had he seen it happen to his friends on Wall Street? Enough to know what happened when times got tough.

"Duncan and the rest of the volunteer committee for the gala are meeting tonight at seven here in the medical building. You're more than welcome to attend and see for yourself how the planning is going," Mark offered. "Better yet, you can offer your services. The committee can always use extra people."

If Duncan needed help, Shane was about to volunteer.

The community college Shane wanted to attend next semester required six months of EMT on-the-job experience as a prerequisite for acceptance into their paramedic program. Sure, there were other programs in the state that didn't make such requirements, but they were already full for the fall.

If he lost this job now...

No. He'd worked hard to get this far and he wasn't about to let his dream slip away now.

Shane would do what needed to be done to ensure he kept this position. No matter what.

Have a last-minute committee meeting for the gala this evening. Can't make our weekly game after all. Layla sent the text to Elle. Grabbing her purse, she slid from the car. A gust of wind blew and she shivered. Zipping her jacket, Layla quickened her pace as she strode toward the entrance of the EMS building.

Stepping into the empty main hall, she stopped

in front of the wall containing the years-of-service plaques. She still got a kick out of seeing her grandfather's plaque on the top row with the five other founding members.

"I remember working with Joe when I first started here. Your grandfather was a great paramedic."

She jumped and whirled around to face the newcomer. "Oh. Hi, Mark."

"Sorry. I didn't mean to startle you," the EMS director said.

"No. That's okay." She gestured to the wall behind her. "I like seeing his picture up there." She was proud of his contributions to the community. Even after he'd retired from the EMS department, he'd continued his support.

"I see you're following in his footsteps."

Brows furrowed; she cocked her head to the side. "What are you talking about?"

"Allowing us to use your restaurant for the fundraiser. Joe hosted at least one EMS event a year when he owned the place. I can't wait to see what you've done now that you've taken over."

She beamed a warm smile at him. "Don't wait until the ball. Come by anytime. Tell your friends, too."

"Will do."

"We should get going." She gestured down the hall to where the community rooms were located. "The fundraiser meeting will start soon."

"I can't make it tonight. I have a family commitment. It was nice seeing you, Layla. Thanks again for helping with this event. It's people like you and the rest of the committee that make it possible for us to raise the money we need to better service the district."

"You're welcome. I'm glad to help." Giving was important. A responsibility as far as her parents and grandparents were concerned, for everyone. If you can't give financially, find another way, Gramps would say.

How could she have lost track of those values over the last few years? Antoine's image appeared in her head. The fact that he didn't share her beliefs should have been a red flag. Yet she'd dismissed the facts, choosing to see what she wanted. *Foolish, all right.* Layla wouldn't make that mistake again.

She continued down the hall and stopped at an open door on the right. The fundraiser team sat inside on either side of two long banquet tables which stood side by side. She grabbed the last open chair.

Her eyes widened when she caught a glimpse of the man to her right. What was Shane Kavanaugh doing here? He seemed as surprised to see her as she him.

Duncan Cruz rose and called the meeting to order. "Thanks for coming, everyone. We're a little less than a month and a half from our event. I have something I need to share with you, but first, I want to introduce a new committee member." Duncan gestured to Shane. "For those of you who don't already know him, this is Shane Kavanaugh. He joined the department about a month ago."

Mr. New York Stock Exchange was an emergency medical technician? *Like Gramps?* No. That couldn't be right. He wasn't anything like her beloved grandfather.

He was a Wall Street Wolf. Wasn't he?

Shane cringed when Layla walked into the room. Wasn't it just his luck she'd be involved with the benefit? He couldn't catch a break.

He straightened and gave a little wave to acknowledge Duncan's introduction.

"Let's get started." Duncan explained the situation with the town budget and how they needed to generate as much revenue from this event as possible. "I'm looking for ideas we can easily implement since we don't have much planning time left."

Hal Smith raised his hand. "What if we changed the seating to family style instead of individual tables?"

Shane nodded. "Great idea. We can seat more people that way, which means we can sell more tickets."

"Can we do that, Layla?" Duncan asked.

"Sure. I don't have long tables, but we can string several of the small ones together and create the same effect."

Duncan grinned. "I like it. What else?"

"What if we do a themed event?" Layla said.

Duncan pursed his lips as if considering. "What did you have in mind?"

"We'll go upscale. Black tie for the men, fancy dresses for the women."

Faith nudged her husband. "Looks like I'm going shopping."

The group chuckled.

Layla grinned. "We'll have fairy lights, gold candelabras on the tables. Lots of glitz and glamour."

"We decorated the fire trucks with white lights for the parade last Christmas," Quinn Cain said. "I'm sure the chief will allow us to use them."

"Sophisticated Blooms can donate flower arrangements," Sophie Bloom added.

A round of *yeses* and *sounds goods* ensued.

Layla's eyes lit with excitement. "We can even do an ice sculpture in the main entry."

An ice sculpture? Seriously? Talk about over-the-top.

The rest of the group agreed with him if their silences were anything to go by.

"You don't have to answer now." Layla laced her fingers together and rested her hands on the table. "Just think about it."

He rolled his eyes skyward. Man, she was just too much.

"While I love your enthusiasm," Duncan started, "and I'm not saying we shouldn't go ahead and snazz things up a bit—because I think we should—our ultimate goal is to generate as much cash as we can. I'm not sure a themed event would bring in the extra money we need."

"Not to mention we'd exceed our budget to pull it off." Faith sighed. "I'm still shopping for a fancy dress." She winked at Layla.

"Me, too." Sophie smiled. "And I'm still willing to donate the flower arrangements."

"I'll string the lights," Quinn added.

"Great." Duncan nodded. "What else can we do?"

"What about a silent auction?" Hal suggested.

"That's always a good moneymaker," Shane agreed.

"We can get donations from local businesses," Sue added.

"I can make that work," Layla confirmed. "We have plenty of space."

"Now you're talking." Duncan gave two thumbs up.

"Sue and I will work together." Hal pointed to his wife sitting next to him. "But we'll need other volunteers to help."

Shane raised his hand along with several other members of the group.

"Tina and Yvonne." Duncan pointed to the two women who sat closest to him. "Sally and Tom." He indicated two others who'd raised their hands. He scanned the group. He pointed to him. "Shane. You team up with Layla."

Work with Layla? For crying out loud. Can't catch a break, indeed. He slanted his gaze in her direction. She seemed less than thrilled with their pairing. Shane straightened his shoulders and held his head high. Well, that was too damned bad. He was as good a partner to work with as any of the others in the room.

Deal with it. He would.

So, they'd spend a few hours together collecting donations. No big deal. The fundraiser would generate the extra revenue they needed. He'd keep his job.

What could go wrong?

Chapter Three

Layla glanced at her watch. They closed at nine on Friday evenings in the winter—no use staying open when the whole town shut down early—but she'd leave the front entrance open so Zara could get in.

Something was up with her sister and Layla was worried.

Zara's call last night had set her on edge when she'd told her she was on her way to New Suffolk. This week should have been a Zoom call according to their schedule of weekly remote meetings and one face to face a month, but she'd insisted on meeting in person.

Even more bizarre, she'd pressed Layla to meet today. They always held their in-person meetings on Saturdays. That way Zara wouldn't miss a day of work.

And the thing with her showing up here late this afternoon and insisting they perform the review immediately was *really weird*. She'd seemed…almost panicky when Layla couldn't drop what she was doing and accommodate the request.

"Layla," her sous-chef called.

"Coming." She hoisted the case of Château Lafite Rothschild Pauillac into her arms and strode toward the bar. Lifting the four remaining bottles from the cardboard box, she set each one atop the glossy wood surface.

"Oh, here you are." Olivia approached. "The kitchen's all set. I'm heading out now."

"Okay, thanks. See you tomorrow." Layla brushed a stray lock of curly hair from her sweaty face.

"Oh, the mailman delivered a certified letter earlier. Couldn't find you so I signed for it and left it on the chair in your office."

That was weird. Who would send her a certified letter? "Okay, thanks for letting me know." Layla headed down the back hall toward her office. She flicked on the light. Sure enough, a large manila envelope sat propped against the back of her brown leather swivel desk chair.

Her brows furrowed as she read the letterhead in the upper left corner. It was from the private lender who'd issued the loan she'd taken out to finance opening the restaurant, using the mansion as collateral. Grabbing the envelope, she tore it open and dropped into the cool seat.

Layla removed the letter and scanned the first page. Her eyes bugged out. "What the hell?"

"Hey, Layla. Where are you?" her sister called.

She rushed out of her office, through the empty

restaurant to the front entrance to meet her. "What is this?" Layla clenched the document in her hand.

"What is what?" Zara asked.

Layla thrust the document at Zara. "Notice of Default." She shook her head. "I don't understand. They're going to force me to sell the mansion to pay off the loan in full if I can't make the loan current by the end of the first week of April." She lifted her gaze to Zara's. "Why would they believe the loan isn't current?" Her finances might be a little tight, but she hadn't missed a payment.

Zara wouldn't answer. She just stood there with a deer-in-the-headlights expression on her face.

Layla sucked in a lungful of air and tried to relax. Yelling at her sister wasn't going to straighten out this mistake. Zara was obviously as surprised by this as Layla. They'd figure it out together.

She walked into the bar. Setting the document aside, she pulled two wineglasses from the rack and set them atop the glossy bar top. "Red or white," she asked when Zara sat in a chair on the opposite side of her.

"Doesn't matter," Zara grunted.

Layla opened a bottle of her favorite Bordeaux and poured two glasses.

"I'm sorry—" She and Zara spoke at the same time.

Layla heaved out a sigh. "Let me go first. I shouldn't have yelled at you. I'm just…in shock, I guess." She drew in a deep breath and let it out slowly. "Do you have any idea what's going on? How could the lender make such a mistake?"

"It's not a mistake." Zara's voice held a note of panic.

Layla stiffened. Her eyes went wide. "Excuse me? What do you mean? There must be some kind of processing error." If there wasn't... Nausea churned in her stomach and burned a path up her throat.

Zara scrubbed her hands over her face. "I couldn't cover the loan amount due in January or February."

The shaking started in her hands and spread like wildfire throughout her body until she shook from head to toes. But she tried to keep calm. "Why would you miss two payments?" How could that happen? She would have noticed the discrepancies during their weekly finance reviews except... An image of her sister's washed-out face formed in her head. "Oh, my God. You've been hiding this from me. Were you even sick, or was it all a sham so you could keep the truth from me?"

Tears formed in Zara's eyes.

Layla rubbed at her temples and started to pace back and forth behind the bar. "Why would you do such a thing?"

Zara's head lowered and her voice shook when she spoke. "I wasn't... I didn't think..."

She marched over to where Zara sat. Her hands clenched into tight fists. "Why couldn't you make the payments?"

"You're not making enough money."

"Are you kidding me?" Okay, yes. The tourists who'd filled her dining room to capacity every night last summer had departed at the end of the season, but still...

"These days, you barely make enough to cover day-to-day operating expenses." Zara sounded as if she were dealing with a stubborn child who refused to listen.

The image of a nearly empty dining room popped

into her head. Her shoulders slumped. "Why didn't you tell me when we missed the first payment?"

"You didn't seem worried when things slowed down after the holidays and I figured we'd make up the missed payment in February."

"But we didn't, and still you said nothing. And how the hell would I make it up in the off-season, of all times?" A heavy weight settled in her chest making it hard to breathe. "For God's sake. You agreed to manage the finances, Zara. I *trusted* you."

The color drained from Zara's face. "I know. I'm trying, but managing *your* restaurant isn't anything like what I did for Gramps, or what I do for the nonprofit. You have so many more moving parts to juggle, new suppliers every week. Just when I believe I'm caught up, you surprise me with another invoice to pay. That coupled with the fact that I hadn't anticipated the steep decline in business in January and February meant I wound up short when the loan payments were due.

"I'm sorry. I really am." Zara's crushed spirit tore at her insides. "I spoke to the lender yesterday. They told me about the letter. I wanted to tell you myself this afternoon. It's why I came up."

Layla scrubbed her hands over her face. She didn't know what to say.

"Please don't hate me," Zara pleaded.

Her heart squeezed. This was her sister—her best friend through thick and thin—not archenemy number one. She wouldn't have made it through those initial days after her split from Antoine without Zara's love and support.

Lord, what a mess they'd made of this.

Zara wiped tears from her eyes. "I never thought it would come to this."

"But it has." Her breaths came in short, sharp gasps. Everything she'd worked for. All her dreams. Gone.

Done. At last. Shane yawned. He couldn't wait to hit the hay. He pushed the door open and exited the EMS building. Stars twinkled in the dark sky and the full moon negated the need for lights as he strode through the parking lot to his truck.

Once there, he tossed his duffel bag on the passenger seat and hopped inside. Shane pulled out of the parking lot and headed east. He drove through the now silent town and turned left at the light and headed toward home.

The bright lights shining at La Cabane de La Mer surprised him. He wouldn't have guessed the restaurant would be open at this hour. Of all the people on the gala committee, wasn't it just his luck he'd end up paired with Layla? Shane blew out a harsh breath. Now that his work schedule was set for the next two weeks, he needed to speak with her and set up a time they could collect the rest of the silent auction donations. Now was as good a time as any. He made a U-turn and headed back.

The parking lot was empty when he pulled in. Maybe he'd been wrong, and the restaurant was closed? He was here, so he may as well check. Shane hopped out of his truck and walked toward the entrance.

Silence greeted him when he stepped inside. "Hello? Is anyone here?" A loud crash came from the room to his left. "Who's there?"

"We're closed," a female voice yelled.

He moved toward the sound but couldn't find anyone. "Hello," he called again.

"I said we're closed." The sound came from behind the bar.

"Layla?" Shane walked over and peered over the marble countertop. She sat in a heap on the floor with three broken wine bottles beside her and spilled red wine on the floor. He rushed to her side. "Oh, no. What happened?"

She shot an accusing glare at him. "It scared the heck out of me when I heard your voice and I knocked over the bottles that were sitting on the bar top. How did you get in?"

"The front entrance was open. Here, let me help you." Shane extended his hand and pulled her to her feet. "Are you okay?" He scanned the length of her to make sure she didn't have any visible cuts.

"What are you doing here?" Oh, yes. She was mad at him all right.

"I saw the lights were still on, and I wanted to talk to you about the silent auction donations we're supposed to—"

The look on her face had him stopping midsentence.

"What's wrong?" Maybe she'd been injured after all? "Are you sure you're not hurt?"

"Not hurt." She shook her head and looked away. "Letter..."

Shane couldn't understand. "What are you talking about?"

She turned to face him. Her distraught expression stole the breath from him. "Close down... Lose everything."

She wasn't making any sense. Maybe he should leave and come back another time.

A single tear fell from the corner of her eye. "What am I going to do?"

Her vulnerability tugged at his heart. "Come on. Let's go sit down, and you can tell me what's going on."

He walked to the closest table and Layla sat.

"Would you like a glass of water?" he asked.

She scrubbed her hands over her face. "Y-yes, please."

"Okay. I'll be right back." He stepped behind the bar. Shane picked up one of the broken bottles. He let out a low whistle when he read the label. *Château Lafite Rothschild Pauillac.* A bottle went for six hundred dollars, maybe more. He couldn't imagine anyone in New Suffolk spending that kind of money on a bottle of wine with dinner. The wealthy tourists who summered in their quaint little beach town, maybe, but the locals who catered to those vacationers... Most couldn't afford such luxuries, especially during the slow season.

Shane tossed the bottles in the trash. He'd help her clean up the rest of the mess later. It was the least he could do, considering he'd been somewhat responsible for creating it. *First things first.* Grabbing a glass from the shelf, he filled it with water and returned to the table. "Here you go."

"Thanks." Her large watery eyes gazed at him. Layla sipped from the glass and set it back down on the table.

"Now tell me what's got you so upset." Shane sat in the seat across from her.

She blew out a breath and recounted the story.

Shane stared at her wide-eyed. "Most banks give you more than thirty days before they make you liquidate your collateral."

Layla nodded. "I used a private lender my sister, Zara, was acquainted with."

Sounded more like a loan shark to him. *Wait.* Thirty days would put them at the end of the first week of April. "What about the gala?"

"We'll have to cancel." Tears welled in her eyes again.

"No way." The EMS department was counting on the funds this event would raise. He was counting on the money to ensure he'd keep his job. "We've sold almost all the tickets, and it's too late to find another comparable venue."

"What do you want me to do?" Layla jumped down from the chair and started pacing back and forth across the room. "We don't have the money needed to make the loan current."

"I can help you." The words erupted from him before his brain could engage.

"How?" She stopped walking midstride and turned to face him.

Shane expelled a resigned sigh. It was either help her or risk getting cut from the EMS team. "Former business investment consultant here. I can review your finances and make some recommendations on how you can make more money." Eliminating the purchase of six-hundred-dollar bottles of wine came to mind for starters.

She studied him, a hopeful glint in her gaze. "You would do that for me?"

"Yes. You have enough for the March payment, right?"

"I'll make sure of it." A tentative smile formed on her face.

"Great. We'll find a way to keep your restaurant open." At least he'd try to make that happen.

Layla walked back to the table and sat in the seat she'd vacated moments ago. "Why would you want to do this? What's in it for you?"

He wouldn't pull any punches with her. "We both know the EMS department needs the money the gala will generate. I want to make sure it happens. It's a win-win for both of us. So, what do you say?"

"Okay." Layla extended her hand to him and he shook it. Sparks of electricity sizzled through him the moment his palm touched hers.

He jerked his hand away and shoved it in his jeans pocket. What had he gotten himself into?

Layla pulled her car into the driveway of the 1930s Cape-Cod-style home on Monday evening and peered around. Strategically placed spotlights brightened the sweeping snow-blanketed front lawn. She imagined what it would look like in spring, the beds of bright fragrant blooms in a multitude of species with green Hosta and tall beach grass intermixed.

The calming ebb and flow of the ocean waves crashing on shore filled her Mini Cooper, even with the windows closed. She took several deep breaths, willing herself to stay calm.

Layla grabbed her purse and the thermal take-out bags from the passenger seat and exited the car. She walked up the blue stone walkway and rang the doorbell.

Minutes passed and no one answered the door. Had Shane forgotten he'd told her to stop by tonight? They hadn't spoken over the weekend. She should have texted him this afternoon and confirmed. She turned and started back down the walkway to her car. The snick of the lock had her stopping. She whirled around.

The door opened.

Shane appeared wearing a pair of black sweatpants slung low on his hips and… Oh, dear Lord, nothing else. No socks, no shoes. No shirt. Holy moly. She swallowed. *Perfection personified.*

"What are you doing here?" he asked.

Yes. He'd forgotten, all right. Layla cleared her throat. "You asked me to stop by tonight and bring the restaurant financial information with me. Remember?"

"Right." He nodded. "Come on in." Shane stepped aside and gestured for her to enter. "Sorry, I just got off shift and was in the shower." He shrugged into the sweatshirt she hadn't noticed in his hand.

Layla stepped inside. "Oh, my gosh. This is an amazing home." She could see through to the opposite side of the house where floor-to-ceiling windows and sliding glass doors lined the outside wall.

His gaze narrowed and every bone in his body stiffened. "It might not be much now, but wait until the renovations I have planned are complete."

"No, no." Layla shook her head. "I wasn't being sarcastic. This place is gorgeous. You must have an amazing view of the ocean from every room in the house."

He stared at her, a curious expression on his face. "Sorry. I guess I'm a little sensitive when it comes to this place. Like I said, it needs work. And yes, the views are stunning. They're what sold me on the place. The rest I can fix."

"You're doing the work yourself?" At his puzzled expression she added, "Right. Of course you are." How could she have forgotten? TK Construction had reno- vated her grandparents' apartment. It was where she'd met him all those years ago. Where she'd experienced her first real crush. Oh, who was she kidding? She'd fallen head over heels for him, but how could she com- pete with all of those Bay Beach Club teenage beauties who flirted relentlessly with him when she couldn't master the art of speech in his presence?

At least she'd finally conquered that particular phobia—funny how the threat of losing everything that mattered to you gave you something else to focus on. She had bigger problems to worry about than making a fool of herself in front of him.

That's what she'd always been afraid of, but it didn't matter anymore.

"Want a quick tour before we get started?" he asked.

Her eyes widened. She wouldn't have expected him to offer such a thing, to be so…friendly. He'd made it clear from the start he was only helping her because it benefited the EMS department. "A win-win," he'd said. That was fine with her. She expected nothing more. Still, her curiosity got the better of her. She couldn't resist now that he'd offered. "Yes. I'd love to hear what you have planned for each room."

"Follow me." Shane walked past the staircase on the right and moved into the interior.

Layla stood in the center of the home and peered around. A large kitchen sat on the right in front of the staircase and a gigantic living room with a wide fireplace on the left. "Oh, wow. I love how all the spaces are open to each other and the view you have...spectacular."

"It wasn't that way when I bought the place. Each room was separate."

"You've done an amazing job making it so open." She wondered why he'd decided to pursue careers in finance and medicine when he obviously possessed the skill and talent to excel at the kind of work his family had been doing for years.

"I'm going to add an island in the kitchen."

"I can picture it there. In front of the dining table." She pointed to the open floor space in front of where the wall of cabinets stood. "A long, wide one with lots of counter space." The perfect place for preparing a meal.

Shane smiled and nodded. "That's exactly what I'm thinking."

She turned toward the living room. "What will you do in here?"

"I'll rip out the nasty carpet. There's hardwood underneath that matches the rest of the flooring on this level."

"Sounds perfect. All you need is a comfy sectional in front of the fireplace and a huge TV over the mantel and you're all set."

"You're reading my mind." Shane stared at her, a stunned expression on his face. "There's not much else to see on this level. We'll work at the table." He turned toward the fridge.

"Wait, please." She placed a hand on his arm to stop him.

He faced her. "What is it?"

"I just wanted to thank you again for helping me. My restaurant is…" She hesitated. How could she explain what La Cabane de La Mer meant to her? "It's more than just a job. Cooking is a part of who I am. To be able to do that on my own terms… It's a dream come true."

He studied her for long intense moments before saying, "I'm glad to help. Go ahead and grab a seat." Shane pointed over his shoulder in the vicinity of the table. "Want something to drink?"

"Actually, I brought you dinner and a bottle of red wine. I figured it's the least I could do." Layla handed him one of the thermal takeout bags and pulled a wine bottle from her purse.

His mouth gaped. "You did?"

Layla beamed a tentative smile. "You mentioned you had to work until six. I figured you wouldn't have much time to eat before we got started, so I thought we could eat while we worked."

"Thanks." A puzzled expression crossed his face. "Where's your meal?"

"Right here." She held up a second bag.

"What'd you bring?" Shane jiggled the bag in his hand.

"Burgers. I hope you don't mind." She'd been in the mood for one. Sometimes you just got a craving for something greasy.

His eyes widened, and was that excitement in his astonished gaze? "Are you kidding? I love burgers."

Layla laughed. "Looks like we've got something in common because I love them, too."

"Thanks again for bringing this." Shane went straight for the table and sat. He unzipped the warming bag and slid the clear container from the bag. "It looks amazing."

"I stuffed the meat with Gaperon cheese and we had extra brioche rolls this evening."

"You made it?" Shane yanked the lid off one-handed. He stared at the burger as if he'd found the holy grail.

"Of course I did. Like I'd serve you fast food from—" She stopped midsentence when he grabbed the burger and took a bite.

"Oh my God." His eyes closed for a moment and a look of ecstasy crossed his handsome face. "It *is* delicious. You're an amazing cook."

A rush of warmth flooded through her. "Thanks."

"Is this on your menu? If not, you should add it." Shane bit into the burger again.

Was he kidding? Of course he was. She owned a gourmet French restaurant, for goodness' sake. "Right." Layla grinned.

"This is really fantastic."

Layla gawked as he consumed the rest of the burger in one bite.

"Sorry." His cheeks flamed bright red. "I, ah… missed lunch and dinner." He lifted a napkin from the holder perched in the center of the table and dragged it across his mouth.

"Why did you miss lunch and dinner?"

His blue eyes sparkled and…he looked like a kid at Christmas.

"I became a godfather today." A wide happy grin spread across his face.

"A godfather?" She frowned. "Did someone have a baby?"

"Yes." His smile grew brighter and his eyes… Holy cow. They danced with delight. "I delivered my first baby this evening," he added at her confused expression.

Work. Of course. "What happened?"

"Woman was alone at home and in labor. She couldn't reach her husband and called 9-1-1." Shane grabbed a fry from the container and munched. "She was one hundred percent dilated when we arrived. No time to get her to the hospital so we delivered the baby at her home. I'm happy to say mother and son are doing great."

He'd brought a new life into this world. Helped someone when they couldn't help themselves. "That's incredible." Now she understood why he'd chosen this profession. He loved his work.

"It really is." His look of wonder made her smile.

Amazing home renovator, successful Wall Street career, EMT extraordinaire, lover of burgers. Let's not forget those fabulous abs and biceps. So many layers to this complicated man. What else made him tick? Layla wanted to know.

"The parents made me an honorary godfather."

She grinned. "Congratulations."

"Thanks." Shane stood and walked to the fridge on the far side of the room. He returned a moment later carrying a bottle of ketchup.

"Oh, you don't need that. There's some in the bag."

He set the bottle on the table and lifted the small cup filled with the dipping sauce she'd included. "This doesn't look like ketchup." He tilted the plastic cup for her inspection.

"That's the honey mustard mayo. The curry ketchup is in the other container."

"Curry ketchup?" He shot her a dubious look.

"It's good. Trust me."

Shane dipped a fry and stuck it in his mouth. His eyes opened wide and a look of surprise crossed his face. "You're right. I thought it sounded a little weird to mix curry and ketchup, but this is great."

"I'm glad you like it." She grinned.

"Okay." He licked the salt from his fingers, grabbed his laptop from the counter and brought it back to the table. "It's time to get to work. Are you ready?"

Layla reached inside her purse, withdrew the Jump-drive containing the restaurant financial records and handed it to Shane. "Let's do this."

Don't miss
A Taste of Home *by Anna James,*
available now wherever
Harlequin Special Edition books and ebooks are sold
www.Harlequin.com

#2989 THE MAVERICK'S SURPRISE SON
Montana Mavericks: Lassoing Love • by Christine Rimmer
Volunteer firefighter Jace Abernathy vows to adopt the newborn he saved from a fire. Nurse Tamara Hanson doubts he's up to the task. She'll help the determined rancher prepare for his social service screening. But in the process, will these hometown heroes find love and family with each other?

#2990 SEVEN BIRTHDAY WISHES
Dawson Family Ranch • by Melissa Senate
Seven-year-old Cody Dawson dreams of meeting champion bull rider Logan Winston. Logan doesn't know his biggest fan is also his son. He'll fulfill seven of Cody's wishes—one for each birthday he missed. But falling in love again with Cody's mom, Annabel, may be his son's biggest wish yet!

#2991 HER NOT-SO-LITTLE SECRET
Match Made in Haven • by Brenda Harlen
Sierra Hart knows a bad boy when she sees one. And smooth-talking Deacon Parrish is a rogue of the first order! Their courtroom competition pales to their bedroom chemistry. But will these dueling attorneys trust each other enough to go from "I object" to "I do"?

#2992 HEIR IN A YEAR
by Elizabeth Bevarly
Bennett Hadden just inherited the Gilded Age mansion Summerlight. So did Haven Moreau—assuming the two archenemies can live there together for one year. Haven plans to restore the home *and* her broken relationship with Bennett. And she'll use every tool at her disposal to return both to their former glories!

#2993 THEIR SECRET TWINS
Shelter Valley Stories • by Tara Taylor Quinn
Jordon Lawrence and ex Mia Jones just got the embryo shock of their lives. Their efforts to help a childless couple years ago resulted in twin daughters they never knew existed. Now the orphaned girls need their biological parents, and Jordon and Mia will work double time to create the family their children deserve!

#2994 THE BUSINESS BETWEEN THEM
Once Upon a Wedding • by Mona Shroff
Businessman Akash Gupta just bought Reena Pandya's family hotel, ruining her plan to take it over. Now the determined workaholic will do anything to reclaim her birthright—even get closer to her sexy ex. But Akash has a plan, too—teaching one very headstrong woman to balance duty, family *and* love.

HSECNM0523

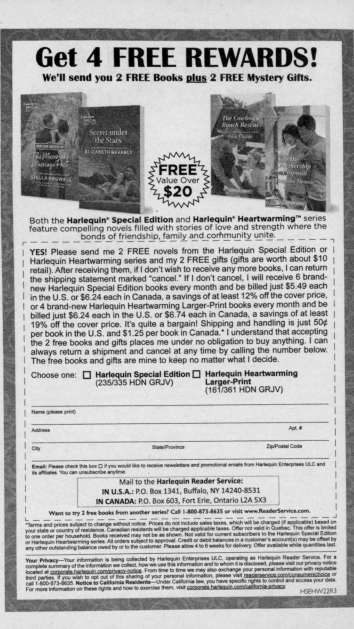

HARLEQUIN
PLUS

Try the best multimedia subscription service for romance readers like you!

Read, Watch and Play.

Experience the easiest way to get the romance content you crave.

Start your **FREE TRIAL** at
<u>www.harlequinplus.com/freetrial</u>.